Angel's Child

To/ all at S.M.A.B.

Best Wishes

from

Laraine

Angel's Child

LARRAINE S HARRISON

Copy Editor: Kate Campbell
Photography: Kerry Harrison
Design: Debby Lewis-Harrison
All illustrations by Esther Campbell
except p.223 by Ivy Campbell

Matador
9 Priory Business Park,
Wistow Road, Kibworth Beauchamp,
Leicestershire. LE8 0RX
Tel: 0116 279 2299
Email: books@troubador.co.uk
Web: www.troubador.co.uk/matador
Twitter: @matadorbooks

ISBN 978 1838593 780

British Library Cataloguing in Publication Data.
A catalogue record for this book is available from the British Library.

Printed and bound by CPI Group (UK) Ltd, Croydon, CR0 4YY
Typeset in 11 pt Minion Pro Regular by Troubador Publishing Ltd, Leicester, UK

Matador is an imprint of Troubador Publishing Ltd

MIX
Paper from responsible sources
FSC® C013604
FSC
www.fsc.org

Contents

What Children Said About *Angel's Child*

I found the story very interesting and once I started reading I couldn't stop.

Alicia Robinson

It was very mysterious and I wanted to keep on reading to find out what happened next.

Imisi Greensides

I found the story very interesting because every time something major happened, it grabbed my attention and I always wanted to read a lot more past that point.

Ben Bayliss

The way the author described the characters helped me to create a picture of them in my mind.

Millie Gulliford

I found the story interesting because the poem grabbed my attention and it held on.

Mia Jones

It is the best adventure story I've ever read.

Nibaa Fahim

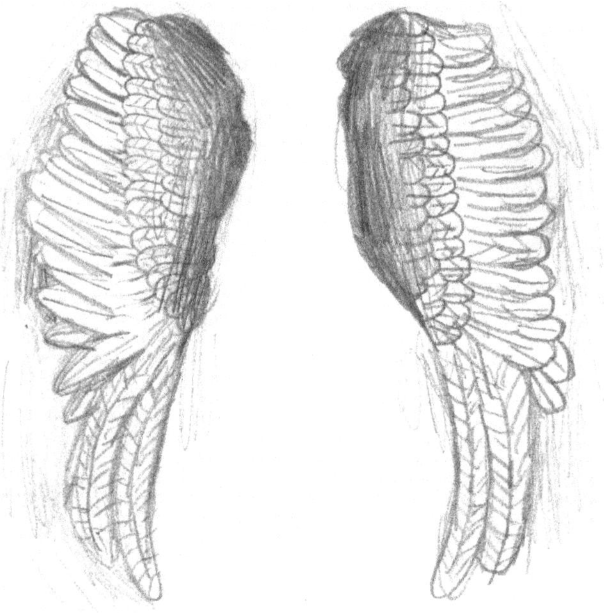

Angel
Wings By Amber
Henry

ANGEL'S CHILD

In an April storm at the close of day
The Bella Rose sank off Legna Bay.
But watching not so far away
Was the Angel of the Sea.

As a mother and baby jumped in the tide
There came a voice from the water-side.
'The sea shall never take them,' cried
The Angel of the Sea.

When the mother died upon the beach
The Angel kissed the baby's cheek.
'This child shall now be mine to keep,'
Said the Angel of the Sea.

The child was happy and wished to stay
But the Islanders took the child away.
'You've stolen my child and you will pay,'
Cried the Angel of the Sea.

On stormy nights, when the tide is high
You can hear the Angel's bitter cry.
'Return my child or you will die,'
Cursed the Angel of the Sea.

Granny's jewellery box

By Amber Henry

1

Cry of the Thunder

One April evening, just before dark, two strangers knocked on Grandad Charlie's door.

Bang! Bang! Bang!

Amber was upstairs unpacking. By the time she got to the bottom of the stairs, a man and a woman were standing in the hallway, their black coats dripping with the rain. The man was tall and well built, with a bald head and a rugged face. 'We're looking for Katrin Morgan,' he said, peering down at Charlie through his gold-rimmed glasses. 'We've knocked next door but she's not in.'

Charlie frowned. 'Has something happened?'

The woman glanced at Amber as she pulled down her hood and shook out her long black hair.

She spoke softly. 'We need to talk to her. Do you know where she is?'

'She's in hospital,' said Charlie. 'She fell in the garden this morning and banged her head.'

The man sighed impatiently. 'When will she be back? Tonight? Tomorrow? In a few days? When?'

Amber thought his words sounded like a machine gun.

Charlie took a step back. 'I've no idea.'

The man moved as if to leave, but the woman caught hold of his arm. 'Wait a minute.'

She turned back to Charlie. 'That's an expensive car on Katrin's drive. Is that hers?'

‘It’s Dave’s.’

The woman looked surprised. ‘Dave? Who’s Dave?’

‘Her boyfriend.’

The man’s face twitched slightly, as if he’d had some bad news. ‘Does anyone else live there? We need to know.’

Amber moved closer to her Grandad. They were alone in the house and these people were making her nervous.

‘No-one else lives there,’ said Charlie. ‘Who are you anyway? Why are you asking me all these questions?’

The woman smiled faintly. ‘Nothing for you to worry about.’

‘I didn’t say I was worried,’ Charlie said. ‘I just want to know why you’re so interested in my next-door neighbour. She happens to be a friend of mine.’

‘You should be more careful who you make friends with,’ muttered the man.

‘What’s that supposed to mean?’ said Charlie.

The man’s eyes flashed as he raised his voice. ‘Katrin Morgan is a thief and a liar!’

Charlie opened the door. ‘No-one talks about my friend like that. I think you’d better go.’

‘We’ll be back,’ said the man, pointing his finger at Charlie.

‘Sorry,’ murmured the woman as they left. ‘He’s a bit upset.’

* * *

Amber raced into the lounge and looked through the window, just in time to see the couple climb into a blue camper van and drive away. ‘Why did you let them in if you didn’t know them Grandad?’

Charlie shrugged his shoulders. ‘I couldn’t leave them standing in the rain could I?’

Amber looked out at the darkening sky. ‘Do you think they could be the police?’

'No. They would have told us if they were.'

'Not if they were undercover.'

Charlie laughed. 'You always did have a wild imagination.'

Amber closed the curtains. There was nothing more to see except the rain. 'I wonder why they want to talk to Katrin.'

'I don't know,' said Charlie, slumping into his armchair, 'but I didn't like what the man said. Katrin's not been here long but she's the best neighbour I've ever had.'

A sudden flash of light took Amber by surprise as it lit up the room.

'Storm's on the way,' said Charlie, picking up a newspaper.

Amber sat on the lumpy sofa and threw her head back against one of the cushions. 'Why does it always rain in the Easter holidays? It was the same last year.'

She sat and watched her Grandad as he read the paper and thought about how she used to dread it when he came to visit them. With his bushy silver beard, bushy eye brows and twinkling blue eyes, her friends called him Santa, but it was his long silver hair tied back with a black ribbon that made them laugh. In the winter he wore a brown leather hat with a feather, and in the summer he wore a white one. Unless it was very hot, he always wore the fisherman's jumper that Granny knitted him. It was called a gansey. Her Granny told her that the pattern on it was different for each fishing village, so if there was a shipwreck you could tell where the fishermen came from when they were washed up on the beach. Grandad had never been a fisherman but his grandfather was, so he was proud to wear the gansey from the Island of Legna, with its special diamond pattern down one side. Amber still found his unusual appearance embarrassing, but secretly she felt proud that he wasn't afraid to be himself.

A low growl rumbled in the distance. Charlie looked up from his paper. 'The Angel's crying for her child again,' he said.

‘What?’

‘She’s angry.’

‘Who is?’

‘The Angel.’

‘It’s only thunder Grandad.’

‘She put a curse on the Island,’ said Charlie. ‘Bad things have happened because of that curse.’

Amber laughed. ‘You’re the one with the wild imagination. You’ve just made that up.’

She looked at her Grandad but his face was deadly serious. ‘It’s not made up. It’s based on something that really happened, right here on the Island of Legna.’

‘Like what?’

‘I don’t want to scare you.’

‘I’m twelve years old Grandad. A story about an angel’s curse isn’t going to scare me.’

Charlie walked over to his vast collection of CDs and books. ‘I’ve got a book about it somewhere.’

Amber stifled a yawn. ‘It’s OK. I’ll read it some other time.’

‘That’s strange,’ said Charlie, tracing his finger along the line of books. ‘It’s called *The History of Legna*. It should be under *H* but I can’t see it.’

Another flash lit up the lounge, followed by a much louder clap of thunder. Amber looked up as the lights flickered. A large spider dangled from the lampshade on a thin thread. She shuffled further along the sofa in case it fell near her feet.

She used to love this room with its high ceilings and shiny brown furniture. It was full of unusual ornaments and old photos in silver frames. When she was much younger she used to play with the little brass animals on the shelf above the bookcase: two ducks, a cat and a small dog with sparkly eyes. They used to be lined up in a row but now they were pushed to the edge of the shelf as if no-one cared about them. Even her Grandad’s precious guitar was propped against the wall, covered in dust. The whole room looked gloomy and grubby. Mum said Grandad never cleaned it, although he said he did. Right now she wished she was back in her own house.

Charlie picked out a book from the bookcase and brought it back to his chair.

'Have you found the one you were looking for?' asked Amber.

He shook his head. 'No. This is a book I used to read as a boy. It's about old fishing boats and trawlers.'

Amber was hoping her Grandad wouldn't show it to her as she wasn't interested in boats, but she needn't have worried. He only looked at a couple of pages before putting it down. 'I'll look at it later.' His eyes closed briefly as he lay back in his chair, then he sat up and rubbed his hands together.

'Switch the fire on Amber. It's getting cold in here.'

Amber was surprised. 'I thought that gansey kept you warm all the time.'

'It usually does but there seems to be a draught in here tonight.'

Heaving herself off the sofa, Amber reached for the switch on the side of the old electric fire, but as she did so her eyes glanced at the glass shelf beside it. 'Where's Granny's jewellery box? It used to be on that shelf.'

'I've given it to Katrin.'

'But Granny's father gave it to her. She used to keep her rings in it. We all loved it.'

'Well Katrin loved it too.'

'I thought you promised it to Mum.'

Charlie didn't answer. He was reaching for something under his chair. 'Here they are,' he said, holding up a packet of jelly babies. Gripping the top of the packet with both hands, he tried to tear it open. 'Why do they seal these packets up so tight? It's impossible to open them.'

Amber held out her hand for the packet. 'Shall I try?'

'No. I can do it. Get me the scissors will you? They're in that bottom drawer over there.'

He pointed to a dark brown chest of drawers in the corner of the room. She noticed that the old clock and the wooden lion that used to sit on top of it were no longer there. The drawer was full of papers, but on the top, next to a roll of tape, was a large pair of scissors.

'These look dangerous,' said Amber.

Charlie took hold of the scissors and snipped the top off the packet with one cut, before handing them to Amber. 'Better put them back. I don't want Katrin telling me off for being untidy.'

Amber watched as her Grandad took a yellow jelly baby from the bag and placed it carefully on the table next to his chair. Then he took out another yellow one and another, until there was a row of yellow jelly babies lined up on the table.

'What are you doing?'

'I like the yellow ones best,' he said. 'I eat those first.'

Amber pulled a face. 'That table's really dusty.'

'Stop fussing,' said Charlie. 'A bit of dust never hurt anybody.'

Amber said nothing more, but she thought her Grandad's behaviour was a little strange. No wonder her Mum was worried about him.

* * *

'Is it still raining?' asked Charlie.

As Amber pulled the closed curtains to one side, sharp slants of rain cut across the window like gashes. She looked at the clock on the wall. Her Mum and Dad had been at the supermarket for over two hours. Maybe she should phone them.

'Why is there never any signal here?' she said, thrusting her phone back into her pocket. 'I was going to phone Mum.'

Charlie took another yellow jelly baby from the row on his table and popped it into his mouth. 'Those mobiles are useless. Try the proper phone.'

The landline phone was in the hall on a small table next to a spiky plant that scratched your hands if you came too near. Once white, the phone was now a grubby pale yellow colour with dirty black buttons. Amber picked up the handset, but there was no dialling tone. Carefully avoiding the plant, she put the handset back, but beside the plant was a small pad with a message on it:

WED 6th APRIL
BE READY BY 1PM

Charlie was still eating his yellow jelly babies when she returned with the pad.

'I found this message Grandad. Is it important?'

Charlie took the pad from her and peered at it through his glasses. 'I suppose it must be. What date is it today?'

'April 1st.'

'That's good. I haven't missed it then. Whatever it's about.'

'Don't you remember writing it?'

'Katrin will have written it. She tries to make sure I don't miss any appointments. You'd better put it back by the phone or she'll go mad.'

Amber had never met Katrin but she was beginning to dislike her. It seemed odd that a neighbour would be telling her Grandad to keep the place tidy.

'You don't have to do everything Katrin tells you to Grandad. She's only a neighbour.'

'Well that's where you're wrong,' said Charlie. 'She's more than a neighbour. She's family.'

'What do you mean?'

'Wait 'til you hear what I've found out Amber. It's unbelievable.'

Charlie took the last yellow jelly baby from the table and chewed it slowly.

'Come on then Grandad. Tell me what's so unbelievable.'

'Oh yes,' Charlie said, as if he'd almost forgotten what he was going to say. 'Katrin was very interested in the jewellery box. She said she'd seen one on that antiques show on the telly. When I told her it was a present to Granny from her father William Jackman, she started to laugh.'

'Why did she do that?'

'She said her mother's family were also called Jackman. That means she's related to your Granny and we never knew. It's unbelievable.'

'It certainly *is* unbelievable,' said Amber. 'Is that why she wanted Granny's box?'

'She didn't *ask* for it,' said Charlie. 'I gave it to her. Her parents have died and she has no brothers or sisters, so I thought it would be nice for her to have it.'

'But Grandad, you don't know if any of that's true.'

Charlie leant forward in his chair, his face flushed and angry. 'Are you saying she's a liar?'

Amber was shocked. This wasn't the Grandad she knew. She couldn't remember him ever raising his voice like this. He was like another person.

'I'm not saying she's a liar Grandad, but you need to look at birth certificates to find out if you're related to someone. Like Mum did when she was doing our family history last year. Don't you remember?'

Charlie sat back in his chair, nervously rearranging the cushions behind him. 'Well I don't remember promising Granny's box to your mother.'

Amber swallowed hard. Talking about her Granny made her realise how much she missed her. There was a photo of her Granny on her bedroom wall at home. It was taken two years ago, just before she died. Amber looked at it every night before she went to bed.

'It was Granny's special box,' she whispered.

'Katrin's been like an angel to me since she moved in,' snapped Charlie, 'and if I want to give her the box as a thank you, no-one's going to stop me.'

He picked up his newspaper and began to flick rapidly through the pages, but Amber could tell he wasn't really reading it. She sat on the edge of the sofa, staring at the dirty marks on her Granny's best blue flowered carpet. She couldn't believe her Grandad had given Granny's jewellery box to someone he hardly knew.

She picked up the new sketchbook she'd brought on holiday with her. She had written her name 'Amber Henry' in red letters on the white cover and she was looking forward to filling it with lots of sketches. There wasn't much else to do here except draw but she didn't mind because drawing was her passion. It made her feel better when she was worried and it helped her to think. One of her teachers said she was a talented artist, which made her Mum and Dad really proud, but she drew because she loved it.

Turning to the first blank page, she began to sketch Granny's box from memory. It wasn't a problem because she knew it so well. She used to come to Legna every summer and always loved the jewellery box. She used to love coming to stay with her grandparents but things had changed since her Granny died. Her Grandad's strange behaviour was making her feel uncomfortable and now she was beginning to wish she hadn't come.

* * *

After some time Charlie put down his paper and looked at his watch. 'Your Mum and Dad have been gone a long time. Have they gone to that new supermarket by the bridge?'

Amber put the finishing touches to her sketch and closed the book. 'Yes. Mum said she wanted to see what it was like. I hope they haven't got lost.'

'How can they get lost when there's only one bridge from the Island to the mainland?' said Charlie. 'Milly will have bumped into someone she went to school with. You know how your mother can talk!'

'I wonder where she gets that from Grandad.'

Charlie laughed. 'Are you saying I talk too much young lady?'

Amber leaned back on the sofa, relieved that her Grandad had calmed down. She didn't like upsetting him.

'Do you know what they used to call your mother at school?'

'No. Tell me.'

'They called her Milly the Mouth, because she used to talk all the time!'

Amber grinned. 'She didn't tell me that.'

Charlie sat up in his chair. 'There was a song I used to play on the guitar:

There was an old owl lived in an oak.
The more he saw, the less he spoke.
The less he spoke, the more he heard.
So take a tip from this wise old bird.'

Amber laughed. 'I've not heard that before. Does Mum know it?'

'Of course she does, but it never made any difference. I could tell you all sorts of things about your mother,' said Charlie. 'Like the time when she…'

But before he could finish, a sudden avalanche of hailstones pelted against the window like bullets. Amber rushed to open the curtains. 'Wow. Look at that.'

Charlie reached for the TV remote. 'I'm sure this wasn't forecast.'

A newsreader appeared on the screen:

> *'Extra police officers have been drafted in, and search and rescue teams have been mobilised. Police are warning that Legna Island is now cut off from the mainland, following the collapse of the bridge a short while ago. Hurricane force winds of 70 to 90 miles per hour are sweeping across the...'*

Then everything went black.

Bonzo

By Amber Henry

2

Sounds in the Dark

'Power cut!' shouted Charlie. A rising sense of panic welled up in the pit of Amber's stomach as she took out her phone. There was still no signal but it gave some light.

'What are we going to do Grandad? If the bridge has broken, Mum and Dad can't get here. What if they were driving on the bridge when it collapsed? They could be injured, or worse.'

'Calm down,' Charlie said. 'We don't know anything yet. Go and get the torches. They're in the kitchen under the sink.'

Heavy rain clattered against the front door as Amber passed through the hallway, but she hardly heard it. Her mind was racing with thoughts about what could have happened to her parents. She passed through the dining room without noticing the chilly breeze lifting the edges of the cloth on the table, so when she got to the kitchen, she was surprised to find the back door swinging back and forth in the wind, splashing the floor with rain. Making a grab for the door, she slammed it shut. The key was still in the lock, so she turned it. But then she stopped. There was a strange sound.

Scratch Scratch Scratch

She shone her phone light back into the dining room. Although she couldn't see much, she knew there was something there. She could sense it. She listened again. The room was silent.

'Amber,' called Charlie. 'Have you found those torches yet?'

Finding anything under the kitchen sink wasn't easy. The whole cupboard reeked of damp. She held her breath as she pulled out a bottle of bleach and a metal bucket with a dirty cloth in it. Diving in again she reached to the back and found two torches. The biggest torch was one of those heavy ones; the sort that holds lots of batteries. It shot a bright beam through the kitchen and lit up the dining room as she walked through. In the corner, beside the dining room table, was a tall thin cupboard with its door wide open. She wondered how that could have happened. She was sure it wasn't open when she walked through earlier. The cupboard was empty, apart from a peg bag hanging on the inside of the door, so she closed it and went to join her Grandad.

'Katrin's always telling me to lock the back door,' said Charlie, when Amber told him what had happened, 'but no-one locks their doors on Legna.'

'It wasn't just unlocked Grandad. It was swinging open.'

'Maybe I didn't close it properly.'

'It could be a mouse or something that got in,' said Amber.

'We'll put some cheese down in the morning,' said Charlie. 'See if we can lure it out.'

Amber looked at her phone again. There was still no signal. 'I can't stop thinking about Mum and Dad. What if they were on the bridge when it collapsed?'

'They'll be fine,' said Charlie. 'Lots of people will be stranded on the mainland if the bridge is out of action. Try phoning them again. The proper phone might be working now.'

Amber took a torch and went to the hall, but the landline was still dead.

* * *

Tap Tap Tap

She jumped. 'There's someone else at the door Grandad.'

Charlie wandered in from the lounge. 'I hope it's not that couple again.'

Tap Tap Tap

'Who is it?' he called.

'It's Emil,' said a boy's voice.

A boy aged about fourteen wearing a parka coat and boots stood on the doorstep. He was carrying a large torch. Charlie opened the door wider. 'Come in out of the rain Emil.'

Amber remembered meeting Emil when he moved in across the road last summer, but it was the day they were going home so she had only said hello.

He glanced at Amber as he stepped into the hallway. 'Have you heard about the bridge? It's collapsed. My Mum's still over on the mainland. I've no signal on my mobile and the phones are down so I can't contact her. I'm really worried.'

'My Mum and Dad are on the mainland too,' Amber said. 'They went to the supermarket by the bridge over two hours ago. Do you know if anyone's been hurt?'

'I haven't heard anything,' said Emil. 'My Mum has a café on the mainland. There was a flood alert so she went to put sandbags outside. We've put some outside our house as well.'

Charlie gave a short laugh. 'You won't need sandbags. I've lived on this island all my life and Cliff Road has never flooded before.'

Emil shrugged his shoulders. 'The weather forecast said this is going to be the worst storm on Legna for over a hundred years, so anything could happen. Have you got any sandbags just in case?'

Amber could sense her Grandad's increasing irritation. 'Of course I haven't. I told you we've never had any flooding here. Why would I have sandbags if we've never had any flooding?'

Emil looked a little surprised at such an outburst. He turned towards Amber. 'I've got some spare ones in the wheelbarrow if you change your mind,' he said quietly. 'Do you think Katrin will want some?'

'She's not there,' said Amber. 'She hurt her head this morning and had to go to hospital.'

'Oh, that explains it,' said Emil. 'I saw her going out in a taxi. I wondered why she didn't use Dave's car.'

Amber wanted to ask him what he knew about Katrin, but this wasn't the right time.

A blast of cold wind filled the hall as Emil opened the door. 'If you hear the flood siren you need to go upstairs, in case the water does reach here.'

'Are you on your own?' said Amber.

'Yes, but I'll be alright.'

'You can stay here with us if you're worried, can't he Grandad?'

Charlie's irritated face softened a little. 'Of course he can.'

Emil thought for a moment. 'I was a bit worried when I heard we were cut off, but I think I'll be OK.'

Charlie patted Emil on the back. 'You know where we are if you change your mind.'

'Thanks,' said Emil as he left. 'I'll let you know if I hear anything more.'

'Don't look so scared,' Charlie said as he closed the door. 'The storm will be over soon. If we can't use the bridge for a while they'll have to bring the ferry back.'

'I'm not bothered about the bridge Grandad. I'm worried about Mum and Dad.'

Charlie walked back towards the lounge. 'They'll be fine.'

Amber felt annoyed. Her Grandad didn't seem to be taking things seriously. How could he be so sure everything was going to be alright? There was another flash of lightning as she entered the lounge. The storm wasn't over yet.

'Do you think we should move things off the floor Grandad?'

'What for?'

'In case we get flooded.'

Charlie threw open the lounge curtains, like an actor on a stage. 'We won't get flooded. Look at that storm Amber. It's spectacular!'

Amber had to agree. She had never seen a storm like it. The rain fell in sheets. Thunder boomed and lightning cut zig zags across the sky. But in that brief moment, Amber had a strange feeling that something even more terrible was about to happen.

* * *

'I'm hungry,' said Charlie closing the curtains. 'Make us a sandwich will you Amber? My eyesight's not good in this light.'

'How can you think of eating when things are so bad?'

'We don't know if things are bad yet.'

'How bad do things have to get Grandad? Even if Mum and Dad are alright, we've no light, no heat and no phone, and Mum said there's hardly any food in the kitchen.'

'I'm sure there's enough to make a sandwich. There's no point starving is there? And anyway it'll take your mind off things.'

Amber took a torch and stormed off to the kitchen. Pretending everything was alright was hard to take. Then there was another small problem. Despite having a packed lunch every day at school, making sandwiches was not something Amber had ever done. It's not that she didn't know how to make them, it was just that her Mum always did it. There was a time when she would ask to help in the kitchen, but Mum and Dad were always too busy to show her how to do things, so she gave up asking.

It wasn't hard to find her way round the kitchen in the dark. It hadn't changed in all the years she had been coming to her Grandad's house, so even though she'd never prepared any food in there, she knew exactly where to find the bread bin. Opening it up she discovered half a loaf of white sliced bread with curled crusts. She took out four slices and placed them on the nearby bread board, but when she looked in the fridge for something to put on the bread it was almost empty. All she found was a packet of cheese, a stick of limp celery, a carton of milk and a jar of jam. She didn't find it too difficult to make two cheese sandwiches, even in the torchlight, but as she put them on the plates she heard a thud, like someone had bumped into something.

'Grandad? Is that you?'

She listened hard. There was no answer.

Back in the dining room, she shone the light on the cupboard, but the door was shut, just as she had left it.

It didn't take Charlie long to finish his sandwich, but Amber didn't feel like eating. She was too nervous, and anyway the bread smelt strange and the cheese was dry and tasteless.

'You'd better take the plates back to the kitchen if you've finished,' said Charlie. 'And make sure you wash them up, otherwise Katrin will be on to me.'

'I'll take them back later.'

'Well make sure you do.'

Charlie sat uneasily, drumming his fingers on the arm of his chair. 'Shine that big torch over here Amber. I need a drink.' He got up and took a bottle of whisky out of a cupboard and poured some into a glass. Then he took out a large bottle of lemonade. Amber watched his hand shaking as he tilted the heavy bottle towards the glass and filled it to the brim. Drops splashed onto the carpet as he carried it back to his chair, but he didn't seem to notice.

They sat in silence. All they could hear was the sound of the rain against the window and the never-ending tick of the clock on the wall. There was nothing else to do but wait.

* * *

Then it happened. The piercing wail of the flood siren. A sound so shrill it made their ears hurt.

'The sea wall's broken!' shouted Amber. She leapt to her feet. 'We'd better go upstairs,' she said, grabbing her precious sketchbook.

Charlie remained in his chair, folding his arms defiantly. 'I'm not going anywhere. The flood won't reach here.'

She didn't know what to do. She had never known her Grandad be so stubborn before. There was a few minutes of silence, but when the water started to gush along Cliff Road, he changed his mind. 'Maybe we'd better go upstairs after all.'

Shining their torches out of Charlie's bedroom window, they stood close together, watching the water flowing along the street like a raging river. It reminded Amber of a giant serpent, licking it's tongue into every corner of the gardens, consuming everything in its path. Neither of them spoke, but they both knew that if the water broke into the house, there would be no-one around to help them.

It was Charlie who first noticed a change. 'Look. The rain's stopping.'

Slowly, very slowly, the water began to lose its power. The wave of water that had swept so violently along the road, gradually began to disappear. And that's when the siren stopped.

'Thank goodness,' said Charlie. 'That siren was ear-splitting. It's given me a headache.'

'At least the house was saved,' said Amber, closing the curtains.

'I've never seen anything like that water,' said Charlie. 'It's shaken me up seeing that. Let's go down and make a cup of tea.'

'We can't do that Grandad. The power's off.'

CRASH

Charlie gripped Amber's arm. 'What was that?'

'It sounded like it was coming from the dining room,' said Amber.

Charlie reached for the walking stick propped against his bedroom wall. 'I don't know what's down there, but with a crash like that, it's definitely not a mouse.'

Holding the stick in one hand, and a torch in the other, he led the way down the stairs. The dining room door was ajar. Using his foot, he slowly pushed it open. Then, holding the stick up ready to strike, he burst into the room only to find there was nothing there.

They stood still and listened. There was another sound. One that Amber recognised.

Scratch Scratch Scratch

Charlie put his head round the open kitchen door. 'Amber. Look at this.'

In the middle of the kitchen floor, beside the over-turned metal bucket, was a large brown rabbit with long floppy ears and huge eyes. It looked tense as it sat there making a little grunting noise.

Charlie gently scooped it up and held it against his shirt. 'And where have you come from my little friend?'

'So that's what I heard earlier,' said Amber.

Charlie stroked the rabbit's furry body. 'You're someone's lovely pet, aren't you, but I've no idea who you belong to.'

'It's got a collar on,' said Amber. She read out the name. 'BONZO.'

Although a little thin, the rabbit seemed well cared for and made no effort to escape from Charlie's arms. He handed it to Amber. 'Here, you hold it while I find something to put it in. We don't want it running round the house.'

'*I* can't hold it. I don't know anything about rabbits.'

'It's easy. I'll show you. Hold it under its hind quarters and support it's back, then put its feet against your chest. They feel more secure with four feet against something.'

Its softness surprised her as she took it with awkward hands.

'Hold it more firmly,' said Charlie. 'So it feels safe.'

'How do you know all this Grandad?'

'I used to have a rabbit many years ago.'

Charlie emptied some things out of a large plastic box he found in a cupboard. Then he put some newspaper inside the box and placed a bowl of water at one end, before putting in the celery from the fridge.

'It'll probably jump out after a while,' he said, as Amber lowered the rabbit into the box. 'But if we close the kitchen door tonight it won't come to any harm.'

They watched the rabbit nibbling the celery. It seemed to be enjoying it.

'What if there's another flood?' said Amber. 'The water might get into the house next time. We can't leave the rabbit down here.'

'We'll put it upstairs in the back bedroom if you're worried. There's no bed in there at the moment, so there'll be room.'

'What's happened to the bed?'

'I sold it.'

'Why?'

'I needed space for all my new boxes.'

'What boxes?'

‘Katrin packed all my ornaments in boxes. She wrapped them in that bubbly stuff. She said I had too many ornaments and the house looked cluttered.’

‘But you like all your ornaments.’

Charlie shrugged his shoulders. ‘Some of them are worth a lot of money. They’ll be safer in boxes.’

‘So where are Mum and Dad going to sleep?’

‘I’m sure they’ll be fine on the sofa. It opens out into a bed.’

Finding the rabbit had taken her mind off her parents for a while, but once it was safely upstairs in the back bedroom with the door closed, Amber began to worry again.

‘Do you think Mum and Dad are alright?’

‘I’m sure they’ll be fine,’ said Charlie stepping into his bedroom. ‘You’ve left your book on the bed.’

Amber took the sketchbook from him. ‘Should we see if Emil is OK?’

‘He’ll be alright. He’s a capable lad. Don’t worry. If the phone’s working tomorrow we can ring your Mum.’

He handed Amber the biggest torch. ‘It’s late and we need to get some sleep. Take this and be careful. Those attic stairs are really steep.’

* * *

Amber always slept in the attic bedroom when she came to stay. She liked being high up in the roof like a bird looking down from the sky. If she looked out of the window, she could see into her Grandad’s back garden and the garden next door and if she looked way into the distance, she could see the sea.

She used to look forward to sleeping in the attic – it was so cosy and warm – but tonight, as she climbed the narrow stairs, she began to wish she could sleep somewhere else. There seemed to be no air and everything smelt of dust, making her cough. When Granny was alive she used to keep the house so clean.

Placing her sketchbook and the torch on the bedside table, she went across to the window and pulled at the catch. For a moment she thought she wouldn't be able to open it but after a while it began to move, letting in a waft of fresh air.

Thinking she probably wouldn't sleep, she kicked off her shoes and leant back against the thin pillows on the bed. The attic room looked the same as it always did: the wonky pink wardrobe in the corner, the little desk and chair that had once belonged to her mother, the white dressing table. She looked again. The antique mirror with the flowery handle and the china cat with the sparkly blue eyes were missing from the dressing table. She wondered if Katrin had packed them up in one of the boxes. At least the paper wings were still hanging on the wall. Her Grandad had made them one summer when she slipped on some rocks and broke her leg. He made them for her while she was in hospital. She remembered how Granny had pushed her in the wheelchair to his shed, so she could see what he had made.

'You may not be able to walk for a while,' he said as he lifted the wings up to the sunlight. 'But if you look at these wings, your mind will fly like an angel.'

They were too fragile to take home, so Grandad hung them on the wall. They still looked beautiful even though they were now old and gathering dust. Maybe she would try to sketch them. It wouldn't be easy and they might not look exactly like the ones on the wall, but she liked to sketch difficult things. Maybe tomorrow. She turned off the torch and closed her eyes. The wind sounded like it was singing.

* * *

The next thing she remembered was waking up feeling cold. She took out her phone and looked at the time. It was half past three in the morning. The wind still moaned through the open window, but underneath the wind she heard another sound: a clawing, scraping sound, as if someone was trying to get in. She looked towards the window and blinked hard. Was that a shadow behind the curtains? A shadow in the shape of a hand?

She sat up and turned on the torch. 'It's just my imagination,' she said to herself. But the sound of the scraping made her skin prickle and the shadows on the window made her stomach lurch. There was no way she could sleep until she found out what it was. Taking a deep breath, she slid off the bed and went towards the window. Then with a sudden movement she grabbed one of the curtains and yanked it to one side. There was a rip as the thin material tore away from the pole, but outside in the waving wind she saw the tip of a branch, scratching its long bony fingers along the glass. *Scrape Scrape Scrape.*

With a sense of relief, she closed the window and changed into her pyjamas, telling herself off for being so stupid. Turning off the torch she snuggled under the duvet and tried to go back to sleep, but it wasn't long before her thoughts turned to her parents again. She tried to imagine what it would be like if she became an orphan. Who would look after her? Charlie was her only grandparent but he wasn't well and she had no aunts or uncles.

Tossing and turning in the little bed, all she could do was listen to the wind as it moaned outside the window and hope that her parents were safe. At least she thought it was the wind she could hear, but as she lay there in the darkness, it began to sound like something else – something that could have been the wind, and yet it was somehow different. Was the wind playing tricks on her again?

She tried her best to ignore it, but when it became even louder she sat up and listened more carefully. This was definitely a different kind of sound. It was more like a human sound, like someone crying. It sounded as if it was very near and yet how could it be? On and on it went. She thought it would never stop. She lay back down and pulled the duvet over her ears. Maybe she was wrong. Maybe it was the wind after all.

Face at the Window

By Amber Henry

3

Face at the Window

'Amber!' called Charlie. 'Where's the rabbit?'

She woke with a start.

'Amber. Come down here.'

Squinting at the bright daylight, she leapt out of bed and ran down the stairs. Charlie was in the back bedroom staring at the empty rabbit box.

'What have you done with the rabbit Amber?'

'I haven't done anything with it.'

'It's nowhere in this room. Are you sure you haven't been in here since we closed the door last night?'

'I'm absolutely sure.'

'Well the door was wide open this morning and a rabbit can't open a door on its own, can it?'

Amber froze. 'Are you saying someone's been in the house?'

'You stay here.' said Charlie. 'Put something heavy against the door and don't open it until I tell you to. I'm going to search the house. Whoever came in last night could still be here.'

Amber could hear her heart beating a little louder than usual. 'Why would anyone still be here?'

Charlie lowered his voice. 'Why would anyone steal a rabbit? There are some strange people around these days and I'm not taking any chances.'

'I don't want to stay here on my own,' said Amber.

‘OK,’ said Charlie. ‘But keep behind me and if we find anyone, I want you to run out of the house as fast as you can. Do you understand?’

Amber nodded.

‘Grandad,’ she whispered. ‘Is the phone in your bedroom working? We should call the police.’

‘They can’t get here if the bridge is broken Amber. We’re on our own. Keep close.’

Amber tried to ignore the churning in her stomach as she followed her Grandad down the stairs.

There was no-one in the hallway and no-one in the lounge, so they made their way back across the hall to the dining room. Nothing had been disturbed. There were no broken windows and no smashed doors. Everything seemed to be as it should be. But when they reached the kitchen, they noticed the back door swinging open in the wind, just as it had done the night before. The cold breeze wafted over Amber’s skin, making her realise she had been sweating.

‘That door was definitely locked last night,’ she said.

Charlie shut the door and locked it. ‘It looks like they’ve gone.’

‘How did they get in if the door was locked?’ said Amber. ‘There’s no sign of a break in. They must have already been inside the house when you locked the door. That’s the only explanation.’

‘Which means they were in the house when we had the power cut.’

The thought of someone watching her in the darkness sent a shiver down Amber’s spine. Then something else occurred to her. ‘The door to that tall cupboard in the dining room was open after I found the torches Grandad. Could someone have been hiding in there?’

Charlie went into the dining room and opened the cupboard door. ‘If the person was small enough then maybe…’

Amber stepped inside the cupboard. 'I can get in easily. If I pull on the peg bag on the back of the door, I can close it from the inside. It's beginning to make sense now.'

'It makes no sense at all to me,' said Charlie. 'Why would anyone go to all that trouble just to steal a rabbit?'

'Maybe they didn't steal it.'

'What do you mean?'

'Maybe it was their rabbit. It's not stealing if you take back what belongs to you is it?'

'In that case, why didn't they knock on the door and ask for it?'

'I don't know,' said Amber.

'It may be nothing to do with the rabbit,' said Charlie. 'They might have been trying to steal my ornaments in the back bedroom and left the door open.'

'A burglar?'

'Exactly. But I tell you something Amber. Whoever was here last night will still be somewhere on this Island. Now the bridge has collapsed there's no way anyone can leave.'

'You'd better see if anything is missing from the boxes.'

Charlie bent down in front of the washing machine. 'I need to check something else first.'

Amber looked puzzled. 'What are you doing?'

Reaching far back into the drum of the machine, Charlie took out a large red biscuit tin and placed it on the work surface. When he opened the lid, all Amber could see were bank notes: bundles of twenty pound notes, bound together with elastic bands.

Charlie smiled. 'I knew this was a good place to hide my savings.'

Amber had never seen so much money. 'Why have you done that Grandad? It needs to go in a bank.' She was trying hard to keep calm, like her Mum always did when things went wrong, but her Grandad was making things difficult. 'It's not safe to keep all that money in a tin.'

'That's not what Katrin said.'

'Katrin? Does she know about the tin?'

'Of course she does.' Charlie put the lid back on the tin. 'She was the one who told me to take my money out of the bank. She said you can't trust banks these days. We had to take it out of the bank in small amounts, so the bank staff wouldn't ask difficult questions.'

'Does Katrin know where you keep it?'

'Oh yes. She told me off. She said I should give it to her to look after. I might do that the next time I pay her.'

'Pay her? What do you pay her for?'

'She gets my shopping and does the cleaning,' said Charlie. 'I don't know what I'd do without her. She's an angel.'

Amber was amazed. The house didn't look as if Katrin had cleaned it and if she'd been shopping for food, there wasn't much of it left.

'Come on,' said Charlie, putting the tin back in the washing machine. 'Let's check the boxes.'

Amber's mind was reeling as they headed for the back bedroom. The more she heard about Katrin the less she trusted her.

'Are they still sealed up?' said Amber, picking up a box. 'This one's sealed but it feels empty.'

'Katrin took some of the ornaments away for cleaning,' said Charlie. 'There may only be a couple in that box.'

'Cleaning? Why would she need to take them away to clean them?'

Amber picked up another box. 'This one's the same. How many ornaments did she take away?'

'She had a couple of bags full when she left. I expect she'll be bringing them back soon.'

Amber had a horrible feeling that all the boxes were empty.

'I don't think anyone's been in here,' said Charlie. 'Why don't you get us some breakfast while I check the other rooms.'

* * *

Breakfast was easy to make but not so easy to eat. The only thing left was stale bread and jam.

'There's nothing to eat here,' said Amber.

'Is there nothing in the freezer?' said Charlie.

Amber opened the freezer door. 'Only ice cream, but the power's been off so it might not be good to eat.'

'I'll make some tea?' said Charlie.

'You can't Grandad.'

Charlie looked confused. 'What are you talking about?'

Amber sighed. 'The power is off. You can't boil the kettle.'

Charlie chuckled to himself. 'My memory's getting bad.'

Amber knew he couldn't help it, but having to remind her Grandad about everything was getting very annoying.

There was a knock at the front door. Amber got up. 'I'll get it.'

It was Emil.

'I've brought this cool box full of food from Mum's café,' he said. 'She brought it home the other day. It needs eating up and there's too much for me.'

'Thanks,' said Amber as they walked to the kitchen. 'We're really short of food at the moment.'

She put the box on the kitchen table to show her Grandad, but he wasn't pleased.

'That's kind of you Emil but we don't need all this food. We've got plenty in the freezer.'

Amber sighed. 'There's none there Grandad. We've just looked.'

'Have we? Never mind.' said Charlie. 'Someone will start the ferry boat again soon, so we can get to the shops on the mainland. That's what they used years ago, before the bridge was built.'

'OK. I'll leave the food anyway. See you later,' said Emil. 'I'm going down to the sea front, to see if I can find out what's happening.'

Then he paused. There was a faint whirring sound in the distance.

They ran out of the kitchen door and up the garden path, leaving Charlie filling the kettle for tea.

Amber pointed upwards. 'It's a helicopter. There it is.'

They waved as the speck in the sky came closer, but within seconds the helicopter swerved back towards the sea and disappeared into the clouds.

A high hedge separated Charlie's garden from Katrin's, but from the end of Charlie's garden you could see the backs of both houses. Amber looked up at Katrin's attic window and thought how bright the curtains were compared to the dull beige ones in her own window. But then, out of the corner of her eye, she thought she saw the bright curtains twitch. She blinked. Maybe she had imagined it. Then she thought she saw something else. Something that looked like a small face at the window. It was only there for a second and then it was gone. At least she thought that's what she saw.

'Maybe we'll get some help now the helicopters are coming,' said Emil.

'What?' said Amber. 'Oh, er. Yeah.'

'What's wrong Amber? You look like you've seen a ghost.'

'I was wondering... Could anyone else be in Katrin's house?'

'Only Dave but he's away at the moment. Why?'

'Nothing.'

'What? Tell me.'

'You'll think I'm stupid.'

'No, I won't. Tell me.'

'I thought I saw a face in Katrin's attic window.'

Emil looked up at the window. 'It was probably the light playing tricks on you.' He paused. 'Or maybe it was the ghost of the Angel's Child.' He grinned as if he was joking, but Amber saw the look in his eyes.

'I'd better go,' he added, walking away rather too quickly.

Amber ran after him. 'No wait Emil. What did you mean about the Angel's Child?'

'I had you scared then didn't I?' he said. 'It's just an old story. Katrin's house is supposed to be haunted. The Angel's Child died there. Ask your Grandad. He'll tell you all about it.'

* * *

Amber couldn't believe how much food was in the cool box. There were pasties, pizza slices, samosas and salad, and a box containing the most delicious looking iced buns.

'It's really kind of Emil to give us all this,' said Amber, as she sunk her teeth into her second slice of pizza. After eating her Grandad's stale bread, every mouthful of cheesy pizza tasted like heaven even if it *was* cold.

Charlie wasn't impressed. 'It's only left-overs from Julia's café.'

'Well he didn't have to share it with us, did he?'

'I suppose not.' He took a pasty from the cool box. 'I used to have these when I went to Julia's café. I used to walk over the bridge every Saturday morning, have a pasty and a chat with Emil and then walk back.'

'Don't you go any more then?'

'I don't go out much these days.'

'Why not?'

I'm not good at finding my way around. That's why I need Katrin. She takes me places and helps me with things.'

‘I’m sure Mum and Dad would help you if you asked them.’

‘How can they help when you live 200 miles away?’

‘Mum phones you every night doesn’t she?’

‘That’s very nice but it’s no good if I need someone to drive me to the bank is it? Do you want one of these iced buns?’

Amber kept thinking about the face in the window, but she had been waiting for the right moment to ask her Grandad. She took a bun. Now seemed to be a good time.

‘Is there anyone staying with Katrin and Dave at the moment?’

‘Not that I know of,’ said Charlie. ‘Katrin’s there on her own most of the time. Dave’s away a lot. He’s a deep-sea diver on the oil rigs. It’s dangerous work but Katrin says he earns lots of money. They’re saving up to buy a bigger house.’

Charlie bit into his bun as if it were the best thing he had ever tasted. Amber noticed how thin he was and wondered if he was getting enough to eat.

‘Dave’s not from Legna,’ he continued, ‘but his family used to live here many years ago. His great great grandfather used to be the lighthouse keeper. Of course there were more cottages here then – mostly fishermen and their families. Anyway, Dave wanted to buy Lighthouse Cottage up on the cliffs. He was going to do it up and then live in it but he changed his mind.’

‘Why?’

‘He found out it was in danger of falling into the sea. But Katrin didn’t like it anyway.’

‘I don’t remember seeing a lighthouse on the Island,’

‘The lighthouse itself fell into the sea years ago,’ Charlie said through mouthfuls of cake. ‘One minute it was there and the next it was down the cliff. Coastal erosion they call it. They say one day the whole island will disappear into the sea.’

‘Do Dave and Katrin ever have any visitors?’ said Amber, trying to keep her thoughts on track.

‘I’ve not seen any,’ said Charlie, helping himself to another bun. ‘Why?’

‘I thought I saw someone looking out of Katrin’s attic window.’

Charlie put down his bun and stared ahead of him. He looked deep in thought. ‘I knew she was still there,’ he whispered.

Light house cottage

By Amber Henry

4

Tears on the Cliff

The ring of the landline phone sent Amber rushing to the hallway.

'Mum? Mum?'

The sound of her mother's voice made her want to cry, but she fought back the tears. 'Yes. Yes. We're fine Mum. Are you OK?'

By now Charlie was standing beside her, craning his neck to hear what was being said. Then the line began to crackle. 'What? I can't hear you very well. What did you say about Dad? OK. Bye Mum. Love you too.'

'What's happened?' asked Charlie.

'They're both in hospital,' said Amber holding back the tears. 'They were driving towards the bridge when it collapsed. Another car crashed into the back of them. They're both injured but Dad is worse. He's going to have an operation this afternoon and I can't even get there to visit him.'

'How bad is he?'

'I don't know. The line was crackly and Mum said she had to go. She's going to ring tomorrow if the phone's still working.'

Charlie put his arm round Amber. 'Don't worry. Your Dad's in good hands.'

Amber brushed away a tear. 'Mum said we had to stay here and look after each other.'

‘And that’s exactly what we will do,’ said Charlie. ‘The weather’s brightening up a bit. Let’s go for a walk and see if we can see what’s happening with the bridge.’

* * *

The sun broke through the clouds as they set out along Cliff Road towards the sea and although there was a strong breeze, it felt mild. After taking his waterproof jacket from the peg by the door, Charlie put on his white hat with a big brim, which he held with one hand to keep it from coming off in the wind. Amber put on the new jacket that her Dad had bought her before they left home. She loved it because it was her favourite camouflage pattern, but today she loved it even more because it reminded her of her Dad.

‘What better way to spend a Sunday afternoon?’ said Charlie.

‘It’s Saturday Grandad.’

‘Is it? Katrin gave me a calendar, but I seem to have lost it.’

‘Mum says things always seem better when the sun shines.’

‘Milly’s right for once.’

After walking a short distance down the road, they came to a sign for a footpath.

‘We can turn off here,’ said Charlie. ‘You get a better view of the bridge from up on the cliffs.’

‘I don’t think I’ve ever been on this path,’ said Amber.

‘It’s not safe for children that’s why. But you’re older now. You’ll be fine.’

The path was flat and wide at first but as they approached the edge of the cliffs it became steep and narrow. Tiny loose rocks skidded under their shoes as they climbed.

Charlie squashed his hat into his jacket pocket as the sun went behind a cloud. ‘Be careful Amber. Look where you’re going and take your time.’

It made Amber realise how her Grandad had changed. Only last summer she had struggled to keep up with his giant strides, but now his body was thinner, his steps careful and measured. Amber was now the one leading the way.

As they reached the highest point they found themselves standing between two bays. The wind was stronger here. Whining and whistling, it came in gusts that made their eyes water.

'Stay in the middle of the path,' warned Charlie. 'It's dangerous near the edge in this wind.'

To their left was a small sandy bay, with rocks jutting out on either side. To their right was a larger bay with holiday homes along the sea front and a road that led to the bridge. Even from high up on the cliffs they could see the damage caused by the flooding. Garden bins had been flung on their sides and the roof of one of the houses had a huge hole in it.

'Look across to the mainland,' said Charlie. 'You can see the end of the bridge dangling in the sea. Anyone going over that when it broke wouldn't stand a chance.'

Amber thought about her parents. She couldn't wait to see them again.

'Why do you think it collapsed Grandad? Was it very old?'

'It was built during the last war,' said Charlie. 'Legna Island was a lookout post. There was a hut on the cliff top used by the soldiers. They built it where the fishermen's cottages used to be, but it's gone now.'

'Let's walk on a bit further,' said Amber. 'I don't want to look at that bridge anymore.'

Turning their backs on the larger bay, they continued along the path until they were directly above the smaller bay. Although it felt good to be out of the house, the path was steep and rugged and it wasn't long before Charlie became breathless. Amber stopped. Ahead was a wooden bench.

'Do you want to sit down a minute?' she asked.

Charlie paused, steadying himself against the wind. He stared at the bench, but he didn't answer.

Amber looked at his troubled face. Something was wrong but she wasn't sure what. 'Are you alright Grandad?'

He stepped slowly towards the bench and sat down. His breathing was fast and shallow. 'I'm fine.'

Amber turned away, her eyes drawn to the sparkling waves on the beach below them. 'It's so beautiful.'

'Legna Bay,' said Charlie after a while. 'It may be beautiful but it's deadly.'

'How can something so beautiful be deadly?'

It was several seconds before Charlie answered. 'You can walk to Legna Bay when the tide's out, but the sea comes back in very quickly. There are rip tides that will cut you off and leave you stranded on the rocks.'

Amber took a step closer to the cliff edge, but that was as far as she dare go. 'What's that down there in the sand? It looks like the ribs of a huge whale.'

'It's the wooden timbers of the Bella Rose. Many lives were lost when that ship went down.'

'Was it a sailing ship?'

'Yes. It was taking Irish families to America, but it crashed on the rocks and they never got there. I used to know a song about it but I've forgotten it now.'

'Why were they all going to America?'

'There was a famine in Ireland. They had nothing to eat. America was a land of plenty, or so they thought.'

'It seems a shame to leave it buried like that.'

'There are quicksands around the ship. Anyone trying to dig it out would be swallowed up by the sand.'

'Did all the people drown?'

'Most of them did,' said Charlie. 'If you're not rescued

quickly from the sea you'll die of cold, but a few people survived. The most famous was a mother who managed to swim to the rocks with her baby daughter on her back before she died.'

'That's sad. What happened to the child?'

'She was rescued by an angel who lived in the cave down there in the rocks.'

Amber pulled a face. 'I thought this was a true story.'

'It is,' said Charlie. 'The Angel named the child Bella, after the ship. She made a home for the child in the cave, but when the Islanders found out, they took the child away. The Angel became angry and put a curse on the Islanders. She said unless Bella was brought back, anyone entering the cave would die.'

'She wasn't a very nice angel then was she?'

'She just wanted her child back.'

'But it wasn't her child,' said Amber. 'I know it's only a story, but just because you save someone's life, doesn't mean you own them.'

'Whenever there's a thunderstorm,' said Charlie, 'you can hear the Angel crying for her child.'

'That's silly Grandad. Thunder doesn't sound anything like someone crying.'

'It's not that sort of crying,' said Charlie. 'It means she's crying out in anger.'

'So is this a story or was there really a child rescued from the ship?'

'Stories always have some truth in them if you look hard enough,' said Charlie.

'Yes, but was there really a child whose mother died?'

'Oh yes. A little girl.'

'What happened to her?'

'She was given to a couple living at number 3 Cliff Road.'

'Katrin's house?'

'That's right.'

'So the child was OK in the end then?'

'Not really,' said Charlie. 'They say she loved the Angel and died of a broken heart.'

'So that's why Emil said Katrin's house was haunted,' said Amber.

'The ghost of the Angel's Child still lives in that house,' said Charlie, 'and until someone takes the ghost of that child back to the cave, the curse remains.'

'That doesn't make sense. How can you take a ghost anywhere?'

'Have you ever seen a ghost?' asked Charlie. 'There's more to them than you may think.'

Amber thought about the face in Katrin's window, but she didn't believe in ghosts.

'Can I ask you something Grandad? Was there anyone staying at Katrin's house when she fell over and banged her head?'

Charlie didn't answer. He was crying.

'Grandad what's wrong?'

He stood up to reveal a small brass plate fixed to the back of the bench. Amber read the words engraved on it.

'IN LOVING MEMORY OF BENJAMIN JONES.
Taken from us too soon.'

'Who's Benjamin Jones?'

Charlie took out a tissue and blew his nose. 'He was my big brother.'

'I didn't even know you had a brother.'

'I don't like to talk about it. It was a long time ago.'

'How old was he when he died?'

'Twelve.'

Amber waited. She sensed he was about to say more and she was right.

'Benny was obsessed with the Angel. He was always drawing wings and writing poems about the Angel's Child.'

Charlie's face lit up as he continued to talk about his brother. 'He was a clever boy. He taught me how to make the most beautiful paper wings. He was the one who took me to Angel's Cave. It was our secret place. No-one else dare go in there because of the curse, but we didn't believe in it.'

Amber couldn't understand why anyone would want to play in a cold dark cave. 'What did you do in there?'

'We used to draw things and write secret messages on the walls.'

'How did you manage to draw in a dark cave?'

Charlie grinned. 'We once tried to sneak a torch out of the house but Mum saw it and wanted to know what we wanted it for. In the end we got some candles. I loved the candles. They made the cave look wonderful.'

Charlie licked the corner of a tissue and wiped some marks off the brass plate.

'How did he die?' asked Amber when he had finished.

'The Angel's curse.'

'You can't die from a curse Grandad.'

'That's what we thought when we played in the cave, but we were wrong.'

'What exactly happened to him?'

Charlie dropped his voice and stared out to sea. 'I can't tell you.'

'Why not?'

'Because I can't remember. I was only a young boy when he died. I know his body was found at the foot of the rocks beneath Angel's Cave, but I can't remember anything else. My mother would never talk about it. She was convinced it was the Angel's curse that killed him.'

'That doesn't make sense,' said Amber. 'If you went into the cave with Benny, why didn't the curse kill you as well?'

But Charlie wasn't listening. His eyes were still wet with tears. There was nothing more Amber could say. She found it hard to imagine her Grandad as a little boy, with an older brother and parents. She put her arm through his and squeezed it gently as they sat together on the bench, watching the waves tumbling back and forth on the beach below. But it was too cold to sit for long and the wind was getting stronger. 'We should go Grandad.'

'I keep trying to remember what happened to Benny,' said Charlie. 'I think I might have been there when he died.'

'What makes you think that?'

'I can picture him lying on the beach but the details are missing. It's like my memory has a black hole in it.'

'I'm sure we can find out what happened to him.'

'How can we do that? It was years ago.'

'It must have been in the papers. You can look at old copies online now.'

Charlie stood up. 'We'll talk about it later. Let me show you Lighthouse Cottage before we go back. It's at the end of this path.'

* * *

They carried on along the edge of the cliffs until the path came to an end beside a small cottage. Amber knew the cottage was old but she wasn't expecting it to look so sad. The roof sagged like some large creature had sat on it, its windows banging in the wind. It seemed so lonely and bleak, like the world had forgotten it.

Crunching their way through rubble and broken glass, they walked round the building until they came to a door with peeling paint. Nailed to the door was a sign saying *DANGER KEEP OUT* in large letters. It creaked as Amber pushed it open.

'Better not go in,' said Charlie. 'It's not safe.'

Amber peered inside as the wind whistled through the gaping windows, crying like someone precious had gone.

She shivered. 'I don't want to go in.'

'It's been empty for as long as I can remember,' said Charlie. 'Benny and I used to play in there if the weather was bad.'

'I don't know why you'd want to play in there. It's creepy.'

'We thought it was an exciting place.'

'It doesn't look very exciting now does it?'

'It was once used by smugglers,' said Charlie. 'There are tunnels leading down from the cellar to Angel's Cave. The Islanders used the tunnels to bring brandy and rum from the ships, so no-one would see them.

'Why did they do that?'

'The government was trying to raise money to go to war, so they made everyone pay them something for each barrel of brandy or rum they brought into the country on the ships. It's called a tax.'

'So people tried to sneak the barrels in before anyone from the government could ask them for money?'

'That's about it.'

'So everyone on Legna was a smuggler?'

'Not everyone. It was too risky. The customs men used to come to the cottage looking for the stuff. The smugglers would be sent to jail or worse if they were caught.'

'So where did they hide it?'

'In the graves.'

Amber was horrified. 'What? In graves with dead bodies in?'

Charlie laughed. 'No not real graves. They buried it all in holes the size of graves and just as deep. It took them a long time but there were more people living here then and they would all help, even the kids. In fact the kids had a really important job to do.'

'Like what?'

'If you bury something, the ground gets disturbed and there would be footprints round it. Anyone looking at the ground the next day would be sure to find where they'd been digging. So when they finished burying the stuff, they got the kids to dance all over the ground, so there were lots of footprints everywhere.'

'Wow. I'd like to have seen that. I bet it was fun.'

Charlie laughed. 'Maybe it was, but it usually happened in the middle of the night so the kids must've been tired the next day. Someone wrote a song about it called 'Mulberry Smuggler.' It's in that book I've lost.'

'Why were they called Mulberry Smugglers?'

'That's the song the children used to sing while they danced on the ground: 'Here we go round the mulberry bush.'

Amber smiled. 'I used to love that.'

She turned her back on the cottage. 'So where was the lighthouse?'

Charlie pointed to the edge of the cliff. 'It was over there until the sea took it.'

Buffeted by the strengthening wind, they stood together, staring out across the vast ocean.

'Is this where the soldiers were in the war?' said Amber.

'That's right. They built their hut on the site of some derelict cottages that used to be here. It's a good lookout point. You can see for miles.'

Amber shielded her eyes with her hand. 'It looks like it goes on forever.'

Charlie looked up at the sky. 'We'd better set off back. I don't like the look of those clouds at all.'

Campervan
By Amber Henry

5

Blood on the Floor

Charlie was right. As they set off back along the cliff path, the sky blackened and the wind hurled giant waves against the rocks. Amber tied her hood tight around her face, against the sudden icy chill. Charlie led the way but as he walked Amber saw his legs tremble with each step and when he finally stopped by the bench, she heard the wheezing of his breath.

'Wait a minute,' he said, fumbling for a tissue. 'I can't see the path. There's rain in my eyes.'

Amber looked up. There was no rain. But the sky told her it was on its way.

'You walk in front,' said Charlie. 'But don't go too near the edge. People have died falling from this path.'

* * *

It wasn't long before Amber felt the first spots of rain on her face. By the time they reached the end of the cliff path the clouds hung heavy like a black blanket, bringing large raindrops that bounced off the ground.

Charlie pulled out a key on a silver key ring as they approached the house.

'Hurry up Grandad. I'm soaking.'

'This isn't my key,' he said as he tried to push it into the key hole.

'Well whose is it then?' said Amber, bending her head to avoid the rain.

Charlie stared at the key. 'I think this is the key Katrin gave me before she went in the taxi. She said I needed it to look after the Angel's Child. I wondered where I'd put it.'

'What? Why did she say that?'

Charlie fished in his pockets again, pulling out a different key. 'This is mine.'

He unlocked the door and walked in. 'Now where did I put my slippers?'

Amber flicked the light switch in the hall. 'Hurray,' she cried. 'The power's back on.'

She was about to close the door when she heard the sound of a car engine. Seconds later, the same blue camper van from the other day came to a stop outside the house. The woman put down the window as the rain finally stopped.

'Hi,' she called. 'Have you heard from Katrin yet?'

'Not yet,' said Amber.

'Who is it?' said Charlie, returning in his slippers.

'It's those people in the camper van.'

'Don't you know the bridge has broken,' shouted Charlie, walking down the wet path towards them. 'Katrin's probably stuck on the mainland with everyone else.'

The man leaned across the woman from the passenger seat.

'How can we get off this island? We can't get any information. We can't even get a phone signal.'

Charlie leaned towards the window. 'This isn't London. It's a small island. We don't have much luck with phone signals and sometimes the landlines don't work either.'

'Well it's not good enough,' said the man.

'Are there any ferries?' asked the woman.

'They'll probably send a small boat from the mainland when the weather improves,' said Charlie.

The man sighed impatiently. 'We need one big enough to take the camper van.'

Charlie laughed. 'You might have to wait a bit longer for that.'

'Thanks,' said the woman as they drove away.

Charlie walked back to the house and hung up his wet coat. 'They're getting to be a nuisance,' he said.

'Look at your slippers,' said Amber. 'They're soaking wet.'

Charlie sat on a stool in the hall and slipped them off. 'They'll be OK. I'll dry them in the oven.'

Amber ran after him as he headed for the kitchen. 'You can't put slippers in a gas oven. They might catch fire.'

But Charlie wouldn't listen. Ignoring Amber's warning, he put his wet slippers on the kitchen table and opened the oven door. 'Stop fussing Amber. You're getting like your mother.'

Reaching inside the oven, he lifted out a large pan and placed it on the table, next to the slippers.

'Is that a chip pan?'

'That's right. We used to have fish and chips every Friday. I think there's still some oil left in it.'

Amber lifted the lid off the pan. The oil was black. There was a hiss as Charlie turned on the gas oven. Amber didn't know what to do, but then she had an idea.

'Why don't you put your slippers on the radiator? It seems a shame to use the oven when you don't need to.'

Charlie thought for a moment. 'You're right,' he said, turning off the gas. 'I'll put them on the big radiator in the lounge.

When her Grandad had gone, Amber took a few plates out of a low cupboard to make room for the chip pan. She didn't know much about fire risks, but she knew that keeping a pan of dirty oil in a gas oven wasn't a good idea. Things were becoming very difficult with her Grandad. She just wished her parents were around. But until they were, she would just have to do the best she could.

When she heard her Grandad switch the TV on in the lounge, she decided to make a start at sketching the wings in the attic. It was more difficult than she had first thought but she persevered until she was happy with the result. She held her sketch up to the wings on the wall. They weren't exactly the same but they did look like angel wings.

She closed the book and went downstairs to check on her Grandad. When she returned to the lounge, he was asleep in his chair. He must have managed to open a new packet of jelly babies because there was another row of yellow ones on the table beside him.

This was the moment Amber had been waiting for. She took the scissors and tape from the drawer and went up to the back bedroom. It would only take a couple of cuts through the tape to open each of the boxes. Then she would know if they were empty.

Starting with the nearest box, she cut the tape holding the flaps. Bubble wrap sprang out as she plunged her hand inside. All she could feel was more bubble wrap. She resealed it and picked up the next box. The same thing happened. It didn't take her long to discover that all the boxes were empty. She flung the scissors down beside her as she knelt on the floor. How could Katrin trick her Grandad like this? There would be such a lot to tell her parents when they came back.

Picking up the scissors, she looked around the floor for the tape but it wasn't there. Thinking it must have rolled under the chest of drawers beside her, she reached into the small gap underneath. It wasn't long before her fingers located the tape, but as she pulled it out she felt something else. Reaching her fingers back underneath, she hooked out a tiny tin, covered in dust. Despite it being rusty with age, Amber could still make out a picture of a bird on the lid. Digging her nail under the rim she carefully prised it open. Inside were two glass marbles, a small blue button in the shape of a fish and a tightly folded piece of paper.

'Amber. Where are you?' her Grandad called from the hallway.

'Upstairs.'

'I thought we were having something to eat.'

She slid the scissors and tape under the chest of drawers, then put the lid back on the tin and put it in her pocket.

'Coming,' she called.

* * *

The afternoon darkened with more black rain clouds as Amber and her Grandad sat together in the lounge eating pasties. She could feel the tiny tin in her pocket and planned to take it to her bedroom as soon as she had finished eating.

Charlie put down his plate. 'Make some tea will you Amber?'

'I'm not very good at making…' she began.

The phone rang.

She ran to pick it up. 'Mum? How's Dad?'

The line wasn't very clear but Amber managed to find out what she wanted to know in the few minutes before it went dead.

'That was Mum,' she said as she returned to the lounge. 'Dad's operation went well and he's back on the ward. That's good isn't it?'

But Charlie was fast asleep.

Emil was coming up the path as Amber went to close the curtains. He handed her a container. 'I've brought you a cake.'

'Thanks. That's lovely,' said Amber as they went into the kitchen. 'Have you found out any more about the bridge?'

'There's no-one around to ask,' said Emil. 'Most of the holiday homes are empty this time of year, but I did see two people driving round in a camper van.'

‘I know who they are,’ said Amber. ‘Well, I don’t actually know who they are, but I know why they’re here.’

Emil listened carefully as Amber told him what had happened.

‘My Mum thinks Katrin’s a good person,’ said Emil, ‘but I’ve never liked her. She used to work in the café until Mum caught her stealing money from the till.’

Amber wasn’t surprised. ‘Did your Mum report her to the police?’

‘No.’

‘Why not?’

‘She told Mum she’d taken the money to pay for her sick sister to be looked after.’

‘That’s strange,’ said Amber. ‘I thought Grandad said she had no family. So what happened?’

‘Katrin offered to pay the money back, but Mum felt sorry for her and let her keep it.’

‘And what about Dave? Do you know much about him?’

‘He used to come in the café a lot. He moved here so he could be near Lighthouse Cottage. He was going to buy it and do it up but then he changed his mind.’

‘I know. Grandad told me.’

‘Anyway not long after that, Dave and Katrin got together, she left the café and moved in with Dave.’

‘Has Dave got lots of money?’

‘Well he drives an expensive car and he’s planning to buy a big house, so I suppose he must have.’

‘I wonder if Katrin’s living with Dave so she can get his money.’

‘Do you think that’s why Katrin’s helping your Grandad? So she can steal his money?’

‘I do, but the trouble is, Grandad thinks Katrin is an angel.’

‘My Mum likes her too,’ said Emil.

Amber was glad to talk to someone her own age. She loved her Grandad, but he had changed. Something was wrong with him. He was behaving oddly and he kept forgetting things.

Amber took the lid off the container. 'Wow. Thanks. I love chocolate cake. I'm going to have a piece now. Do you want some?

Emil sat down at the kitchen table and cut himself a slice of cake.

'Emil, can I ask you something?'

He took a bite of cake. 'Yeah. What?'

'Do you know anyone on Legna who has a pet rabbit?'

Emil spluttered on his cake. 'A rabbit! I thought you were going to ask me something serious.'

The more Amber tried to explain, the weirder it sounded, but eventually Emil understood why she wanted to know.

'Some kids in the holiday homes might have had a rabbit,' said Emil taking another piece of cake, 'but they've all been empty since last summer.'

'Hey I thought you brought that cake for us,' teased Amber.

Emil looked embarrassed. 'Sorry.'

'I was only joking. Of course you can have another piece.'

'I'll make you another cake.'

'Don't lie. Your Mum made it.'

'No, I made it,' said Emil. 'I do lots of baking. I want to be a chef when I leave school.'

'I wish I could cook.'

'Have you ever tried?'

'No. My Mum does it all.'

'Well how do you know if you haven't tried?'

Emil's next bite of his cake sent several large crumbs tumbling onto the kitchen floor.

'Sorry,' he said as he bent down to pick them up. Then he stopped and stared into the drum of the washing machine. 'Is that a biscuit tin in there?'

Amber wondered whether she ought to keep her Grandad's savings a secret, but she didn't know how else to explain the tin.

'Wow,' said Emil when he saw what was in the tin. 'How much money is in there?'

'I don't know, but Katrin has offered to look after it for him.'

'If she does look after it, Charlie won't see it again.'

'She's already taken some of his ornaments and now it looks like she'll have his savings as well.'

'Do your Mum and Dad know about this money?'

'They wouldn't let him keep it in a tin if they did.'

'Why has he let her take his ornaments?'

'She said she was getting them cleaned but I don't believe her.'

'Are they very old; like antiques?'

'I think they must be. Dad once said this house was like an antique shop.'

'Some antiques are worth a lot of money. She might be planning to sell them. Do you know what she's taken?'

'I wish I did. Then I could make sure she gives it all back.'

'I wonder if they're still in her house?'

Amber thought for a moment before she replied. 'There's only one way to find out.'

She opened a drawer and pulled out the key on the silver key ring.

'What's that?'

'It's Katrin's door key. She gave it to Grandad so he could look after the Angel's Child.'

Emil's eyes widened. 'Why did she say that?'

'She'd had a bump on the head. She probably didn't know what she was saying. We'd be doing her a favour, keeping an eye on the house while she's away.'

'You mean we should go in and look round?'

'Why not?'

'That's not a good idea Amber.'

'Why?'

'You never know what you might find.'

'I know why you don't want to go to Katrin's,' said Amber.

'Go on then. Tell me if you're so clever.'

'*You* think there's a ghost in there don't you? The ghost of the Angel's Child.'

Emil jumped off the stool. 'No I don't.'

'Yes you do. I saw how scared you looked when I told you I'd seen a face at Katrin's window.'

'It's alright for you. I've got to keep out of trouble.'

'What do you mean?'

Emil sat back on the stool and looked at the floor. 'I was expelled from my last school.'

'What for?'

'Fighting.'

'It must have been bad if you were expelled. What happened?'

'Two boys were making fun of my name.'

'What's funny about Emil?'

'No they were laughing at my last name.

'Why what is it?'

'It's Wysocki. My Dad's Polish.'

'So did you hit them?'

'I don't want to talk about it. I just don't want to get into any more trouble that's all.'

'You won't get into trouble Emil. We're just checking Katrin's house, like good neighbours. I'll say it was my idea if you're worried.'

Emil stared out of the window.

'Have you started at another school then?' asked Amber, trying to fill the awkward silence.

Emil nodded.

'Do you like it?'

'It's OK.'

'I hate my school,' said Amber.

'Why. What's wrong with it?'

'Nothing I suppose. I wanted to go to the high school my friends went to, but it was full, so I had to go to a different school.'

She stood up to put the key back in the drawer.

'If you want to go to Katrin's then let's go,' said Emil.

'OK, if you're sure,' said Amber. 'I'd better leave Grandad a note in case he wakes up while we're gone. I'll say I've gone out with you and we'll be back soon.'

* * *

They decided to knock on Katrin's front door first, in case there was someone there, but when there was no answer, they turned the key and stepped into the hallway.

'I don't like empty houses,' said Emil. 'They're spooky.'

Their feet sunk into the plush white carpet as they crossed the hallway into the lounge. 'It's very clean,' said Amber. 'Everything's white, even the sofa and the curtains.'

Emil pointed to a painting of a bright yellow flower. 'Apart from that.'

Amber was shocked. 'That's Grandad's painting. It was in his bedroom.'

'Shall I take it down?' said Emil.

'No. He might have given it to her.'

'I bet he hasn't.'

They moved back through the hallway into the dining room. Red petals from a vase of dying roses lay scattered across the white table.

'It doesn't look real in here,' said Emil. 'It's like something from a magazine.'

Amber's eyes darted around the room. Something on the window sill caught her eye. 'That's Grandad's clock. Mum bought it for him when he retired.'

'You should take it back.'

'I can't.'

'Why not? It belongs to your Grandad.'

'I don't understand you Emil. You say you don't want us to get into trouble, but now you're telling me to take things without asking.'

'Well what have you come for then?'

'I told you. I want to find out what Katrin's taken.'

'OK I get it,' said Emil. 'Let's have a look in the kitchen.'

The white worktops and cupboards gleamed as they entered the kitchen, but Amber's eyes were fixed on something on the floor by the back door. 'Is that a rabbit cage?'

Emil wandered over to take a closer look. 'It's a bit small but it could be. Maybe that's where your mystery rabbit came from.'

Amber was confused. How could the rabbit have come from here when the house was locked up, and if it did, where was it now?

The kitchen wasn't as tidy as the other rooms. There was an open packet of cereal on one of the worktops, alongside a dirty bowl and spoon. To the side of this was an apple core and next to that was a biscuit tin.

Emil picked up the tin. 'This looks like the one your Grandad keeps his savings in but this one's sealed up.'

'It is,' said Amber. 'It's identical.'

She took a closer look at the empty bowl. 'Someone's living here Emil and it's not Katrin.'

'How do you know?'

'The dish is still wet.'

Emil picked up a half-opened packet of cheese on the worktop beside the sink and then dropped it. 'Amber,' he said. 'I don't want to frighten you, but that looks like blood.'

In the sink was a pair of scissors with red smears on the blades.

'It could be Katrin's blood,' said Amber. 'Maybe she was trying to cut up a bandage for her head.'

'Look at the floor,' said Emil. He bent down to take a closer look at the shiny red drops on the white tiles. 'It can't be Katrin's blood. It's still wet.'

He stood up and walked towards the door.

'Where are you going?'

'Something's not right here Amber. I think we should go.'

'No we can't go yet. I keep thinking about the face in the window. It was small, like a child's face. What if there's an injured child here, left all alone? We need to have a look.'

'There aren't any children here,' said Emil. 'If there were, I would have noticed.'

'Would you Emil? I'm not so sure.'

'I live across the road. Of course I would notice.'

'Unless you spend all day looking out of your front window, you could easily miss a child coming or going.'

'OK so I don't look out the window every moment of every day, but I did see Katrin going out in Dave's car several times last week and there was no child with her then.'

'Maybe she left the child at home.'

'No-one would leave a child in a house on their own. Anything could happen.'

'Grandad said Katrin asked him to look after the Angel's Child. I thought she was confused after she hit her head, but maybe there really is a child here.'

There was a pause before Emil spoke. 'What if it's the Angel's Child?'

Amber stared at him. 'I can't believe you're saying that. Even if there were such things as ghosts, they don't eat cereal and take bites out of apples do they? And they don't bleed either.'

'Well that's where you're wrong,' said Emil. 'I once saw this horror film where the spirit of a Victorian child entered the mind of this boy and he never knew.'

'That was a film Emil. Not real life. Someone's in this house and if it is an injured child, we need to find them.'

Emil headed for the door. 'We don't need to do anything. It's none of our business.'

Amber followed him into the hallway. 'You don't care do you?'

'Care about what?' yelled Emil. 'You're talking like you know there's a real child here, but you don't know anything.'

He put his hand on the door handle.

'Wait. Listen,' said Amber.

It wasn't very loud but they could both hear something. It was the same sound Amber had heard the night before; a high-pitched sobbing, like a young child in distress.

She pointed shakily up the stairs. 'Someone's up there.'

Emil's face turned pale. 'Come on Amber. Let's go.'

Amber didn't move. 'We need to find out who it is.'

'If you're mad enough to go up there Amber, you can go on your own, 'cos I'm leaving right now. Are you coming or not?'

'Please Emil. I'm scared too, but someone needs our help.'

Emil's face hardened, 'I'm not scared.'

'Then come with me.'

'I'm the oldest,' he said. 'I'm the one who'll get the blame if something goes wrong. We need to tell someone.'

'Like who? My Grandad's too confused and everyone else is on the mainland.'

'I don't care,' said Emil. 'It's crazy to go up there when you don't know what you might find. Are you coming or not?'

Amber followed Emil out of the door in stony silence. She was angry with Emil but she felt even more angry with herself because she was too scared to stay.

'Katrin will be back as soon as there's a ferry,' said Emil as they hurried along the path. 'If there is a real child in there, they won't be on their own for much longer.'

'You're just saying that to make yourself feel better,' snapped Amber. 'We don't know when Katrin will be back. How long can a young child survive on their own?'

'You don't know if it is a child. It could be anyone hiding in there,' said Emil.

'What you mean like a ghost?'

'You go back in there if you think I'm so stupid,' said Emil, 'but I'm going home.'

As Amber marched up her Grandad's path, she could hear the sound of the sobbing inside her head.

* * *

Charlie was still asleep in his chair when she got back. She thought about trying to ring her Mum, but didn't want to worry her any more than she already was, so she decided to go up to the attic and sketch something to make her feel better. It was then she remembered the little tin in her pocket. She sat down on the bed and opened the lid. The paper inside was folded very tight. It was yellow with age and very fragile. Carefully unfolding it she saw it was covered in faint writing. As she smoothed it out she realised it was set out like a poem but the words didn't make any sense.

She tried to read the title out loud, to see if it sounded like anything.

'DLIHC S'LEGNA'

One of the words had Legna in it but she had no idea what the other letters meant.

Struggling through the next four lines, she read them letter by letter, word by word, to see if they sounded like anything she recognised.

yad fo esolc eht ta mrots lirpA na nI
.yaB angeL ffo knas esoR alleB ehT
yawa raf os ton gnihctaw tuB
.aeS eht fo legnA eht saW

She put down the paper. It was useless.

She thought maybe she would sketch something but she couldn't concentrate. However much she tried, she couldn't stop thinking about the crying. She didn't know what to do. Should she tell her Grandad? Should she wait to tell her Mum? Gazing absent-mindedly around the room, she looked at the glass of water by her bed. Her Grandad had once told her that you can hear things through a wall if you put a glass up against it and listen. Something about the sound being magnified. It was worth a try.

She drank the water and then cleared away her bags so she could stand right up against the wall next to Katrin's attic. Taking the glass in her hand, she held it against the wall and pressed it to her ear. There was a whooshing noise like the sound you hear when you put a sea shell to your ear, but after a while she heard something else. It was very faint but she could definitely hear it.

That same crying sound. As if someone was in deep trouble.

She slammed the glass down on the table. 'Why am I always such a coward? I'm sick of being scared of everything. I'm going back to Katrin's house, even if I have to go on my own.'

Grandad's

White hat

By Amber Henry

6

Silence of the Child

After checking on her sleeping Grandad, Amber took Katrin's key from the drawer and made her way next door. Still fired up from her outburst, she felt braver than she had ever done before and it felt good. When she entered the house there was no sound. No crying. Nothing but the sound of her own breathing. For a brief moment she thought about going back. Her bravery was beginning to desert her. She felt unsteady on her feet, almost dizzy, but it had taken all her courage to come this far and after a few seconds she decided she wasn't going to give up.

The softness of the carpet dulled her footsteps as she crept up the stairs. The door to the back bedroom was open but there was nothing much in there, apart from two large supermarket bags. Amber wondered if these contained more of her Grandad's ornaments but there was no time to look. She glanced into the front bedroom as she passed. Shoeboxes jutted out from under the bed, but her eyes were drawn to the jewellery box on the dressing table. It was made of wood, with swirly patterns of leaves and flowers on the lid and it belonged to her Granny.

Just at that moment, somewhere in the house, a child began to sob. The sobbing was deep and urgent. Too urgent to ignore. She tried to work out exactly where it was coming from. It was louder than before. She listened again. It sounded like it was coming from the attic bedroom.

Standing at the bottom of the attic stairs, she stared up into the darkness. If it was the same as her Grandad's house, there would be a door at the top of the stairs, but it was too dark to see. Wishing she had brought a torch, she hovered her hand over the light switch. She tried to ignore the little voice inside her that kept telling her to turn back. It would be so easy to run away, but the sobbing was driving her forward.

As soon as she flicked the light on, the sobbing stopped. Whoever was in that room knew she was there. She looked up. The door at the top of the stairs was closed.

Taking a deep breath, she set off up the stairs, but by the time she reached the top step she felt sick and her mouth was dry. Wiping her sweaty hands on her jeans, she took hold of the door handle and turned it slowly. One gentle push opened the door wide enough for her to enter but she hesitated. 'Careful now,' she said to herself. 'Go slowly. Go very slowly.'

Silently taking a couple of steps into the darkened room, she stood still, waiting for her eyes to become accustomed to the dim light. A few thin rays of light shone through the partly opened curtains onto a pale coloured carpet, and on the other side of the room she could see another door. It was slightly open, revealing the edge of a small washbasin. Not far from this door she could see a small dressing table and a chair with some clothes draped over the back of it. She took a few more steps into the room, but as she turned towards the far wall she felt her breath catch in her throat. There was a bed against the wall and on the bed was a small dark shape. Her legs trembled as she took a step nearer, blinking her eyes as she strained to see. There on the bed, silent and still, was the curled up figure of a little girl with long unruly hair covering her face. Amber's heart gave a thump as she looked closer. One of the girl's hands was wrapped in a white tea towel, but in her arms she was holding a rabbit.

The girl whimpered.

‘It’s OK,’ said Amber softly, ‘I’m not going to hurt you.’

Hair still covered part of the girl’s face as she looked up, but Amber could tell she was only young. Maybe six or seven years old.

Amber took a step towards her then stopped. She didn’t want to frighten the child. The rabbit twitched and squirmed as the girl tightened her grip.

‘I’m staying next door with my Grandad,’ said Amber, inching a little closer. ‘I heard you crying and I’ve come to help.’

The girl looked back but said nothing.

Amber looked at the tea towel wrapped around the girl’s hand. Even in the dim light, she could see it was streaked with blood.

She moved closer to the bed, kneeling beside it. ‘Have you cut your hand?’

The girl nodded.

‘We can find a plaster for it if you like.’

The rabbit wriggled again and, with a sudden leap, jumped out of the girl’s arms and onto the floor causing the girl to cry out in pain as she clutched the tea towel round her hand. Amber watched as the rabbit disappeared under the bed.

‘I’ll get him,’ she said. ‘My arms are longer.’

She couldn’t see a thing but when her hands brushed against the rabbit’s soft fur she grabbed it.

‘Ow! It nipped me.’

She tried again. Slowly this time, she tried to feel for the rabbit’s fur, but as she did so, it darted out and headed towards the door to the bathroom. Thinking it was probably more scared than she was, Amber waited until it was still before she crept over and gently picked it up. Holding it like her Grandad told her, she smiled triumphantly. ‘Come on. Let’s take your rabbit to see if there’s a plaster in the kitchen.’

Amber had never put a plaster on anybody else before and she had no idea if there was one in the kitchen, but she wanted to get the child out of the dark attic so she could take a closer look at her.

* * *

By the time they got to the kitchen, Amber's heart was beating normally again. The child still hadn't spoken but she seemed less frightened.

'What's your rabbit's name?' Amber asked. But she already knew what the rabbit was called. This was the same rabbit that had appeared in her Grandad's kitchen. Taking hold of the rabbit's collar, she pretended to read it. 'Bonzo. That's a lovely name for a rabbit. Shall I put him on the floor so we can wash your cut hand?'

The girl shook her head and looked up, her eyes still red from crying. Amber was desperate to ask her more questions. Was this little girl the intruder that came into her Grandad's house and took the rabbit? And if so why? But when she looked at the girl's tear-stained face, she decided this was not the right time to ask. She walked towards the cage in the corner of the kitchen. 'I'll put Bonzo in here while I sort out your hand.'

Once the rabbit was safely in the cage, the child seemed to relax a little, so Amber found some soap and ran the tap. 'Wash your hands and then I'll put a plaster on.'

Trying frantically to remember the first aid training she'd had at school, Amber took a look at the girl's hand. There was a long cut across one of her fingers and it was still bleeding. 'Did you do this with the scissors?'

The girl nodded.

Taking a clean tea towel from the drawer, Amber made a pad and pressed it firmly over the cut to stop the bleeding. She sat the girl on a chair and held her finger up high, like she had been told to do and waited. In the corner of the kitchen, they could hear Bonzo scratching around in his cage. As the child turned towards the sound, Amber noticed how matted her long hair was and how her t-shirt and cardigan were creased and grubby.

'It'll stop bleeding in a minute,' said Amber. 'I don't think it's a deep cut.'

The girl brushed her hair away from her face with her free hand, revealing a bright red mark.

'What have you done to your face?'

The girl frowned and shook her head. Amber looked again at the mark. She had seen something like this before. 'Is it a birth mark?'

The girl nodded.

'There's a boy at school who has one,' said Amber. 'When he was young his Mum used to say he'd been kissed by an angel.' She smiled at the girl but got no reaction.

'Are you here on your own?'

The girl nodded again.

'So where is your Mummy?'

Still no reply.

'Is Katrin your Mummy? '

The girl looked up with blazing eyes and shook her head.

Amber persisted. 'Well is Dave your Daddy then?'

There was still no response. Maybe Dave was her father, but if the child wouldn't talk, there was no way of finding out. The little girl either wouldn't or couldn't speak. Amber wasn't sure which. Right now, there was only one thing she was certain of. Someone had left this child all alone, with only her rabbit for company.

She lowered the girl's hand. 'Let's see if your finger's stopped bleeding.'

The cut was drying up nicely so Amber searched for a plaster. 'There's some in this drawer. That's lucky.'

She was trying to sound cheerful as she put the plaster on the little girl's finger, but it didn't seem to do any good. 'Would you like to stay with me at my Grandad's house next-door? You can bring Bonzo.'

The girl shook her head.

'You can't stay here on your own,' said Amber sitting down next to her. 'It's not safe.'

The girl pointed to Bonzo's cage.

'I'll get him out now,' said Amber. But as she stood up, the girl jumped off her chair, kicking it over so it fell in front of Amber. Then grabbing another chair she tipped it onto the first one, trapping Amber behind both of them.

'Wait,' yelled Amber as the girl ran out of the kitchen, but by the time Amber had moved the chairs out of the way, she had gone. Amber dashed after her, catching her up as she ran up the stairs.

She made a grab for the back of the girl's t-shirt but the girl swung her arm round, hitting Amber in the face with her elbow. Staggering backwards with the force of the blow, Amber grabbed the hand rail to steady herself as the girl fled up the second flight of stairs towards the attic, leaving Amber with a trickle of blood running from her nose. The girl's behaviour had taken her completely by surprise. She felt shaken and upset. After all, she was only trying to help.

Wiping her face with a tissue, she guessed the child was probably very frightened and decided to take things more slowly.

She climbed the stairs to the attic, her steps careful and slow, until she stood in the doorway. Taking a few more steps into the room, she paused. The girl was sitting on the bed, hugging a toy that looked like a rabbit. Fearing she may run away again, Amber kept her distance, speaking as calmly as she could. 'You can't stay here on your own. You can't cook for yourself. What will you eat when you run out of cereal and apples?'

There was no reaction at first but when the girl sniffed loudly and buried her face in the toy rabbit, Amber had an idea.

'Bonzo will get hungry if you stay here. If you come to my Grandad's house we can make sure he has enough to eat.'

The girl looked up from the toy rabbit as if she was thinking about what Amber had said, which gave Amber some hope.

'You can bring your toy rabbit,' said Amber quickly. 'Then you'll have two rabbits.'

There was a brief pause before the girl swung her legs off the bed and stood up. Amber moved away. She didn't want to be attacked again, but when the girl took a coat from the back of the chair and put it on, she knew her idea had worked.

* * *

Five minutes later, Amber and the little girl walked into Charlie's kitchen, along with the toy rabbit and Bonzo in his cage.

'Grandad,' called Amber. 'I've brought some visitors!'

There was no reply.

'I expect he's still asleep in the lounge.'

But his chair was empty. His jacket and his white hat were missing from the hook in the hall and his shoes were gone. Amber ran around the house calling his name but he wasn't there.

She dashed out of the back door. 'He might be in the garden.'

The girl waited by the cage, clutching her toy rabbit but it wasn't long before Amber came back. 'Maybe he didn't see my note and he's gone to look for me. He's probably just down the road.'

She was trying her best not to panic but inside she was shaking. 'I'm going to look for him. You stay here with Bonzo. I won't be long.'

The girl shook her head vigorously, her eyes widening with fear. Amber didn't have time to argue. She had to think fast.

'You'll have to keep up if you're coming with me,' she said, taking the two torches from under the sink. 'We need to find him before it gets dark.'

They crossed the road to Emil's house and ran up the path.

'Emil,' said Amber, shouting through the letter box. 'It's Amber. Open the door. My Grandad's gone.'

'Who's this?' said Emil as he opened the door.

'I don't know. I went back to Katrin's and she was in the attic room. Grandad was missing when I brought her back with me. He must have left the house because his coat and shoes are gone. I'm really worried. Can you help me find him?'

Emil grabbed his parka. 'Do you know which way he might have gone?'

'He often walks down to the sea front. Let's go there first.'

Emil was curious about the child and tried to watch her without seeming to as they ran, but her face was expressionless and she remained silent.

* * *

It was still light when they reached the sea, but a mass of dark storm clouds were gathering on the horizon. The bright coloured holiday homes stood eerily empty, making the whole place feel like a ghost town. All they could hear was the creak of an open gate as it swung back and forth in the gathering breeze.

'He's not here,' said Emil. 'It's deserted.'

'He might have fallen over and be lying injured somewhere,' said Amber. 'We need to search some more.'

With the sound of the sea roaring in their ears, they walked along the road by the sea front, looking in back yards and behind fences, along alleyways and behind walls, but Charlie wasn't there.

Amber thought they would never find him. She felt bad. If she hadn't left her Grandad when he was sleeping, he would still be at home. What was she going to tell her Mum? She was beginning to feel desperate. 'Where can he be?'

Emil stopped. 'Maybe he went on the cliff path.'

'Maybe,' said Amber.

As they turned away from the holiday homes Emil gazed out across the sands and gave a shout. 'Is that Charlie on the beach over there?'

Walking across the sands in the direction of Legna Bay was a dark figure, stooping against the wind, holding on to a large white hat.

'He's heading for Legna Bay,' said Amber.

Emil set off running towards the beach. 'The tide's coming in. He'll be cut off if he doesn't come back soon.'

'Grandad!' shrieked Amber. 'Grandad come back!'

But he was too far away to hear.

Soft sand tumbled into their shoes, dragging down their steps like weights as they ran along the beach, calling, shouting. But their voices mingled with the cry of the seagulls and disappeared into the wind. And all the time the silent little girl clung on to her toy rabbit, running as fast as she could to keep up.

When Charlie rounded the headland, he disappeared from sight, but by now they had reached firmer sand and were making better progress. Racing round the rocks into Legna Bay, Amber called him one last time. 'Grandad! Stop!'

This time he heard them. 'Hello,' he said calmly.

Amber tried to catch her breath as she took him by the arm. 'I don't know what you're doing here Grandad, but we've got to go back right now or we'll be cut off by the tide.'

Charlie shook her off. 'I'm not going back. I've come to find Benny. He's gone missing but I know where he is.' He pointed towards the steep rocks ahead of them. 'He's in Angel's Cave. I'm going to take him home.'

A cold chill ran through Amber's body as she realised that her Grandad's mind had gone back to the past. He thought he was a young boy again, going to fetch his missing brother from Angel's Cave. She looked at his face. It looked the same, but when she looked into his eyes, all she saw was emptiness.

Emil glanced back at the approaching tide. 'Come on Charlie, we've got to go back now.'

'Don't tell me what to do,' said Charlie. 'You can go back if you like, but I'm going to get Benny.'

Emil grabbed Charlie by the arm and pulled him hard. 'Charlie we've got to go. Come on.'

Charlie spun round, lashing out at Emil, then somehow he lost his balance and fell down in a heap on the sand.

'Leave him alone Emil,' said Amber helping him up. 'Forcing him like that isn't going to work.'

'Well what *will* work then?' yelled Emil. 'Because if we don't move soon we're all going to be in trouble.'

Amber picked up her Grandad's hat and handed it to him, but when she glanced back towards the sea, she realised it was too late.

'The tide's come in too far,' she cried. 'We can't get back.'

She looked up at the white rocks, layered with shiny grey quartz and she looked at the sign saying *Danger Falling Rocks,* but there was no other way. The sea was coming in fast. If they didn't find somewhere higher than the sea, they would drown. The ledges halfway up the cliffs were too high to reach but tucked away at the base of the cliff further along the beach was a small opening.

'Grandad, is that Angel's Cave over there?'

'That's it,' said Charlie. 'Are you going to help me get Benny back?'

There was no time to convince her Grandad that Benny had died long ago, so Amber didn't even try.

'Grandad listen. This is important. Does the water get into the cave when the tide comes in?'

'Yes, but if you go back far enough into the cave it's higher and stays dry,' said Charlie. 'That's where the Angel took her child.'

Patches of seaweed squelched and slid beneath their feet as they ran along the beach in the direction of the cave. The little girl hung firmly on to her toy rabbit as Amber took hold of her other hand, pulling her along as fast as she could. She wished she'd made the girl stay at home with Bonzo. It would have been safer, but it was too late to worry about that now.

Ahead was the skeleton of the Bella Rose with its wooden ribs peeking out above the sand, but as they came closer, something changed. Amber noticed the sand becoming sticky under her feet. It took longer for them to walk and each step was an effort. The sand was like a suction pad, pulling their feet towards it. Then everything happened so quickly. A gust of wind took Charlie's hat across the sand towards the Bella Rose, where it landed beside one of the wooden ribs.

'I'll get it,' said Emil, running towards it.

'Stop,' yelled Amber. 'Look.'

She pointed to a sign high up on the rocks near the ship. *Danger Quicksand.* But Emil had already started running, his feet sinking down a little further with each new step.

Amber tried to shout again but her voice came out shrill and high pitched. 'Quicksand Emil. Come back.'

He stopped and turned towards them, frozen with fear as Amber watched the sand slowly covering his ankles. 'Move Emil. You need to move now before it gets worse.'

The sound of Amber's voice jolted him into action. He wrenched one leg out of the sand and put it down in front of him.

'Keep going,' yelled Amber.

'He lifted up another leg and put it down, then another and another until his steps became easier and his feet lighter. Then with a sudden rush he hurled himself towards them, breathless and exhausted. Amber wanted to hug him but she resisted. 'Are you OK?' was all she said.

'I didn't see the sign,' he said, trembling.

'You were lucky you didn't run any further,' said Amber. 'We must be just at the edge of the quicksand.'

She looked behind her. The sea was closing in.

Charlie looked annoyed and spoke sharply. 'You shouldn't be walking here. It's not safe. Everyone knows you have to walk further along the beach to avoid the quicksands.'

'Why didn't you tell us that before?' said Emil. But Charlie was already walking away.

The sand was still sticky underfoot, but after a while it became firmer and they were able to walk a little faster.

'I can see the mouth of the cave now,' said Amber. 'If we can make it across those flat rocks we'll be there.'

Crossing the rocks was not as easy as it looked. Each one was black and slippery and in between them lay shallow pools of water as clear as glass. Amber had played in pools like these in the past, but today they were something to get over as quickly as possible.

'Benny calls these rocks sleeping sea monsters,' said Charlie.

'Be careful,' said Emil as the little girl wobbled.

Then *splash*. Her foot went into a pool but still she said nothing. She just stepped out and carried on.

Amber was pleased the girl didn't make a fuss but Emil found her silence strange and unsettling.

Charlie took a long time to cross the rocks, pausing to catch his breath each time before moving on. When Amber looked back as they waited for him, the tide was roaring up the beach like a crazed animal.

Once over the small rocks, they stood on a sandy strip, where the mighty cliffs loomed above them, grey and jagged. The entrance to Angel's Cave was now in front of them. High above the cave entrance Amber could see the grassy edge of the cliff path with the brown clay beneath it. It seemed to be overhanging, as if a small push or a sudden vibration would bring the whole clifftop crashing down. If the cliff fell when they were inside the cave... She shuddered at the thought.

They paused a moment in front of the cave, looking back at the sea. The entrance to the cave was a narrow opening between the rocks, dark and forbidding.

'I'm not so sure about this,' Emil said. 'But I don't know what else we can do.'

Amber hated the dark but when she saw the huge swell of the ocean and the waves coming in so fast towards the rocks, she knew they had no choice.

'How long have we got before the tide goes back out again Emil?'

'I don't know,' said Emil, 'but look how fast it's coming in. It won't be long before it reaches the cave entrance.'

'Are you sure we can climb higher than the sea in this cave Grandad?'

'Of course I'm sure,' said Charlie. 'How else did the Angel save the child?'

Inside Angel's cave

By Amber Henry

7

Wings of the Angel

Turning their backs on the sea, they entered the jaws of the cave into another world: dark, cold and still. Amber's knuckles whitened as she gripped her torch. She was trying so hard not to be frightened but the blackness around the beams was darker than anything she'd ever known, the silence quieter than any other silence.

At first the cave seemed fairly dry, but as the daylight disappeared it began to feel damp and cold and it wasn't long before it narrowed into a tunnel. Straight at first, the tunnel soon became twisted. There were places where their coats scraped the walls and places where Charlie and Emil had to stoop to get through, but they kept on moving. They said very little, but when they did speak their voices sounded different. It was easy to imagine things in such a place. The torchlight played tricks on their eyes. Amber thought she saw a bat fluttering, but the fluttering was the sound of her heart.

After a while they began to climb.

'Watch where you're walking,' said Amber. 'There are chunks of rock all over the ground and it's steep ahead.'

Emil walked behind, shining the torch so the girl and Charlie could see where they were going. He watched the child as she walked silently in front of him. There was something about her that disturbed him but he was more worried about the darkness.

At least he had his phone. There would be no signal but it should give some light if the torch batteries failed.

'We need to keep climbing 'til the cave opens out a bit,' said Charlie. 'There's a space further along as big as a room.'

He was right. After they'd been climbing for several minutes, the air seemed fresher, and not long after that the cave opened out into a large dome-shaped space. Amber shone her torch upwards. There was a shaft like a chimney and at the top there was a faint glimmer of light.

'Are those foot-holes?' she said as she splayed the torch beams along the shaft.

'You know what this could be?' said Emil.

'What?' said Amber.

'It could be a Bronze Age well. I saw a programme about one in a cave in the south of England somewhere. If it is a Bronze Age well it could be four thousand years old. If those are foot-holes, they must have dug them out to get water for their animals. I wouldn't want to climb down those to get water, would you Amber?'

But Amber wasn't looking at the foot-holes any more. She was shining her torch on something else.

'What is it?' asked Emil.

'Wings,' said Amber. 'Angel's wings scratched onto the wall of the cave.'

Charlie put out his hands and stroked the wings as if they were the most precious thing in the world. He smiled. 'I love these.'

Amber traced her fingers over the wings. 'Did Benny draw them?'

'No, they've always been here. Benny loves them.'

'Wow,' said Emil. 'They could be thousands of years old.'

Amber shone her torch a little lower. 'There's something else below the wings but I can't make it out.'

Emil put his finger on the wall and traced over the marks.

'They're letters. *s g n*.'

'*S g n*,' repeated Amber.

'*Sign*?' said Emil. 'Is it a sign for something?'

'It can't have said *sign*,' said Amber. 'There's a gap for another letter between the *g* and the *n*.'

'Benny wrote them,' said Charlie.

'I thought you said they'd always been here,' said Emil.

'The wings were, but Benny wrote the letters.'

'So what did they say?' said Emil.

Charlie shrugged his shoulders. 'I can't remember. I'll ask Benny when I see him.'

Amber looked at Emil and shook her head. There was no point saying anything.

Charlie leant against the wall of the cave and looked across at the little girl. There had been no time to tell Charlie about her, but no-one expected him to say what he said next.

'This is where you came with the Angel isn't it Bella?' he said. 'She'll be pleased we've brought her child back.'

Emil frowned. 'What are you talking about Charlie?'

'This little girl is Bella, the Angel's Child,' said Charlie. 'She has the mark on her face where the Angel kissed her.'

The little girl bowed her head, covering her face with her long hair.

'We don't know what her name is Grandad,' said Amber. 'She won't speak. But it's not likely to be Bella from that old story.'

Charlie moved away from the wall and stood upright. 'It's not a story. The Angel used to help the smugglers find their way through the tunnels to Lighthouse Cottage.'

'Angels belong in stories,' said Amber. 'This girl is definitely real.'

'Well who is she, if she's not the Angel's Child?' said Charlie.

'We think she's Dave's daughter,' said Amber. 'She's been staying with Katrin while Dave's away and the mark on her face is a birth mark, so will you stop calling her the Angel's Child. You're upsetting her.'

'I didn't know Katrin had a daughter,' muttered Charlie, leaning back against the wall again.

'She's not Katrin's daughter,' said Amber. 'I think she's Dave's.'

'Dave?' said Charlie. 'Whose Dave?'

Amber gave Emil another knowing look. Her Grandad was getting worse.

'Did you say the tunnels in this cave led to Lighthouse Cottage, Charlie?' said Emil, deciding to change the subject.

'That's right,' said Charlie. 'But you have to know the right way. The smugglers dug out false tunnels to fool anyone chasing them.'

'We don't need to worry about tunnels,' said Amber. 'The tide will be going out in a few hours. We can go back the way we came.'

'I'm tired,' said Charlie.

Amber sat down on the rocky floor, leaning her back on the cave wall. 'I think we're safe here. Let's sit down and try to get some rest until it's time to go back.'

The girl sat down next to Amber, beneath the wings. Her tiny body looked so fragile, it almost seemed she would break. Even though she had a coat on, she shivered with the cold as she buried her face in her toy rabbit.

Emil took off his parka and draped it round her shoulders. 'Here. This'll keep you warm.'

There had been times when Amber found Emil annoying, but whatever she thought of him, he was certainly very kind. She looked across at her Grandad sitting on the cave floor, his arms wrapped around himself for warmth. He was going to need all the kindness she could give him, but his forgetfulness was making things very difficult.

Then Charlie suddenly struggled to his feet. 'I don't think Benny's here today. I think we should go home.'

'Sit down Grandad. We have to wait for the tide to go out.'

Charlie hesitated, looked confused and then sat back down. 'Will someone come and rescue us soon?'

'No-one knows we're missing yet,' said Emil, 'and even if they did, they'll never think of looking for us in Angel's Cave.'

'No-one will know Grandad and I are missing unless Mum tries to phone from the hospital tomorrow,' said Amber. 'If she doesn't get an answer she'll probably think we're out for a walk or something.'

Amber looked at the girl. 'And no-one knows Dave's daughter is with us, do they?'

'If she really *is* Dave's daughter,' said Emil. 'We don't know who she is.'

The girl turned her head away and stared at the ground.

'Well if she's not Katrin's child, she must be Dave's,' said Amber. 'Otherwise why was she in that house?'

'There is another explanation that you won't even think about,' muttered Emil.

Amber moved away from the girl, signalling for Emil to follow her. 'If you're talking about ghosts,' she whispered, 'then I don't need to think about it. Everyone knows the stuff you see in horror films isn't true.'

'I'm not talking about stupid horror films,' muttered Emil. 'I'm talking about the Angel's Child. Don't you think it's strange we've ended up in this cave, with an unknown child from the house where the ghost of the Angel's Child lives?'

'No. What's strange is how you think she could be a ghost.'

'What are you two whispering about?' called Charlie.

Amber moved back to sit with her Grandad and the girl. 'Nothing.'

Charlie shuffled to his feet. 'We need to go home.'

‘We can’t go yet Grandad. I told you we have to wait a few hours for the tide to go out.’

‘Are we trapped here then?’ he asked. ‘In total darkness?’

‘Sit down Grandad. We’ll be going soon.’

‘We’ll never get out as long as Bella is with us,’ said Charlie, pacing up and down. ‘The Angel will want to keep her child here.’

Amber didn’t say any more. There was no point going over the same thing again. Her Grandad would only forget. She looked at his face in the dim torchlight and thought about how different he looked from when she was a young child. He was always so strong and clever. Now he seemed like a child himself.

It was several minutes before Charlie sat back down again. ‘You need to find a way out of here.’ he said. ‘I’ve had my life but you’re young. You’ve got a lot of living left to do.’

‘We’re not going to die,’ said Amber, taking hold of Charlie’s hand. ‘We’ll soon be out of here, won’t we Emil?’

But as they huddled together beneath the Angel’s wings, neither Amber nor Emil were certain of anything.

* * *

It was difficult to get comfortable on the cold hard rocks of the cave and even more difficult to sleep. Amber’s hands and feet were numb with cold. Right now she would give anything to be back in her Grandad’s house in her warm bed, even if it was in the dusty attic. Only a few days ago she was a child travelling to Legna with her parents. Now she felt forced into being like an adult. People were depending on her. She hoped Emil would stay strong and stop thinking crazy things about the Angel’s Child. She was going to need some help.

‘Maybe we should turn the torches off for a while,’ said Amber. ‘We need to save the batteries for when we really need them.’

No-one replied at first. Fear hung in the air; the dark like a monster waiting to consume them.

Then Emil spoke. 'Just turn one off.'

'Shall I turn mine off then?' asked Amber.

'OK,' said Emil, 'but keep it close. You never know when we might need it.'

'I'm turning it off now,' said Amber. 'Are you ready?'

With the click of the torch button, the cave became even darker. Emil gripped the handle of his torch and fixed his eyes on its single beam. His hand shook. 'I'm not keen on the dark.'

'It's all in the mind,' said Charlie. 'When I was a boy I kept the bedroom door open at night to let the light in. Shadows became ghosts in my mind.'

'Don't let's start talking about ghosts again,' said Emil.

'Let's talk about something else then,' said Amber. 'Do you remember those boys who were trapped in a cave for days before they were rescued? It was on the news. They talked about their lives to take their mind off things.'

'They talked about their favourite food didn't they?' said Emil.

'You'd think that would make them hungry,' said Charlie.

'Well what shall we talk about then?' said Emil.

Amber looked at the girl. 'Why don't you tell us about Bonzo.'

The child's face brightened up.

'Tell Emil what he's like,' said Amber trying not to sound too keen.

'Is he the same colour as your toy rabbit?' asked Emil.

She shook her head.

'What colour is he then?' asked Emil.

The girl's mouth twitched as if to speak but nothing came out.

Emil tried again. 'Is he green?'

The girl smiled.

'Or is he yellow?'

The girl shook her head and laughed out loud.

'Well let me think. He can't be brown can he?'

The child reached into her coat and pulled out a silver locket on the end of a chain round her neck. She opened it up for them to look inside.

'Shine the torch on the locket Emil,' said Amber. 'That's a lovely photo of Bonzo.'

The girl grinned as they looked at it but when she closed the locket, Amber noticed something engraved on the outside. 'It says *ELLA*. Is that your name?'

The child pulled away, pushing the locket and chain back under her clothes.

Amber tried again. 'We want to know what to call you that's all.'

The girl frowned, her face set like stone.

'I know you don't feel like talking, but you need to tell us what your name is,' said Amber. 'It's Ella isn't it?'

The girl nodded.

Amber could tell by Emil's face that they were both thinking the same thing. Ella's name was almost the same as Bella, the name of the Angel's Child.

Charlie, who had been staring at the wings as if he wasn't listening, pulled a packet of jelly babies from his pocket. 'Do you want a sweet Bella?'

Emil glared at Charlie as Ella took a jelly baby. 'Will you stop calling her Bella. It's freaking me out.'

'Well that's her name isn't it?' said Charlie. 'She's got the mark on her face where the Angel kissed her. She's Bella, the Angel's Child.'

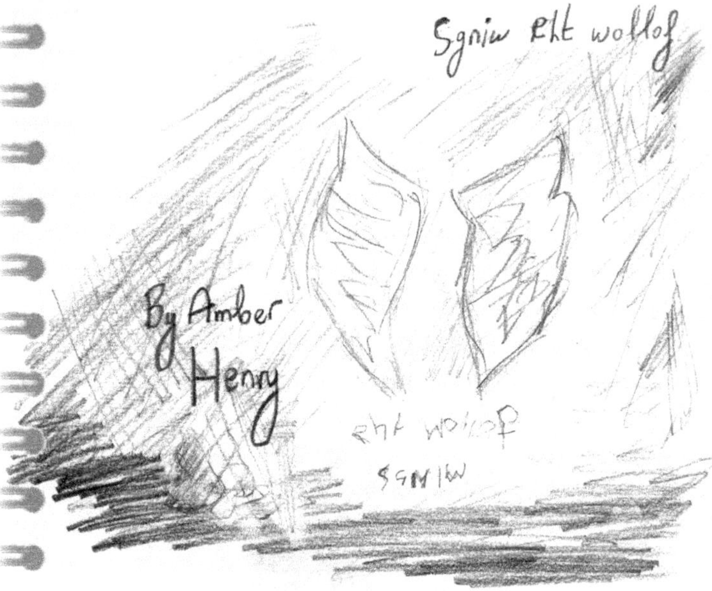
Sgniw eht wollof
By Amber Henry
follow the wings

8

Fall of the Rocks

It was two o'clock in the morning before Emil looked at his phone to check the time. Ella was asleep on the floor with her toy rabbit beside her and Charlie was slumped against the wall with his collar up and his eyes closed.

'Amber. Are you awake?'

'I haven't been to sleep,' whispered Amber. 'Is it time to go yet?'

'We probably need to wait another few hours before the tide goes out fully.'

'Sorry I've got you into this Emil. Grandad would have drowned if we hadn't helped him.'

'What's wrong with him?'

'Mum thinks he may have dementia.'

'Someone came to our school to talk about that,' said Emil. 'It's a disease of the brain isn't it?'

'Yes. Mum wants him to see a doctor, but I don't think he will.'

'Why not?'

Amber smiled. 'He says doctors make him ill.'

'I like Charlie,' said Emil. 'He's got a bit of spirit and he makes me laugh.'

Amber looked over to where her Grandad was sleeping fitfully. 'He's not the same as he used to be. He was always busy doing something. Now he sits all day and does nothing. Part of him has gone. It makes me feel so sad.'

‘I know it’s not the same thing, but I felt sad when my Dad left,’ said Emil.

‘Do you still see him?’

‘He’s gone back to Poland, so it’s a bit difficult.’

‘That must be horrible. Was it a long time ago?’

‘It was when I was at my last school. Mum says that’s why I got into so much trouble. She said I was angry with everyone.’

‘And were you?’

‘I suppose so.’

‘So what’s different here?’

‘I don’t know. The school’s better but I don’t want to let Mum down again.’

‘I’m going to ask my Mum if I can change schools,’ said Amber.

‘We have to get out of here first,’ said Emil. ‘At least Charlie and the girl can sleep a while. I daren’t close my eyes.’

‘I’m the same. I keep listening for the sound of water. I know Grandad said the sea won’t come this far into the cave, but he could be wrong.’

‘I think we’ve climbed high enough to be clear of the waves. But what if the torches stop working?’

‘We’ve still got the lights on our phones.’

‘Yes, but the charge will run out eventually. What will we do if we end up in complete darkness Amber?’

‘Try not to think about it.’

‘There’s something else I’m worried about,’ said Emil.

‘What?’

‘Ella.’

‘What about her?’

Emil lowered his voice. ‘Well she’s not like an ordinary child is she?’

‘How do you mean?’

‘Why won’t she speak? I mean that’s not normal is it?’

‘She’s been left alone in a house Emil. It’s been a shock. That’s probably why she won’t talk.’

Emil stood up and stamped his feet for warmth. ‘What if there really was a curse on this cave Amber?’

‘Don’t be stupid.’

‘It’s not stupid. It all points to being true Amber.

‘What does?’

‘If Ella is the Angel’s Child, we’ve broken the curse by returning her to the cave, but if the Angel wants to keep her here, we’ll never get out. Why didn’t you leave her at home?’

‘I had to bring her Emil. She wouldn’t stay on her own.’

‘Can’t you see Amber. She knew this was going to happen. She wanted to get back to the cave. She’s calling herself Ella but Charlie’s right. Her name is Bella, the Angel’s Child.’

Emil put his head in his hands as if he had given up, but Amber didn’t feel sorry for him. She just felt angry.

‘Stop it Emil. Talking about ghosts and curses isn’t going to get us out of here is it? Just because Ella’s name is like Bella doesn’t mean the story’s true. The curse was probably something the smugglers made up to keep people out of the cave.’

Emil slumped against the cave wall. ‘Then why do I get the feeling we’re never going to get out of here?’

* * *

A few hours later Amber woke up with a jolt. ‘What’s happened?’ yelled Charlie. ‘Where am I?’

Emil scrambled to his feet as Ella started to cry. Amber turned on her torch. ‘It’s OK. We’ll soon be out of here.’

‘We must have both fallen asleep,’ said Emil. ‘Let’s go and see if the tide’s gone out.’

They walked slowly, their limbs stiff with cold, their eyes stinging with tiredness. There were times when Charlie had to be helped along the path and times when he sat down and had to be persuaded to keep going, but somehow they kept him moving.

'I can see daylight,' said Amber after a while. 'We're almost there.'

Heading towards the light, they moved a little faster, until a low rumbling sound took them by surprise.

'What's happening?' said Emil.

Amber put her hand against the cave wall. 'It's moving.'

Within seconds there was a loud crashing sound as huge boulders tumbled across the entrance to the cave, blocking out most of the light.

'Move back,' yelled Emil, grabbing hold of Charlie's arm.

Amber took hold of Ella's hand as dust began to fill the tunnel. There was no time to think, no time to call out. Stumbling back into the blackness, coughing and gasping towards the dome, they followed the hazy beams of torchlight like cars in a fog. Amber could feel Ella shaking as she clung on to her hand, but when she dropped her torch, it was Ella who dived to pick it up.

Finally they approached the dome, where the air was clear and they were able to breathe again.

'Let's stop a minute,' said Amber slumping to the ground. She could feel her heart racing but at least they were still alive. No-one spoke for a while. All was silent apart from the sound of Charlie fighting for breath.

They listened.

'We need to go back,' said Amber after a while. 'We need to get out of here.'

Emil kicked a small rock. 'Are you blind Amber? We're trapped. We can't get out. It's useless. Didn't you see the boulders covering the entrance. I told you this would happen.

We'll never get out of here as long as the Angel's Child is with us. We shouldn't have brought her in here.'

'He's right. This is the Angel's doing,' said Charlie. 'She's trapped us in here.'

'Will you all shut up about the Angel,' yelled Amber. 'I'm sick of hearing about it.'

'Don't talk to me like that young lady!' said Charlie.

'You think you know everything don't you Amber,' said Emil, raising his voice. 'Well you don't.'

'I never said I knew everything,' said Amber. 'But I'm not stupid enough to believe a real live girl is a ghost.'

Ella put her hands over her ears.

'Will you two stop shouting,' said Charlie. 'I've got a headache.'

There was a pause as Emil kicked some more stones around with his foot. Ella held her toy rabbit against her face as Charlie sat down on the ground and leant against a rock.

'What are we going to do then?' said Emil.

'I don't know,' said Amber. 'Maybe we should go back to the entrance and shout for help.'

'Who's going to hear us? There's no-one around.'

'Well if you've got a better idea Emil, let's hear it.'

'I don't know what you're worrying about,' said Charlie. 'We can go back the other way.'

'What other way?' asked Amber.

'The way Benny and I used to go. Up from here through the smugglers' tunnels to Lighthouse Cottage.'

'It's too risky,' said Emil. 'Some of the tunnels might be blocked and we could end up getting lost.'

'What are we going to do then?' said Charlie. 'Because I'm not feeling too good at the moment and Bella needs something to eat by the look of her.'

Despite knowing how ill her Grandad was, his insistence on referring to Ella as 'Bella' was beginning to get to her. She was trying to be understanding, but she could feel the anger rising inside her again. 'Grandad will you stop calling her Bella. None of us are feeling great at the moment.'

Charlie heaved himself up from the ground. 'Well I'm going to Lighthouse Cottage even if you're not. Pass me the torch.'

There was no way Amber was going to give her torch to her Grandad, but she knew that finding a way back through the tunnels was their only hope of getting out.

'We'll put a big pile of stones by the walls every now and again as we go,' she said, 'so we can retrace our steps if we can't find a way through.'

'I hope Charlie's right,' said Emil, 'because if he isn't, we could be down here for ever.'

* * *

Deeper and deeper into the cave they walked until the path became so narrow that Emil's shoulders touched the sides. Amber tried to breathe deeply. She hated being closed in like this, but after a few minutes they were forced to stop. There was a fork in the tunnel ahead of them.

'Which way?' said Amber shining her torch along the left-hand tunnel. 'It looks like there's a path through this one.'

Emil shone his torch along the other tunnel. 'There's a path here as well but it's narrower.'

Charlie pointed at something on the wall. 'Look. Up there.'

Amber could see nothing at first but as she hovered her torch along the wall, the image became clear. Scratched into the surface of the rock on the right-hand tunnel was another pair of wings.

'There's some letters, like the other ones,' said Emil.

'That's Benny's writing,' said Charlie.

Amber read out the letters. They were arranged in groups as if they were words:

'sgniw eht wollof'

Emil went closer. 'Is it some kind of code?'

Then Charlie spoke. 'It's backwards writing. That's how Benny and I write to each other.'

'I don't get it,' said Emil.

Amber stared at the letters again. 'I think I understand it,' she said after a while. 'If you read it backwards, from right to left instead of left to right it makes sense. Start with the letter *f* Emil. Then read from right to left.'

Emil put his finger on the letter f and read the letters from right to left. '*f o l l o w t h e w i n g s*. Oh I get it now. Follow the wings. The wings show the way.'

'Come on,' said Amber, leading the way. 'This right-hand tunnel is the one we need.'

They followed blindly on until the tunnel became so narrow that Emil and Charlie could barely squeeze through. But then it opened out again as they came to another fork with three tunnels to choose from this time.

'Look for more wings,' said Emil. 'They'll be here somewhere.'

Ella tugged Amber's sleeve and pointed upwards. She had found the wings.

The next tunnel was high enough to walk upright but only wide enough to walk single file. Amber felt hemmed in by such a narrow space and rushed ahead in the hope the tunnel would soon widen. When her torch began to flicker she said nothing. If it stopped working there was nothing they could do about it. Breathing deeply to calm her rising panic, Amber hurried on round a bend and then stopped. 'There's something ahead,' she called. 'It looks like a door, but there are rocks in the way.'

Emil caught her up and squeezed past to take a look. 'That must be it,' he said. 'That's the door into Lighthouse Cottage.'

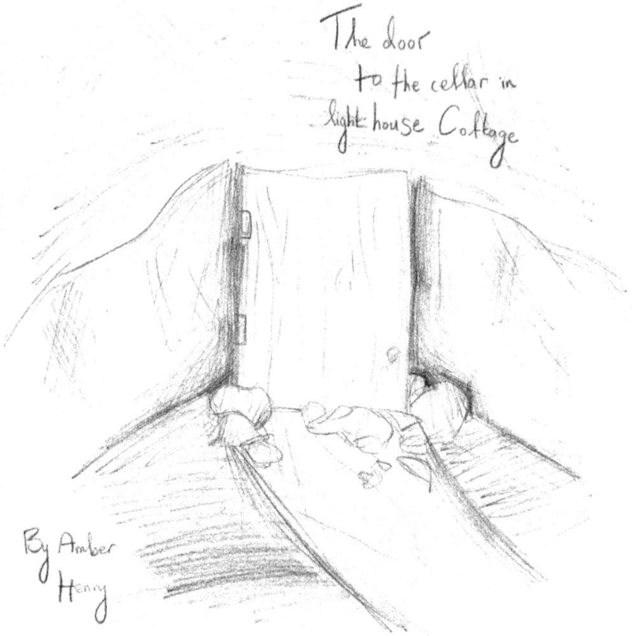
The door to the cellar in light house Cottage
By Amber Henry

9

Out of the Gloom

Emil positioned his torch on a large flat stone so it shone towards the doorway. 'Come on Amber, let's clear these rocks away. We've got to make a way through.'

Amber turned round to give Ella her torch. 'Where's my Grandad?'

Ella pointed back towards the bend in the tunnel.

'Grandad?'

There was no answer. Amber felt a stab of fear in her stomach as she ran back round the bend of the tunnel. If her Grandad had wandered off again he could be lost forever. But he was still there, sitting crumpled up on the floor. She sighed with relief as she knelt down beside him. 'Grandad you need to get up. We've found the door to Lighthouse Cottage.'

He opened his eyes. 'I can't go on any more. I've got a headache and I'm tired. I'll wait here for Benny. He shouldn't be long.'

Emil's voice came out of the darkness. 'Come on Amber. We need some help.'

'Benny wouldn't want you to stay here in the dark,' said Amber, taking her Grandad's arm. She felt bad that she was talking to him as if he was a young boy but it seemed to work. With Amber's help Charlie rose unsteadily to his feet. 'I'm coming Benny,' he whispered.

Amber blinked away the tear stinging her eye. This was not the time to cry.

With Charlie now sitting propped up against the cave wall where she could see him, Amber gave her torch to Ella and went to help Emil. It took some time before they cleared a way through to the door, but there were still several bigger rocks piled high in front of it. Amber rubbed her sore hands and wiped the dust off her face as they stood back and looked at the door.

'We need to keep going,' said Emil.

Shifting the bigger rocks was heavy work. There wasn't much room so they decided to put them in a pile behind Charlie.

'Be careful Amber,' warned Emil picking up a large rock with both hands. 'If we drop one of these we could be badly injured.'

Slowly and steadily they carried the rocks away from the door until finally it was clear.

Emil sat down on the ground. 'We've done it.'

There was a moment's silence before the light suddenly dimmed and Amber let out a cry. 'My torch has gone out.' Taking it from Ella, she flicked the switch on and off several times in the hope she might revive it but it was useless.

'It's alright,' said Emil. 'Mine's still working and we've still got the phones. We'll be out of here soon.'

'The door opens into the cottage by the look of the hinges.'

'Try it then,' said Amber.

Emil took hold of the handle and turned it but the handle came off in his hand. He flung it to the ground saying something under his breath which Amber didn't quite catch, but she knew it was something he probably shouldn't be saying.

'I told you this place was cursed. The Angel wants to keep us here. That's why everything's going wrong.'

Amber ignored him. She wasn't going to give up after all this effort. 'Try pushing it again Emil. It looks like it's opened a bit.'

Emil sighed deeply but then positioned himself between the

walls of the narrow opening and pushed the door as hard as he could with his shoulder. 'It's moving.'

'Keep pushing,' said Amber.

'Ow!'

'What's wrong?'

Emil stopped. 'I've hurt my shoulder.'

'Move back Emil. Let me have a go.'

Emil was right. It was moving, but Amber wasn't as strong as Emil and the movement was only slight.

'Let me try again Amber. I can push with the other shoulder.'

'Let's take turns,' said Amber. 'We might do better that way. We only need it to open enough for us to get through.'

* * *

The door opened a little more each time they pushed. But after a while it stopped, and this time it stopped completely.

'There must be something behind it,' said Emil. 'Did you say this door led to a cellar Charlie? There might be barrels or something behind it.'

When Charlie closed his eyes, they knew he wasn't going to answer. It was obvious to Amber that the opening was too small for either her or Emil to get through. But then she looked at Ella. It was a risky thing to ask a young child to do, but it was their only hope.

'Ella. I want you to be very brave,' said Amber. 'You're the only one small enough to crawl through the doorway to see what's stopping it from opening.'

Ella folded her arms defiantly.

Amber put her arm round the little girl but she knew feeling sorry for her wouldn't help. 'I know it's hard, but if you want to see Bonzo again we need to get through that door.'

Emil spoke gently. 'All you have to do is squeeze through

and try to move whatever's behind it. That's all we're asking.'

'You can come back if you don't like it,' said Amber.

Ella unfolded her arms as if she was thinking about it. Then she took a deep breath and nodded.

'Thanks Ella,' said Amber. 'I'll pass you Emil's torch when you get through.'

'No you won't,' said Emil. 'If you give her my torch, we'll only have the torches on our phones and they're gonna run out soon.'

'We need her to see what she's doing Emil. If the door leads to the cellar there won't be any windows in there.'

Neither of them noticed Ella reaching into her coat pocket until she held up a small green plastic frog and touched a switch on its side, sending out a beam of light.

'Why didn't you say you had a torch?' said Emil raising his voice. 'We could have used it when we were clearing the rocks.'

Amber glared at him. If Ella became upset she could change her mind. 'It doesn't matter now Emil. It's good we've got another torch.'

Emil tightened his lips and tried not to show his anger.

'Right Ella,' said Amber. 'You and the frog torch can help us get out of here so you can both see Bonzo again. OK?'

Ella switched off the frog torch and put it back in her pocket. For a minute Amber thought she wasn't going to go, so she was relieved when Ella finally slid herself through the opening.

They saw a faint beam of light as Ella switched on her torch again.

'What can you see?' asked Amber.

'She won't answer you,' said Emil. 'We're trusting our lives to someone who won't speak.'

Amber ignored him. 'If there's something behind the door Ella, can you move it out of the way?'

There was a pause and then a crash like something falling

on the floor.

'Be careful,' said Amber. 'If you hurt yourself we can't come and help you.'

'Let me talk to her,' said Emil.

Amber shuffled back to let Emil near the opening. 'Make sure you can see what you're doing Ella.'

A dull sound like something being dragged across a hard floor drifted into the tunnel.

'She's moving something,' said Emil, 'but I can't tell what.'

The sounds carried on for some time but when the sounds stopped, they became alarmed.

'Ella?' they both called.

A loud high-pitched scream came from behind the door and echoed back through the tunnel.

'Ella,' shouted Emil. 'Are you OK?'

'Ella! Ella!' yelled Amber.

The terrified voice of a little girl came back. 'A rat!'

'She spoke,' said Emil.

'Has it gone now Ella?' said Amber

There was no reply.

'Stand back Ella,' said Emil. 'I'll see if I can open the door.'

There was a creaking sound as the door jerked forward and then stopped.

'It's moving,' said Amber.

Each time Emil pushed the door, it opened a fraction more, until finally the gap was wide enough for him to crawl through, followed closely by Amber. Ella threw her arms round Amber. Her whole body shook.

'Well done Ella,' said Emil.

Ella looked up at him and smiled. It was only a faint smile but it was the first time Emil had seen her smile. She had seemed so strange to him in the cave, but now she just looked like a frightened little girl.

A pile of broken wooden chairs and stools lay scattered around the cellar floor.

'Were those behind the door?' said Emil.

Ella nodded.

'I'm going back to get Grandad,' said Amber. 'We need to get out of this cottage. It's not safe.'

* * *

Back in the tunnel, Charlie was still sitting propped up against the wall.

'Come on Grandad. We've got through to the cellar.'

Charlie opened his eyes and then closed them again.

'Grandad wake up. We need to get out of here.'

Charlie blinked his eyes open again. 'What? Where are we? Where's Benny?'

'Come on Grandad. Please.'

It took some time to help her Grandad to his feet, but once he was standing she was able to guide him through the open doorway. Emil was waiting on the other side and took his arm as he staggered into the cellar. Then suddenly Charlie's knees buckled and he sank to the floor.

'Grandad,' said Amber, kneeling beside him. She took one of his hands and rubbed it gently. 'I know we're out of the tunnels but we've got to get out of this cottage. It could fall into the sea any minute. You've got to get up.'

'What's wrong Amber?' he asked. 'I'm having a rest that's all.'

Emil shone his torch across the room. 'There's some steps over there, leading up to another door. Can you walk up those steps if we help you Charlie?'

'Of course I can,' said Charlie. 'I'm not dead yet you know.'

This was the old Grandad Amber knew. The man with a fighting spirit who never gave up. She hoped his fighting spirit would last long enough to get him out of the cottage.

It took Charlie a long time to climb the steps, despite Amber holding his arm. His body was stiff from spending time bent over in the tunnels. The door led into a small room with an old white sink in the corner but they had no time to linger.

'Through here,' said Emil. He led the way into another slightly larger room, strewn with broken bricks and glass. There, on the other side of the room, was the door to the outside.

The sharp dazzle of daylight stung their eyes as they left the dimness of the cottage, but as they breathed in the morning air, it smelt sweet as honey. Amber had never really listened to birds singing before, but now she thought it was the most beautiful thing she had ever heard.

'I didn't think we'd get out of there alive,' said Emil.

'Neither did I,' said Amber.

Charlie coughed loudly.

'We need to get him home,' said Amber.

'The quickest way back is on the cliff path,' said Emil, 'but it may be too dangerous after the cliff fall.'

Amber agreed. 'Let's stick to the road then. It'll be easier to walk on.'

Walking either side of Charlie, Amber and Emil linked their arms in his, in case he fell, but Ella was the one Amber was worried about. They had only been walking a few minutes when she started to shiver violently. Amber moved to help her but it was too late. Within seconds she was sick.

Amber tried desperately to comfort her. 'Oh Ella. It's not far now. We'll soon be home and then you can have a nice rest in the warm.'

Ella took the toy rabbit from her coat pocket and held it close. 'I don't want to go back to Katrin.'

To hear her voice saying such a long sentence was a shock, but Amber was pleased she was talking at last. 'You can stay with me until Katrin gets back.'

Ella took a shaky step. 'Katrin's not coming back,' she said. 'She's dead.'

'What?' said Emil.

'She isn't dead,' said Amber. 'She'll be back when her head's better.'

Ella said no more but both Amber and Emil thought it was a very strange thing for a little girl to say.

* * *

It wasn't far but it seemed to take such a long time to walk home. Charlie leaned heavily on Emil, and Amber had her arm round Ella all the way.

'Are we nearly home?' mumbled Charlie as Cliff Road came into sight.

Amber looked towards the three houses. There was a blue camper van parked on the road.

'It's that couple again,' said Amber, taking out her door key. 'Don't tell them anything. I don't trust them. Just keep walking and act normally.'

'You OK?' asked the woman, opening the van window.

'We're fine thank you,' said Amber.

'Well you don't look fine,' said the woman. 'What are you doing out so early?'

Emil wanted to ask them the same question, but he resisted. 'We've… er… been for a walk,' he said.

The woman frowned as she peered at the group. 'You look

exhausted.'

'It was a bit further than we thought,' said Amber. 'We'll be OK.'

'Have you heard anything from Katrin yet?' she asked. 'According to the local radio there's a ferry coming from the mainland later today. We thought she might be on it.'

'Sorry,' said Amber, 'we haven't heard from her.'

'OK. Well take care then,' said the woman as they drove away.

Emil watched them go. 'She seems OK.'

'She might be, but the man scares me,' said Amber. 'He's really mad about something.'

'They must be desperate to see Katrin,' said Emil.

'Yes, but we still don't know why do we?'

Emil shrugged his shoulders. 'Maybe they'll leave the Island if there's a ferry going back.'

'Only if it's big enough to take that camper van,' said Amber.

'I'll help you with Charlie and Ella before I go back to my house,' said Emil. 'Then I'll try and call my Mum again. I got through on the landline yesterday. She might know what's happening with the ferry.'

Charlie went straight to his bedroom to rest, but Ella wouldn't lie down until she'd checked on Bonzo. It seemed like they had been away such a long time, but it was only one night and Bonzo was fine.

Emil yawned as he watched Ella fall asleep on the sofa. 'I think I'll go back to my house now. I can't keep awake any longer.'

'Can you wait a bit Emil? I need to put a note through Katrin's door telling her where Ella is.'

'Why?'

'In case she comes back on the ferry today. It won't take long but I don't want to leave Ella and Grandad on their own.'

She looked at Ella sleeping peacefully with her toy rabbit close to her face. 'I suppose I should take her with me so she can get herself some clean clothes.'

'It's a shame to wake her now,' said Emil. 'I'll come back in a couple of hours.'

'OK. I'll wait til then. I'm really tired as well.'

'That was weird when Ella said Katrin was dead wasn't it?' said Emil as he left.

'She probably thinks that 'cos Katrin didn't come home.'

'At least she's talking now. See you later.'

After Emil had gone, Amber sat in her Grandad's big chair and closed her eyes. Thoughts of what could have happened in the cave whirled around in her mind, but it wasn't long before she drifted into a deep sleep.

* * *

Two hours later, Amber was woken by Emil knocking on the window. 'Didn't you hear me knocking on the door,' he said as she let him in.

'I thought I was dreaming it,' said Amber.

Emil slumped down into Charlie's chair. 'You'd better wake Ella if she's going with you.'

But Ella had already opened her eyes.

Amber smiled at her. 'I'm just going to Katrin's. Do you want to come with me to get some clean clothes?'

'Am I staying here now?' she said.

Amber still couldn't get used to the fact that Ella was talking, but she was very pleased she was.

'You'll be staying here tonight if Katrin doesn't come back on the ferry,' said Amber.

Ella frowned. 'Katrin isn't coming back.'

'You said that before,' said Emil. 'What do you mean?'

‘She’s dead,’ said Ella, ‘and it was all my fault.’

Amber sat beside her and spoke softly. ‘Katrin’s not dead Ella. She’s in hospital with a bad head that’s all.’

‘I know,’ said Ella. ‘But she hasn’t come back, so she must be dead.’

Amber tried to explain that the broken bridge meant Katrin couldn’t get back to Legna, but she wasn’t sure Ella believed her.

‘Why did you say it was your fault?’ asked Emil.

‘Katrin said it was,’ said Ella. ‘But it was an accident.’

‘What was an accident?’ asked Emil.

‘I was playing with Bonzo in the garden when Katrin came out to bring the washing in. He jumped out of my hands. I couldn’t help it.’

‘I don’t understand,’ said Emil. ‘Tell us exactly what happened.’

‘Bonzo ran in front of Katrin and she fell over him,’ said Ella. ‘She banged her head on the garden path.’

‘It was an accident then,’ said Emil.

‘She said I let him go on purpose,’ said Ella. ‘She said Bonzo would be taken away from me and I would go to jail.’

‘How old are you Ella?’ said Emil.

‘Nearly seven.’

‘Seven year olds don’t get sent to jail Ella and it’s not a crime to let go of a rabbit.’

Amber turned to Emil. ‘How could anyone say that to a little girl?’

Emil clenched his fists. ‘Katrin’s the one who should be locked up.’

* * *

Ella held on tightly to Amber’s hand as they walked up to Katrin’s front door. Once inside, they went straight to the attic bedroom to collect a few of Ella's clothes.

Ella took a bag from the chair and waved it in the air. 'Do you like my new bag? It's got a rabbit on it like Bonzo.'

'It's cute,' said Amber. 'We can put your things in it.'

'Look. Daddy put my name in it so I could take it to school.'

Amber read out the name on the inside of the bag. 'ELLA SAVAGE. So that's your name is it?'

Ella wasn't really listening. She was pulling things out of the drawers in the dressing table.

'Do you like my new pyjamas?'

'Let me guess,' said Amber. 'They've got rabbits on them.'

'How did you know?'

Amber smiled. She had never thought about it before, but it must be nice to have a younger sister.

'This was my first rabbit,' said Ella, pulling the toy rabbit from her pocket. Mummy bought it for me when I was a baby. She's called Hoppy.'

'Where is your Mummy then?'

Ella's face became serious. 'She was taken to hospital. She might be there for a long time. I have to live with Daddy until she gets better.'

'So Dave's your Daddy then?'

'Yes. Can I play with Bonzo in your garden tomorrow?'

'You can if it's not raining.'

'You'll have to block up the hole in the hedge though,' said Ella.

'What hole?'

'The one Bonzo ran through after he tripped Katrin up. I crawled through it to look for him after Katrin had gone.'

'Did you go into my Grandad's house?'

'The door was open. I thought Bonzo might be there, so I sneaked in but then the lights went out and I couldn't see.'

‘Did you hide in a cupboard when you heard me coming?’

‘I did, but I didn’t like it. When I heard you leaving the room I went under the table, but I banged my head.’

Now Amber understood everything. Ella was the intruder after all. ‘Did you take Bonzo from the bedroom?’

Ella nodded.

‘There was a power cut,’ said Amber. ‘How did you find him in the dark?’

‘I had Froggy in my pocket.’

‘Why didn’t you just knock on our door and ask for Bonzo?’

Ella’s lip quivered. ‘Because Katrin said if anyone found out there was no-one to look after me, I would have to go to boarding school without Bonzo. That won’t happen will it?’

Amber hugged the little girl. ‘No of course it won’t.’

‘Do you want to see my drawing book?’ said Ella, jumping off the bed.

As Ella fizzed like a bottle of pop, Amber suddenly felt very tired. She was almost aching for sleep.

‘I’d love to see your book Ella. I love drawing too but I need to get home and get some rest first.’

Ella moaned but put the drawing book in her bag. Amber smiled. Ella was like a different child to the one she found bleeding on the bed.

‘Let’s find your toothbrush Ella and then we can go.’

Downstairs a door slammed shut. Ella grasped Amber’s hand. ‘I’ll go and see who it is,’ she said, prising off Ella’s fingers. ‘It’ll be alright.’ But deep down she wondered if it would.

‘Hello,’ she called as she made her way down the attic stairs.

‘Who are *you*?’ said a woman’s harsh voice. ‘And what are you doing in my house?’

Ella's locket

By Amber Henry

10

Words of the Cruel

Katrin was younger than Amber had imagined. She was slim and smartly dressed with long wavy hair and lots of make-up. She had just taken off her high-heeled shoes in the hallway.

'I'm Amber, Charlie's granddaughter. Sorry if I scared you.'

'What are you doing in my house?' said Katrin.

'I found Ella here on her own,' said Amber. 'We realised you were stuck on the mainland so we decided to look after her. We've come back to get some of her things.'

Katrin looked surprised. 'What do you mean you found her on her own? I asked Charlie to look after her while I was in hospital. He said his family were coming to visit, so I thought it would be fine.'

'He didn't understand what you meant,' said Amber.

Katrin picked up her shoes. 'Silly old man,' she muttered.

'He's not silly,' said Amber, trying not to show how angry she was. 'He's not well.'

Katrin placed her shoes against the wall, adjusting them so they were perfectly straight. 'Can you believe the taxi wouldn't come over with me on the ferry?'

She stood on one leg and rubbed her foot. 'I had to walk all the way from the sea front in high heels.'

Amber was amazed that Katrin didn't even ask how Ella was.

'So, the child is staying with you now is she?' said Katrin, looking at her watch.

'She was going to, but now you're back…'

Katrin interrupted her. 'Did she tell you what happened in the garden?'

'Yes, she told me.'

'All because of that stupid rabbit.'

Amber followed Katrin to the kitchen and watched as she took a bottle of wine from the fridge and opened it. 'I tried to ring Charlie to check on the child, but I couldn't get through.'

She poured some wine into a glass and took a big swig, leaving a lipstick stain on the rim.

'Listen,' she said, 'I've some business to see to on the mainland. Could you look after the child until I get back?'

'I'm sure that'll be OK,' said Amber trying not to sound too pleased. 'Should we let Dave know?'

'No need for that,' said Katrin. 'I'll be back in two days.'

'Ella said her Mum's in hospital,' said Amber.

'She was taken ill very suddenly,' said Katrin, 'so Dave had to bring her here. It's alright for him. He's working away. I'm the one who's had to look after the spoilt brat. That's what you get for being so kind hearted.'

'You've been helping my Grandad as well haven't you?' said Amber. 'It's very kind of you to take away all his ornaments for cleaning.'

Katrin frowned. 'Yes, well anyway. I haven't got time to stand here talking. The ferry goes back to the mainland in an hour and I'll have to walk to the sea front.'

Her voice trailed away as she headed for the stairs. Amber was a few steps behind her when they heard a loud knock on the door.

'Katrin,' said a man's voice. 'We know you're in there.'

Katrin grabbed Amber roughly by the arm and pushed her against the wall.

'Quiet,' she hissed.

‘We’ve come for Amy’s money,’ said a woman’s voice.

Amber knew exactly who they were.

Katrin put her finger to her lips and glared at Amber.

‘If you don’t answer the door we’re going to the police,’ said the man.

‘We know what you’ve been up to,’ said the woman.

With every word they spoke, Katrin’s fingers dug deeper into Amber’s arm. When Amber tried to move away, she tightened her grip.

‘Have it your own way,’ said the man. ‘See you in court.’

There was a long silence, followed by the sound of a car engine starting up and driving away. Katrin pushed Amber out of the way and looked through the spy hole in the door. Then she ran into the lounge and peered through the window. ‘They’ve gone. It’s all lies. They’ve got it wrong. They’re stalking me. I’m the one who should be going to the police.’

She moved back to Amber, fixing her gaze with an icy stare. ‘It’s best if you don’t say anything to anyone about this. I know you haven’t stolen anything from my house, but the police might take a different view if I had to tell them things had gone missing.’

Amber was shaking. She knew Katrin was threatening her, but she just wanted to get out.

‘I’ll get Ella’s things,’ she said backing away.

‘Good idea,’ said Katrin. ‘But before you go, I need to tell you something.’

Amber waited.

Katrin lowered her voice. ‘You do know there’s something wrong with the child don’t you?’

Amber was angry that Katrin couldn’t even call Ella by her name.

‘Do you mean Ella?’

‘Yes. Yes of course I do,’ said Katrin. ‘There’s something wrong with her.’

'Do you mean the birth mark on her face?'

'No. Not that.'

'I'm sorry I don't know what you mean.'

'She's a bit odd,' said Katrin. 'A bit strange.'

'What do you mean?'

'She tells lies. She makes things up.'

'Like what?'

Katrin looked at her watch. 'I need to go but I'm just warning you not to believe everything she tells you, that's all. And don't put up with any nonsense from her. Her Dad spoils her. She needs a firm hand.'

Amber guessed Katrin was the one telling lies about Ella but she didn't want to argue. She wanted her to leave as quickly as possible. But then she remembered what her Mum always asked for when she had friends to stay.

'Can you leave your phone number in case anything happens to Ella?'

Katrin sighed. 'I've told you I'll be back in two days. I haven't got time for all this.'

'Maybe Grandad has Dave's number,' said Amber. Katrin grabbed Amber by the arm. 'Stop it. You're hurting me.'

'Don't you dare phone Dave,' she hissed. 'If you breathe a word about what's happened, to Dave or anyone else, you'll be very sorry and so will the child.'

Amber pulled away, rubbing her arm.

'Dave's working at sea and he doesn't need any hassle from you. My number's in a phone book in the kitchen somewhere.'

Amber didn't want to make things worse for Ella, so she said no more and went into the kitchen to look for the phone book. When she couldn't find it, she made her way up the stairs to Katrin's bedroom and peeped in. 'I can't find a phone book.'

Katrin was on her hands and knees pulling boxes out from under the bed. She stopped when she saw Amber. 'It'll be around somewhere. I've got to get on with my packing.'

Amber didn't move. Something on the bed attracted her attention.

'Do you want something else?' asked Katrin.

Amber didn't reply. She was gazing at the thing on the bed. It was Granny's jewellery box.

Katrin took a piece of bubble wrap from one of the shoe boxes and stood up. 'Lovely thing isn't it?' she said, taking hold of the jewellery box. 'Charlie wanted me to have it.'

'It belonged to my Granny's father,' said Amber, her voice quavering. 'Grandad promised it to my Mum but he can't remember because he's got dementia.'

'Is that what you think?' said Katrin sharply. 'How do you know he has dementia? Has he been to see a doctor?'

'No. He won't go.'

'That's right,' said Katrin, folding the bubble wrap round the box. 'He won't go to the doctors, so how can you say he has dementia. Are you some kind of doctor?'

'No but anyone can see he's getting mixed up.'

Amber watched as Katrin carefully placed the jewellery box in the bottom of a large red shopping bag.

'Are you taking it somewhere?'

'To an antique dealer on the mainland. I want to find out how much it's worth.'

'Please don't sell it. I'll ask my Dad to buy it back from you.'

Katrin gave a short, mocking laugh. 'It's mine now so I can do what I want with it. It's about what Charlie wants, not what you want.'

Tears welled up in Amber's eyes as she turned away. No wonder Ella didn't want to be with Katrin.

* * *

She found Ella curled up in a ball on the bed, clutching Hoppy.

'I'm wicked,' she muttered. 'Katrin's going to take Bonzo away.'

Amber sat down on the bed beside her. 'You're not wicked Ella.'

'I am wicked. Katrin said I was.'

'You didn't let Bonzo go on purpose, did you?'

'Not on purpose,' said Ella. 'He slipped out of my hands, but I was glad when she fell. That's wicked isn't it?'

'Look Ella, it was an accident and anyway Bonzo is in my Grandad's house now, so Katrin can't take him away can she?

'No but she will.'

'Bonzo's safe at the moment,' said Amber. 'Katrin's going away for a few days so you're coming to stay with me for a while.'

Ella uncurled herself. 'Can we stay with you 'til my Daddy gets back?'

'When is he due back?'

'I don't know. He works out at sea so he has to stay for a long time. Can we stay 'til he gets back?'

Amber wanted to say yes, but she didn't want to make a promise she couldn't keep.

'We'll see,' said Amber. 'Now let's finish packing your bag. What else do you need?'

They had just finished packing when they heard a stair creak, then footsteps. A strong smell of perfume filled the air as Katrin appeared in the doorway, wearing a white fur coat.

'I'm going now,' she said. 'I'll be back in a couple of days but when I get back I don't want to see that rabbit here. I don't care what you do with it but I don't want it in my house. Is that clear?'

She glared at Ella. 'Answer me child!'

Ella nodded, her eyes wide with fear.

Amber moved as close to Katrin as she dare. She wanted to shout at her but she knew that would make things worse so she spoke politely. 'Is there a reason why Ella has to get rid of Bonzo?'

'If her mother's not better soon,' said Katrin, 'the child will have to go to a boarding school. I've had a nasty fall and I'm not well enough to look after a rabbit as well as a child who tells lies.'

'I don't tell lies,' wailed Ella.

'Be quiet,' said Katrin.

Ella stopped immediately, biting her lip to stop the sobs.

'But you can't take Bonzo away,' said Amber. 'Ella loves him so much.'

Katrin turned her back and started down the stairs. 'Lock the front door when you leave. I'll pick up the key when I get back.'

There was nothing Amber could say to make Ella feel better. She promised to find a good home for Bonzo, but Ella still cried.

When she heard the front door slam, Amber ran downstairs to look through the front bedroom window. Katrin was pulling a big wheeled case down the street, walking confidently in a pair of sparkling white trainers but she wasn't carrying the red shopping bag.

A thought crossed Amber's mind. If she had left the bag behind, Granny's box might still be in it.

She looked around the room. There was no sign of the bag but it must be here. Katrin definitely hadn't taken it with her. She opened the wardrobe and there it was, with Granny's box still inside, staring at her, willing her to take it back. It meant so much to her Granny. She reached out her hand and grasped the box. Whatever happened now, she would face the consequences, but Granny's box was not going to be sold.

As she turned away from the wardrobe, she knocked over a small waste paper basket. A crumpled piece of paper fell out. When she picked it up she realised it was a letter. The writing was spidery, as if the writer had a shaky hand, but at the bottom of the paper she clearly saw a name that made her curious. It was signed by someone called Amy. Placing Granny's box on the bed, she took the crumpled letter in both hands and smoothed out the paper so she could read it more easily.

Dear Katrin,

Thank you for the postcard. I'm glad you have now settled in to live with your sister.

You asked me to send you some more money, but I'm worried it might get lost in the post.

When my son and his wife come to visit, I will ask them to drive over to Legna and give you the money.

I will write again to let you know when they will be coming.

Love Amy xxx

Amber remembered the couple saying they had come for Amy's money, but she didn't understand what it was all about. She needed more time to think. Putting the letter in her pocket, she picked up Granny's box and went back to find Ella.

* * *

Emil was in the kitchen when Ella and Amber returned to the house, but there was someone else with him.

'This is my Mum, Julia,' said Emil. 'She's just arrived on the ferry. I couldn't believe it when I looked out of the window and saw her walking up the road.'

Julia was a small woman with the same blonde hair and bright blue eyes as her son.

'Emil has been telling me how you got trapped in the cave,' she said. 'It must have been terrifying.'

Although Julia spoke perfect English, there was something about the way she spoke that made Amber think she could be Polish like Emil's Dad.

'It was very scary,' said Amber. 'We're lucky to be alive.'

'And this must be Ella,' said Julia. 'The girl with the lovely rabbit.'

Ella smiled.

'What's that in your hand?' asked Emil, looking at the bubble wrapped box.

Amber's face reddened. She didn't mind telling Emil but she didn't want anyone else to know what she had done. 'Oh just something Katrin borrowed from my Grandad,' she muttered, giving Emil a knowing look. 'Katrin came back while we were getting Ella's things.'

'I saw her on the ferry,' said Julia. 'She told me she was in hospital when the bridge collapsed.'

'But Katrin's gone away now so I can stay here can't I Amber?' said Ella.

'That's right,' said Amber. 'But only for two nights until Katrin gets back.'

Julia raised her eyes in surprise. 'Gone away? She's only just come home. Where has she gone?'

'Ella why don't you take your things up to my bedroom in the attic,' said Amber, 'There's some paper and pens up there. You could draw something for us.'

* * *

When Ella had gone, Amber tried to explain what had happened. She told them about the visit from the couple in the camper van and how Katrin had threatened her if she told anyone.

'I expect she was stressed,' said Julia. 'Katrin's been so good to Charlie since she moved in. She's such a kind person. I don't think she meant to threaten you.'

Amber took the letter from her pocket. 'I knocked over a bin and this fell out. Someone called Amy gave Katrin money to live with her sick sister but it's not true. She's living with Dave.'

'We ought to call the police,' said Emil after they had both read it.

'Hang on,' said Julia. 'That letter doesn't prove anything. We don't even know who Amy is. She could be the one telling lies for all we know.'

'If Katrin asked Amy for *more* money, like it says in the letter,' said Emil, 'it means Amy must have already given her some and now she's asking for more'.

'That must be the money the couple wanted her to give back to Amy,' said Amber.

'So Katrin must have stolen it,' said Emil.

'You don't know she stole it,' said Julia. 'Amy could have given her the money. I know Katrin has a sick sister in a nursing home, so maybe the money was towards the cost of that.'

Emil looked again at the letter. 'It says the money was for Katrin to live with her sister, not pay for her sister to stay somewhere else.'

Julia took the letter in her hand and looked at it closely. 'The writing looks shaky like an elderly person has written it. If Amy is elderly she could be confused.'

'But Katrin hasn't got a sister,' said Amber. 'She told my Grandad she had no family.'

Julia handed the letter back to Amber. 'Charlie might have got that wrong Amber. He has been getting things mixed up lately.'

'Well I think she's a thief,' said Emil.

Julia gave Emil a disapproving look. 'It may not be right to ask someone for money but it's not against the law.'

'She left Ella in a house all on her own didn't she?' said Emil. 'That's against the law isn't it?'

'Yes, but she didn't mean to,' said Julia. 'She thought Charlie was looking after Ella. It's not Katrin's fault he didn't understand what she meant.'

'Katrin doesn't care about Ella,' said Amber. 'She's cruel to her.'

Julia sighed. 'You're both making things up. We don't know anything for sure.'

'When Katrin gets back I'm going to make sure we see Ella every day,' said Emil. 'If she's cruel to her again I'll know.'

Julia shook her head. 'Katrin might make mistakes sometimes but she's a lovely person. I can't believe she would hurt anyone.'

Amber could see it was useless to argue. 'I'd better make Grandad some tea,' she said, reaching for the kettle.

Julia put her arm round Amber. 'We know Charlie's not well. Call us if you need anything.'

* * *

The curtains were closed when Amber took the tea to Charlie's room, but she could hear his heavy breathing. She put the cup on his bedside table in case he woke up, but decided to let him sleep. As she turned to leave, she noticed a green notebook lying on the floor. She picked it up intending to put it on the nearby dressing table but the writing on the cover made her stop. She took it out of the room into the light to check she was right. And she was. It said *senoJ ynneB*. This was Benny's backwards writing. This was his notebook. Could this be what prompted her Grandad to go looking for Benny?

She took the book downstairs and sat on the sofa to read it. Page after page of wings and angels lay before her, all beautifully drawn like the ones in the cave. How she wished she could draw as well as this. Then half way through the book she had a shock. There was a portrait of a young girl with long fair hair and a red mark on the side of her face.

The door opened suddenly.

'I've found this in your bedroom,' said Ella, handing Amber a folded piece of paper. 'It looks like that writing in the cave.'

Amber had almost forgotten about the paper from the tin. 'I couldn't understand it when I found it Ella, but you're right, it's backwards writing.'

'I want to write it out in proper writing in my book,' said Ella. 'Then we can find out what it means. Will you help me Amber?

'Yes but not now,' said Amber putting the paper in her pocket. 'I'm looking at this.'

'What is it?'

'It's an old notebook. It belonged to my Grandad's brother Benny.'

Ella stared at the open page. 'Why is there a picture of me in it?'

'It does look a bit like you, doesn't it?' said Amber, trying to sound calmer than she felt.

'It's very dirty,' said Ella. 'Did Benny draw this a long time ago?'

'Yes, a long time ago, before you or I were even born.'

'It must be older than my locket then,' said Ella, 'because I got that when I was born.'

Ella fished around the neck of her t-shirt for the chain. Then her face changed. 'It's gone! My locket's not on the chain any more. It's gone.'

'How can it have gone?' said Amber. 'You showed it to us in the cave.'

‘It’s special. Daddy put that photo of Bonzo in it for my birthday last year. Where can it be?’

Amber put her hand on Ella’s shoulder. ‘Don’t worry we’ll find it.’

* * *

They hunted in all the places Ella had been in Charlie’s house. They looked outside and even went back into Katrin’s house, but the locket wasn’t there.

‘You could have lost it on the road when we were walking back,’ said Amber, ‘but if it’s not there then it must be in Lighthouse Cottage or in the cave. Those are the only places we haven’t searched.’

Ella blinked away a tear as Amber took hold of her hand. ‘It’s getting dark now, but we’ll go back along the road to Lighthouse Cottage first thing in the morning Ella. It’s got to be somewhere.’

That evening they put Bonzo in the spare room and Julia brought an airbed round so Ella could sleep on the floor next to Amber’s bed. When Ella wasn’t looking, Amber put her Granny’s jewellery box under some of her clothes in her drawer. It was best to keep it secret for now.

‘I don’t want to go to sleep yet,’ said Ella, when Amber took Hoppy from her bag.

‘We can stay up a bit longer,’ said Amber, ‘but we need to get up early if we’re going to look for your locket.’

‘I can’t stop thinking about it,’ said Ella.

Amber noticed Ella’s notebook on the floor. ‘Do you want to help me work out that backwards writing, so you can write it in your book? It’ll take your mind off the locket.’

They sat together on the bed for some time as Amber gradually worked out what the words in the poem meant. As she read them out, Ella carefully wrote them in her book in lines and verses, as Amber suggested.

'Now it looks like a real poem,' said Amber. 'Shall I read it to you?'

'I can read it. I'm a good reader.'

'Some of the words are difficult.'

Ella looked at the poem. 'OK. You read it and I'll follow the words.'

* * *

'Who wrote it?' asked Ella after Amber had finished reading.

'My Grandad's brother Benny. It has his initials at the bottom of the page. B J for Benny Jones.'

Ella yawned. 'Do you think we'll find my locket tomorrow?'

Amber handed Ella her pyjamas. 'We'll try.'

Working on the poem had taken their mind off their problems, but as they climbed into bed, Amber couldn't help noticing how sad Ella looked.

'This is like a sleepover isn't it?' said Amber, trying to cheer her up.

'My best friend Ivy had a sleepover on her birthday,' said Ella. 'Me, Ivy and her big sister Esther all slept in the same room.'

'I bet you were talking all night.'

'We were eating sweets and telling jokes.'

'Do Esther and Ivy go to your school?'

'Ivy does, but Esther goes to the high school.'

'It's good to have friends,' said Amber. 'I used to have friends at my primary school but I don't see them anymore.'

'Why not?'

'I go to a different school now.'

'I'm your friend Amber.'

'And I'm your friend too,' said Amber turning out the light. 'Goodnight Ella.'

'Amber, can I ask you something?'

'Of course you can.'

'What's it like in boarding school?'

'I don't know, but it could be fun sleeping with other girls.'

'It's not like a sleepover with your friends though is it? I won't know anyone there.'

'You may not have to go to boarding school Ella, but if you do, you'll soon get to know everyone.'

'What if they make fun of me?'

'Why would they do that?'

'Because of my birth mark.'

Amber had almost forgotten about Ella's birth mark. 'The girls at the boarding school would soon get used to it, Ella.'

They said no more for a while but, in the quiet of the night, Amber could hear Ella sobbing quietly to herself.

'Don't cry,' said Amber. 'Everything will be fine. You'll see.' But it was hard to sound as if she meant it.

'Amber?' said Ella sitting up suddenly. 'Can I tell you a secret?'

'What?'

'I'm not going to boarding school and I'm not leaving Bonzo.'

'What do you mean?'

Ella lay back on the pillow. 'Nothing. I might find my locket tomorrow.'

As Amber closed her eyes, she hoped that Ella's Mum would soon be better. That seemed to be the only way to solve Ella's problems.

Ella's Note

By Amber Henry

11

Pain of the Missing

In the early hours of Monday morning, Amber had a bad dream. She dreamt she was one of the Mulberry Smugglers, dancing round on top of the soil to hide where the goods had been buried. She held hands with the other children and began to dance round and round so fast that the ground beneath them gave way and they fell down – down into a dark grave as dark as the inside of the cave. 'No!' she yelled sitting up with a start.

It was still dark but moonlight shone through the thin curtains onto Ella's airbed. Amber felt pleased she hadn't woken Ella but when she looked at the airbed, something wasn't right. The bed was empty and Hoppy had gone.

She ran down the stairs, hoping Ella had gone to the bathroom, but she wasn't there. The door to the spare bedroom was open. Bonzo's cage was empty. She ran around the house in a frenzy. Where could Ella be and why was Bonzo not in his cage?

The last place Amber looked was the kitchen and it was there she found the answer to Ella's disappearance. There was a folded sheet of paper on the table with the word *Amber* written on it. Snatching it from the table she unfolded it and looked at the words:

rebmA raeD
loohcs gnidrob ot og ot oznoB gnivael ton ma I
emoh semoc yddad lit gittoc eht ta yats lliw I
x allE

Some of the words were misspelt but she marvelled at how clever Ella was to have written this note in backwards writing. But the thought of Ella walking alone to Lighthouse Cottage in the middle of the night gave her a sinking feeling. Taking a torch from the cupboard, she grabbed her coat and ran across the road.

Julia answered the door. 'Amber. What's wrong? Has something happened to Charlie?'

'It's Ella. She's run away to Lighthouse Cottage so she doesn't have to go to boarding school.'

Emil appeared dressed in shorts and a t-shirt. 'What's happened?'

'Get dressed Emil,' said Julia. 'We're going to Lighthouse Cottage.'

* * *

'How long has she been gone?' said Emil as they hurried up the hill towards the cottage.

'I don't know,' said Amber. 'She was gone when I woke up.'

'We need to find her as soon as possible,' said Julia. 'It's not safe for anyone to be out on a night like this, never mind a child with a rabbit.'

Emil marched ahead, setting his body in an arc against the swirl of the wind. 'Hurry up,' he shouted. 'The weather's getting worse.'

Amber and Julia fell behind as he disappeared round a bend.

'Emil,' yelled Julia. 'Wait for us.'

‘We need to move quicker,’ said Emil as he reappeared.

‘Yes, but we need to keep together,’ puffed Julia. ‘It’s getting difficult to see.’

They raced on together, heads against the rain, each hoping Ella would be found safe and well.

‘We should be at the cottage soon,’ said Emil.

‘It’s there,’ said Amber.

Appearing through the mist, ghost-like in the distance, was Lighthouse Cottage.

The building rattled and moaned as they drew nearer. It reminded Amber of a dying animal, fighting for its life. Moving along the side towards the front door, they heard a loud crash.

‘Watch out,’ shouted Emil. ‘Things are falling from the roof.’

‘Keep close to the wall,’ said Julia.

The front door was hanging loosely on one hinge, banging against the wall with each gust of wind. Emil held it steady as the beams of his torch lit up the emptiness inside.

‘Don’t go in,’ said Julia. ‘It’s too dangerous.’

‘Hello. Is anyone there?’ he called.

There was a flutter as something flew out above their heads.

Amber ducked down. ‘What was that?’

Emil circled his torch above them. ‘Probably a bat or a bird.’

‘Call Ella’s name Amber,’ said Julia. ‘She might answer if she knows it’s you.’

‘Ella,’ called Amber gently. There was no reply. She called again a little louder.

‘Ella if you’re there please come out. We can phone your Daddy so you won’t have to go to boarding school. We can sort something out.’

When there was no reply, Amber began to shout louder. ‘Ella! Ella! Are you there?’

There was a rattle as the windows quivered in the wind, but still no-one answered.

'I'm going in,' said Amber.

Julia grabbed her arm. 'It's too risky. The whole place is unsafe. We shouldn't really be anywhere near it.'

There was another creak. The cottage shuddered and shook.

'The ground's trembling,' said Emil.

Julia pulled at his sleeve. 'We need to move away.'

Amber turned to follow Julia and Emil, but as she did so, the beam of her torch lit up something small and shiny on the ground. Even though she couldn't see it properly, she knew what it was. She picked it up and put it in her pocket. Another shudder rippled the ground. Then she heard Julia shouting. 'Run! Run!'

They didn't look back. Running across the road as far as they could, they huddled together, trembling amid the settling dust. But then, from somewhere in the darkness they heard a loud crack, almost like an explosion, followed by a few seconds of silence as if the world was holding its breath. Peering through a haze of dust, they watched in disbelief as one whole side of Lighthouse Cottage began to sag and buckle before their eyes.

'It's falling into the sea!' yelled Emil.

'Keep back,' shouted Julia.

'It's going,' yelled Emil again.

Amber covered her ears as the whole building slid and crashed into the sea, like a slow motion film. Huge clouds of dust billowed into the sky as the sea swallowed up the cottage like prey.

When it was over, all they could hear was the sound of the sea lapping against the rocks, as if it was licking its lips. All that was left was a huge empty space where Lighthouse Cottage had once stood. No-one spoke for a while. It was as if they were in some kind of dream. They couldn't believe what they had seen. Julia put her arms round Emil and Amber and held them close. 'We've had a lucky escape.'

Amber reached in her pocket. 'I found Ella's locket in the doorway. She must have been in there.'

Emil and Amber looked at each other for a brief second as if they both knew what to do next.

'Come back,' shouted Julia as they raced towards the edge of the cliff. 'It's not safe.'

But neither of them listened. Saving Ella was the only thing on their minds, but as they looked down the cliff, all they could see was blackness.

'She could have dropped the locket when we left the cave,' said Emil. 'It doesn't mean she was in the cottage when it fell.'

'It's my fault,' said Amber as Julia pulled them away. 'I should have left Ella in Katrin's house. At least she was safe there.'

'She wasn't safe in Katrin's house,' said Julia. 'She was completely alone. Anything could have happened to her and no-one would have known.'

Emil looked at Amber's dejected face. 'It's not your fault Amber.'

Julia put her arm round Amber as they walked slowly away from the cliff. 'If Ella was in the cottage, there's nothing more we can do.'

Emil walked alongside them. 'We don't know that for sure do we Mum? Maybe she wasn't in there. She didn't answer when we called.'

'You're right Emil. She may not have reached the cottage,' said Julia. 'We need to search everywhere between home and here.'

Amber took out the locket and gripped it tightly. 'Please be still alive Ella,' she said quietly to herself. 'Please.'

'We need to keep calling her name,' said Julia. 'She might be near the road somewhere.'

'I've just thought of something else,' said Emil. 'What if she didn't use the road at all? What if she used the cliff path?'

‘Does she know about the cliff path?’ asked Julia. ‘She hasn’t been here long.’

Amber thought for a moment. ‘Yes she *does* know about the path. We talked about using it when we got out of Lighthouse Cottage, didn’t we Emil? You said it was a short cut but thought it wasn’t safe.’

‘That’s right I did.’

They looked towards the cliff path, where it once came out by the cottage, but the path there had also fallen into the sea. If Ella had taken the cliff path that night, Amber knew the chances of finding her alive were very small.

‘If she did go on the cliff path, she could have turned back when she saw it falling,’ said Amber.

‘It’s no good guessing Amber,’ said Emil. ‘We don’t know anything for sure.’

Amber shone her torch ahead. ‘What’s that? There’s something moving in the grass beyond those small rocks.’

‘I can’t see anything,’ said Julia.

‘I definitely saw something moving,’ said Amber. ‘Ella,’ she called. ‘Ella are you there?’

There was no reply but as they continued to shine their torches on the grass, a small brown furry creature appeared, nibbling the grass by the roadside. And the creature had a collar round its neck.

‘Bonzo,’ called Amber as she scooped him up in her arms.

‘Ella must be here somewhere,’ said Emil. ‘She would never leave Bonzo on his own.’

‘Look behind those small rocks,’ said Julia. ‘It looks like there’s a patch of grass there.’

Clambering over the rocks, they called Ella’s name over and over again until at last they heard something. A tiny voice in the darkness. ‘*Amber? Emil?*’

Out of the dust and the mist came a small figure, limping across the grass towards them.

'She's here,' called Amber. 'It's Ella.'

Amber held on tightly to Bonzo as Ella sank to the ground in front of her.

Then Emil's voice came out of the darkness. 'Is she alright?'

Amber knelt down as Ella reached out her hand to stroke Bonzo.

'What happened?' said Julia, coming to sit beside them.

'Some bricks fell on my leg when I was in the cottage,' said Ella. 'Then Bonzo jumped away from me and I couldn't breathe.'

'We didn't see you come out,' said Emil. 'It was all so dusty.'

Amber was so glad that Julia seemed to know what to do and it wasn't long before Ella's leg was strapped up with her scarf.

'Emil can carry you back,' said Julia. 'Be a brave girl. We'll soon be home.'

Ella took a very squashed Hoppy from her coat pocket and held it tightly as Emil picked her up.

'Wait,' said Amber. 'Look what I found as we ran from the cottage.'

'My locket,' said Ella. 'Thank you.'

* * *

Dawn was breaking as Emil and Julia took turns to carry Ella back to Charlie's house. Amber tried to reassure her that everything would be fine, but Ella sobbed most of the way.

Once they arrived at the house, Julia spent a long time cooling Ella's swollen leg with an ice pack and bandaging it up. Ella had stopped crying by now but every few minutes she would say the same thing.

'Don't send me back to Katrin. Don't let her give Bonzo away.'

It wasn't long before Charlie appeared at the kitchen door, wearing his gansey over his pyjamas.

'What's happening? It's six o'clock in the morning. What's everyone doing here so early?'

Amber tried to explain things to her Grandad and even though he nodded as she spoke, she could tell he wasn't really following it. When she had finished talking, he went to a cupboard and took out a bag of jelly babies.

'These are for you Bella,' he said as he cut off the top of the packet with some scissors. 'The yellow ones are the best.'

Ella took the bag and put a jelly baby in her mouth. 'Thank you,' she whispered.

Charlie patted her on the head. 'Don't cry little one. You'll make both your rabbits sad. The toy one and the real one.'

He picked Bonzo up from the floor and handed him to Ella. 'We'll take him for a run in the garden later,' said Charlie. 'How about that?'

Ella nodded. 'Can I take Bonzo to sleep with me?'

'Bonzo can sleep next to your bed in his cage if you like,' said Amber.

'Oh, thank you Amber,' said Ella taking another jelly baby. 'Do you want one Charlie?'

Ella seemed pleased to share the sweets with Charlie and it wasn't long before they had eaten the whole packet between them.

'Is it time for breakfast now?' said Charlie putting the empty packet in the bin. 'Why is everyone here so early?'

Amber sighed. 'I've already told you Grandad.'

'Have you? My memory's getting bad.'

Julia stood up. 'I think we should all go back to bed for a couple of hours. It's been quite a night.'

Emil carried Bonzo's cage up to the attic, before he and Julia went home, leaving Amber and Ella to wash the dust off their clothes and their bodies.

‘Ella,’ said Amber as they got into bed. ‘Don’t ever run away like that again will you? You could have been killed.’

Amber looked at her phone and yawned. It was seven o’clock in the morning.

‘I’m glad you found Bonzo,’ said Ella.

* * *

They both slept until late morning, when they were woken by the phone ringing. Amber ran downstairs. It was her Mum with news that although her Dad was still very sick, he was recovering well. When her Mum said she would be back in a couple of days, Amber decided to tell her how badly Katrin was treating Ella and her Grandad.

‘I know you mean well,’ said Mum, ‘but we can’t go accusing people of things just like that.’

This was not the reaction Amber expected. ‘Alright, I can’t prove she’s stealing from Grandad, but I know she’s treating Ella badly.’

Mum sounded irritated. ‘You don’t know for sure Amber. It’s only what Ella has told you and she might be making it all up.’

‘She isn’t making it up Mum. Emil thinks the same as me. Why won’t anyone believe us?’

‘I have to go,’ said Mum. ‘We’ll talk about it when I get back. Make sure you tell your Grandad that Dad is going to be alright. He’ll be worried.’

Amber was pleased to hear about her Dad, but she felt so angry about her Mum’s reaction to Ella.

‘Dad’s going to be OK Grandad,’ said Amber walking into the lounge. ‘Mum’s coming home in a couple of…’ But the lounge was empty.

She ran into the kitchen. 'Grandad. Where are you?'

The back door was open so she went outside, shivering in her pyjamas. There was a shed at the end of the garden and the door was open.

'There you are Grandad. What are you doing?'

'I'm looking for that missing book *The History of Legna,*' he said, standing over a large plastic box.

'I think it might be in here.'

'Let's take the box into the kitchen,' said Amber. 'It's cold in here.'

Ella wandered into the kitchen with Hoppy in her hand, wearing her pyjamas. Her face was as pale as her light blonde hair but Amber was pleased to see she was smiling.

'What's that?' she asked, looking at the box.

'Some things from when I was a boy,' said Charlie.

Amber reached inside the box and pulled out a green exercise book, similar to the one she found belonging to Benny. It was marked and faded with age and the staples holding it together were rusty. There was a name on the front cover, written in childish handwriting. It said *Charlie Jones.*

'This is yours,' said Amber, handing it to him.

'I don't want to look at it,' said Charlie as he walked out of the room.

Amber put the book back in the box. She couldn't understand why her Grandad didn't want to look at his own book.

'Go and get dressed Ella,' she said. 'I'll get you some breakfast later. I'm going to see if my Grandad is OK.'

'I'm going to read Benny's poem all on my own,' said Ella.

Benny and Grandad
By Amber Herry

12

Curse of the Angel

Charlie was sitting in his chair in the lounge when Amber came in. He was staring at the floor.

'Are you OK Grandad?'

Charlie reached for the box of tissues next to his chair and dabbed his eyes. 'I remember it all now Amber.'

'What?'

'I remember what happened to Benny.'

'Can you tell me?'

'We were pretending to be soldiers marching along the cliff path, but when we got to the part above Legna Bay, Benny slipped and fell. He went backwards over the edge like a rag doll.'

'What did you do?'

'I ran back along the path and down to the beach. It took a long time and by the time I got there, a woman had already found him. When someone told my mother they'd seen us climbing up to the cave earlier that day, she thought it was the curse that made Benny fall.'

Amber sat with her Grandad for some time, keeping him company. It seemed the only thing she could do. She couldn't change the past.

She had almost forgotten about Ella when she came in carrying her book. 'I've been practising reading the poem about the Angel's Child,' she said proudly. 'Can I read it to you Amber?'

'I don't think my Grandad wants to hear it at the moment Ella.'

'Let the child read it,' said Charlie. 'I can't feel any worse than I do now.'

'What happened to Benny wasn't because you'd been cursed for playing in the cave Grandad. It was an accident.'

'You remind me of your Granny,' said Charlie. 'She was always trying to cheer people up.'

Ella stood up. 'I'm ready to read it now.'

Ella's words sang out across the room as she read the poem. It was as if she had known it all her life.

THE ANGEL'S CHILD

In an April storm at the close of day
The Bella Rose sank off Legna Bay.
But watching not so far away
Was the Angel of the Sea.

As a mother and baby jumped in the tide
There came a voice from the water-side.
'The sea shall never take them,' cried
The Angel of the Sea.

When the mother died upon the beach
The Angel kissed the baby's cheek.
'This child shall now be mine to keep,'
Said the Angel of the Sea.

The child was happy and wished to stay
But the Islanders took the child away.
'You've stolen my child and you will pay,'
Cried the Angel of the Sea.

On stormy nights, when the tide is high
You can hear the Angel's bitter cry.
'Return my child or you will die,'
Cursed the Angel of the Sea.

They both clapped.

'I remember that poem,' said Charlie. 'Benny wrote it.'

'He was very clever wasn't he?' said Ella.

'You're clever, reading all those difficult words,' said Amber.

Ella looked pleased. 'My teachers say I'm very good at reading and writing, but I like drawing best.'

Charlie leaned back in his chair and smiled slightly as he spoke. 'Benny was good at drawing.'

'You thought I was that Angel's Child in the poem didn't you Charlie?' said Ella.

Charlie nodded. 'But you are the Angel's Child in a way aren't you?'

Ella looked puzzled. 'What do you mean?'

'Katrin's like an angel,' said Charlie, 'so if she's been looking after you, then you are the Angel's Child aren't you?'

'Katrin's not an angel,' said Ella. 'She left me on my own and I was scared.'

'That was a mistake Ella,' said Amber. 'Katrin asked my Grandad to look after you but he didn't understand what she meant.'

Ella's lip quivered as if she was about to cry. 'Well what about all those other times?'

'What other times?'

'She left me on my own every time she went out in Daddy's car. She told me to stay in my room 'til she got back. She told me not to answer the door or the phone but she was gone a long time and I was scared and hungry.'

Amber put her arms round Ella and gave her a hug. She couldn't understand how Katrin could have been so cruel. She looked at her Grandad, but his eyes were closed. He had drifted away into the world of his old memories.

'I won't have to go back to Katrin will I Amber?'

Amber didn't know what to say. 'You're safe with us for now Ella.'

'My Daddy's kind like you,' said Ella. 'He'll be back soon won't he?'

'I'm sure he will,' said Amber. But she had no idea when Dave would be back.

* * *

She switched on the TV and managed to find a channel for Ella to watch before returning to the kitchen. The box from the shed was still there. She took out her Grandad's old exercise book and looked inside. There was a drawing of two boys fighting on a cliff. She turned the page to find another drawing of a boy falling down the cliff and one on the opposite page of the same boy lying on the sand with his eyes closed. There was blood on his head. This was a diary in drawings. Her Grandad had drawn the story of Benny's tragic death in this little book and yet something wasn't right. The boys in the drawing weren't marching like her Grandad had said. They were fighting. Had her Grandad accidently pushed Benny over the edge in a play fight? If he had, then she was glad he hadn't remembered it properly. She put the book back in the box as Ella came in.

'Charlie can't remember how to switch the TV off.'

When Amber went back into the lounge, Charlie was standing in front of the TV, frantically pressing every button on the remote. 'It's broken. Can you fix it?'

Amber took it from him and pressed the OFF button. The screen went blank.

'How did you do that?'

'You need to press the button on the top right.'

Charlie looked irritated. 'That's what I was pressing.'

Amber didn't say anything, but she knew there must be something very wrong with her Grandad if he couldn't remember how to turn off his own TV.

* * *

After a late lunch, Amber and Ella spent the rest of the day playing Ludo and some card games that Charlie found in his cupboard. Ella was good at games and didn't seem too upset if she lost. Charlie didn't want to play but he seemed to enjoy watching them. By four o'clock he'd fallen asleep in his chair again.

Amber and Ella were about to start another game when there was a knock at the door. It was Emil carrying a large bag. 'Mum's sent these pies,' he said. 'You need to warm them in the microwave.'

Amber hesitated. 'I've never used a microwave.'

Emil raised his eyebrows in surprise. 'Mum's written the instructions inside, but I can show you if you want.'

Amber took the bag from him. She felt embarrassed and wished she hadn't admitted how useless she was. 'I'll be fine. It's really kind of her.'

Emil followed her into the kitchen. 'My Mum phoned your Mum at the hospital today. She told her we'd look after you.'

'Your Mum's really nice,' said Amber, unpacking the bag.

Emil pulled up a chair and sat down. 'Sometimes she's too nice.'

'How can you be too nice?'

'She let Katrin keep the money she stole, even though she doesn't make a lot of money from the café.'

‘That’s because Katrin is such a good liar. She can fool anybody.’

‘Well she doesn’t fool me,’ said Emil.

‘Nor me,’ said Amber looking in the bag for the microwave instructions.

‘Hi Emil,’ called Ella as she skipped into the kitchen. ‘I’ve won four card games.’

Emil smiled. ‘How many has Amber won?’

‘Only two,’ said Ella.

‘Then you’re the champion,’ said Emil.

Ella giggled. ‘Am I?’

‘If I had a medal I would put it round your neck.’

‘Like the Olympics?’

‘Just like that.’

‘Will you play cards with us Emil?’

‘I’ve got to go home now,’ said Emil, ‘but I’ll come back tomorrow.’

‘OK. See you later. I’m going to tell Bonzo I’m a champion,’ said Ella as she left.

Emil stood up to leave.

‘Are you still going to keep Bonzo in your bedroom Amber?’

‘I will if it keeps Ella happy.’

‘She’s not going to like it when she has to go back to Katrin’s is she?’

‘I’m trying not to think about that,’ said Amber.

* * *

After Emil had gone home, Charlie spent the evening watching TV while Amber and Ella sat on the sofa, drawing things in their notebooks.

‘I’m going to draw me winning the Olympics,’ said Ella. ‘What are you going to draw Amber?’

‘I’m going to draw Lighthouse Cottage,’ said Amber. ‘I’m going to draw it how it looked just before it fell into the sea.’

By the time Amber had finished her sketch and admired Ella’s drawing, it was time for bed and it wasn’t long before she and Ella were sound asleep.

It was midnight when Bonzo moved around in his cage, waking Amber up. She looked at Ella sleeping peacefully with Hoppy and wished she could save her from Katrin. Thoughts were whizzing around her head. She couldn’t get back to sleep, so she went downstairs to the kitchen for a drink of water. There was a pile of ripped pieces of paper on the work surface next to Grandad’s box. She tried to piece them all back together, but there were too many. She guessed what had happened. Grandad had torn up his old exercise book; the one with the drawings of Benny in it. She thought about sticking it all back together but then decided against it. It was her Grandad’s book and he could do what he liked with it, but it still made her sad to think he had ripped it up. She scooped up all the pieces and put them in the bin, before turning out the light.

My attic Window

By Amber Henry

13

Talk Through the Window

The next day was sunny with light clouds drifting across the sky and Ella was up early.

'Amber are you awake? It's sunny. Can I take Bonzo into the garden?'

Amber yawned and wondered if this was what it was like having a younger sister.'

'Can we go now Amber?'

'I've got to put some wood over the hole in the hedge first. We don't want Bonzo running away again do we?'

Parts of the garden were still muddy after the flood, but once Amber had blocked up the hole, Bonzo hopped about happily as Ella chased him around. 'Daddy said I have to watch him in the garden to make sure he doesn't eat anything he shouldn't.'

Amber felt better after speaking to her Mum on the phone the previous night, but today was the day Katrin was due to come back, and that made her feel anxious.

It was about eleven o'clock when Emil came round with a football.

Ella was delighted. 'Oh thanks Emil. Can we play with it now?

'It's a bit muddy to kick it about Ella. But we can throw it to each other.'

'Am I still a champion?' asked Ella.

'Of course you are,' said Emil, bouncing the ball on the garden path. 'Once a champion, always a champion. Put Bonzo back in his cage so he doesn't get in the way and then we can start.'

Amber went inside to check on her Grandad. He was still recovering after the incident in the cave, but he refused to let anyone call a doctor, so she was pleased to see he was sitting in his chair, eating sweets.

'Are you OK Grandad?'

'Of course I'm OK. Why wouldn't I be?'

'Mum might be coming out of hospital tomorrow.'

'Hospital?' said Charlie. 'I didn't know she was in hospital.'

'Yes you did Grandad. She was hurt when the bridge collapsed. Dad is in the same hospital but he's still too ill to leave.'

'Oh yes. I remember now.'

'Shall I put the TV on?'

'No, it's all rubbish. I can't follow what's going on these days.'

'Do you want anything to read?'

'That book on the history of Legna,' said Charlie. 'There's something in it about the Angel's Child. Can you find it for me?'

'I'll try. Maybe it's in your bedroom. I'll have a look later.'

'What time is it?'

'Eleven o'clock. Why?'

Charlie grinned. 'Time for you to make me a cup of tea.'

Amber could hear Ella and Emil laughing in the garden as she put the kettle on. It was good to hear. She hadn't heard much laughter for a while.

'Do you two want a drink?'

Emil took his boots off by the door. 'It's half time Ella. Time for a break.'

Ella's clothes were splattered in mud and her face was red with effort but she was smiling broadly.

'I'm the champion again Amber,' she said. 'Emil can't catch. He keeps dropping the ball.'

'Only because you can't throw it properly,' teased Emil.

Ella tapped him playfully on the arm. 'That's not true. Bonzo knows I can throw a ball don't you Bonzo?'

A knock at the front door stopped their conversation.

'I'll go,' said Emil.

Amber put out some biscuits and waited. She guessed who it was and she was right.

'I've come for the child,' said a woman's voice.

'Ella put down the biscuit she was about to eat as her red faced drained of colour. 'I don't want to go.'

When Emil returned to the kitchen, Amber could tell he was angry.

'It's Katrin,' he said. 'She's in the lounge talking to Charlie.'

Amber looked at Ella. There was real fear in her eyes.

'Can Bonzo stay here?' said Ella. 'Katrin will give him away if he comes back with me.'

'I don't know,' said Amber. 'Charlie's not well. He can't really look after a rabbit and if Bonzo comes home with me you won't see him again. We live such a long way from here.'

'Please take him Amber. Please.'

'I'll take him to my house when Amber goes home,' said Emil. 'You can come and play with him whenever you want to.'

'Thank you,' said Ella throwing her arms around Emil. 'You're my best champion.'

'Hello,' said a cold voice.

The sweet sickly smell of Katrin's perfume wafted into the kitchen as she approached. 'I'm very busy Amber. Can you keep the child until six tonight?'

'Can't I stay longer?' whispered Ella.

Katrin narrowed her eyes as she stared at Ella. 'Your father's going to ring at six tonight and he'll want to speak to you.'

'Can I come back here after I've spoken to Daddy?'

'She can stay here as long as she wants,' said Amber. 'We don't mind.'

'She doesn't deserve to stay with such kind people,' said Katrin. 'Look how filthy she is. Her father paid good money for those clothes and she's ruined them.'

'Ella's a good girl,' said Emil. 'She's been playing in the garden that's all.'

Amber moved closer to Ella and took her hand. It was shaking.

'I don't want Dave saying I'm not looking after his child,' said Katrin. 'She's got to stay with me tonight, but I don't want the rabbit. Set the thing free if you can't get rid of it.'

'Emil's going to look after it,' said Amber.

'Do you want some tea Katrin?' asked Charlie as he joined them.

Katrin's face softened immediately. 'My dear Charlie,' she gushed. 'You are so kind but I need to get back. I've got so much to do.'

'Katrin's always busy,' said Charlie, 'but she finds time to help me.'

'You call me your angel don't you Charlie?'

Charlie leant against the kitchen door. 'I need to sit down. I'm feeling a bit dizzy.'

Amber rushed towards him and guided him to a kitchen chair.

'I'll see myself out then,' said Katrin.

Charlie wanted to sit in his chair in the lounge, so Amber went with him in case he fell.

When she came back, she found Emil and Ella sitting in silence, staring at the floor .

Emil looked up. 'Is Charlie alright?'

'I think so. He's eating his sweets now, so that's a good sign.'

Ella didn't move. She had her head in her hands.

'I'll ask Katrin if you can come here to play tomorrow,' said Amber. 'I'm sure she won't mind.'

'You need to tell your Dad you don't want to stay with Katrin?' added Emil.

'I can't,' whispered Ella. 'She's always standing by the phone when I speak to him.'

'I wish I could talk to him,' said Emil. 'I'd tell him how mean Katrin is.'

'He wouldn't believe you Emil,' said Ella. 'They're getting married as soon as they find a bigger house.'

'Why do they want a bigger house if there's only two of them?' asked Amber.

'It's Katrin who wants it.' said Ella. 'Daddy had to get a new job at sea, so he can get enough money to buy one.'

Emil stood up. 'I don't want to hear any more. It's making me mad.'

'Come on Ella,' said Amber. 'Let's go upstairs and pack your things and then we can play cards.'

'I'd better go,' said Emil. 'I'm helping Mum clean out the café this afternoon. We don't want to miss the ferry.'

'I wish I could come with you. I'd like to visit my Mum and Dad in hospital,' said Amber.

'I thought your Mum was coming back tomorrow.'

Amber shrugged her shoulders. 'It depends on what the doctor says this afternoon.'

'My Mummy's in hospital too,' said Ella. 'I wish she'd hurry up and get better so I can go home.'

Amber put her arm round the little girl, as Emil coughed and pretended to blow his nose.

* * *

After Emil had gone, Amber persuaded Ella to pack but it wasn't easy. All she wanted to do was hold Bonzo. She held him so tight that he finally wriggled out of her arms and hid under Amber's bed.

'He'll come out when I bring his food up later,' said Amber.

'Will you still keep him up here in the bedroom?'

'Is that what you want?'

'Yes. Then when I'm asleep I'll know he's the other side of the wall.'

'I've had an idea,' said Amber. 'If you need to speak to me tonight we can talk though the windows.'

Ella's face brightened a little. 'Can we?'

'The two attic windows are very close. I'm sure we'll hear each other if we speak loud enough.'

'What if Katrin hears me talking?'

'We'll wait 'til she goes to bed. Her bedroom's on the other side of the house so she won't hear us. I'll call you at midnight, just to see how you are. Katrin should be in bed by then.'

'How will I know when it's midnight?'

Haven't you got a watch or a clock in your room?'

'No. Daddy said he would get me a watch when I learn to tell the time but I'm not very good.'

'I'll bang three times on the wall when it's midnight,' said Amber. 'That'll be your signal to open the window.'

* * *

Amber and Ella spent the afternoon playing cards and drawing. Amber decided to draw the inside of the cave. She wanted to show just how dark and scary it was, but Ella's drawing was much more cheerful. Her page was covered with tumbling shapes and patterns which she then coloured in with a pack of felt-tip pens that Amber had given her.

At half past five, Amber took Ella round to Katrin's house, so she wouldn't miss the phone call from her Dad. Ella was reluctant to go and became tearful as they approached Katrin's house, but she cheered up a little when Amber reminded her about their plan to talk through the window.

When Katrin answered the door, her face was thunderous. To Amber's surprise she didn't even look at Ella. Instead she seized Amber by the hair and pulled her inside with such force that she dropped Ella's bags.

'Where is it?' she hissed.

Every part of Amber's body trembled as her head throbbed with the pain.

Ella began to cry. 'Don't hurt her.'

'I don't know what you mean,' said Amber, her voice quivering.

Katrin took hold of Amber's arm and gripped it hard. 'Don't pretend you're little miss innocent. That jewellery box has gone and you are the only one who could have taken it.'

'Let go. You're hurting me.'

'Tell me where it is then.'

'Grandad's ill. He shouldn't have given it to you.'

Lunging towards Ella, Katrin snatched Hoppy from her hand and held it up high so she couldn't reach it. 'If you don't bring that jewellery box back by tomorrow, this is going in the bin.'

Ella screamed as Katrin pushed Amber out of the door and slammed it shut, leaving Amber standing alone outside.

Paralysed with the shock of what had just happened, Amber stood motionless on the doorstep. All she could hear was the sound of Ella's pitiful cries as she pleaded for Hoppy's return. Her mind was in turmoil. Anger welled up inside her like an erupting volcano. No-one should behave like this. Katrin had hurt her. She needed to phone her Mum. But then she thought about it some more. Katrin would probably deny it ever happened. Ella was the only witness and Katrin could say she was making it up. With her legs still trembling, she walked away down the path. She was thinking about what her parents would say if they found out she'd taken the jewellery box. She knew they would say it was wrong, even though they would understand why she had done it. By the time she arrived at her Grandad's house she had decided what to do. Tomorrow she would give Granny's box back to Katrin because, if she didn't, Ella would suffer even more and she couldn't stand that.

She said nothing about the incident to her Grandad as they sat watching TV together. He was too confused to understand and he would probably forget soon after anyway.

'I'm going to bed,' he announced, as the documentary they were watching came to an end. 'I like programmes about sea life but that was too complicated. I can't follow these programmes any more.'

'It's only nine o'clock Grandad.'

'I don't care what time it is. I'm feeling tired.'

'What about your sweets?' said Amber noticing he had left his usual line of yellow jelly babies on the coffee table.

'Leave them,' said Charlie. 'I'll eat them tomorrow.'

Amber had a slight headache and wished she could to go to bed early too, but she was waiting for the phone call from her Mum, and anyway she couldn't stop worrying about Ella. She picked up her sketch pad. It might take her mind off things while she waited. She had just finished sketching the row of jelly babies on Grandad's table when the phone rang.

'It's bad news and good news,' said her Mum. 'What do you want first?'

'The bad news,' said Amber.

'I won't be coming home tomorrow. The doctor said I have to stay another day, but the good news is Dad is improving. He might be well enough to come home at the end of next week. How's Grandad?'

Amber lowered her voice. 'He's getting worse Mum. I don't think he should be living on his own anymore.'

'Julia told me what's been happening,' said Mum. 'We'll talk about it when I get out of hospital. Try not to worry about your Grandad. There's nothing you can do.'

Amber wasn't sure how much Julia had told her Mum, but she felt she needed to tell her about Ella.

'Katrin's treating Ella really bad Mum. I'm scared for her but I don't know what to do.'

'What do you mean *treating her bad*?'

'She makes Ella stay in her room all day and leaves her on her own when she goes out and there's other things as well. I think she might hurt her.'

'Do you know that for sure Amber or is that just something Ella told you?'

'Ella told me but I've seen how scared she is of ...'

Her Mum interrupted her. 'You have to be careful with young children. They can make things up.'

The phone line began to crackle. 'I'll phone you tomorrow Amber. Love you.'

Amber loved her Mum but she felt disappointed and angry with her. Ella was in trouble and no-one except Emil was willing to help. She switched off all the lights, checked the doors were locked and went upstairs. As she passed her Grandad's room she could hear him snoring.

Once in the attic bedroom, she opened the window ready to talk to Ella when the time came. She took Granny's box out of the drawer and unwrapped it, tracing her fingers over the leaves and flowers across the lid. She had a lump in her throat thinking about losing it but she had to take it back. Ella was in enough trouble without this. She wrapped it up again and put it back in the drawer, She was so glad she had sketched it.

As she lay on the bed staring at the wings on the wall, a light breeze from the window blew through them, making a soft whispering sound. It was hot in the room despite the breeze and it wasn't long before Amber closed her eyes and drifted into an uneasy sleep.

It was the sound of breaking glass coming from the garden that woke her up. She rushed to the window and peered out. In the half-light of the moon she could see the figure of her Grandad standing in the greenhouse. 'Grandad! Are you OK?'

'Milly?' he called. 'Is that you?'

She ran downstairs and out into the night. If her Grandad thought she was her mother Milly, she knew he was in one of his confused moods.

'I've put my walking stick through the greenhouse,' said Charlie as he stepped over the broken glass. 'Not sure how I came to do that.'

'What were you doing?' Amber said as she led him inside.

'Getting tomatoes.'

'What? In the middle of the night?'

'I thought it was time to get up. What time is it then?'

Amber looked at the clock on the wall. 'Eleven thirty.'

Then she remembered. She had promised to contact Ella at midnight. It was lucky Grandad had woken her up.

* * *

It was one minute past midnight by the time Amber returned to her bedroom. She stood against the wall and knocked three times. Then she waited. Nothing happened. Maybe she didn't knock loud enough. She tried again.

Bang Bang Bang

The reply came instantly. *Rap Rap Rap*

Amber ran to the window and pushed it open a little wider. 'Ella are you there?'

There was a creak. Then a small voice. 'Amber? Can you hear me?'

'Yes, I can hear you. Did your Daddy phone?'

'Yes, but Katrin was standing with me.'

'Did he say anything about boarding school?'

'He said I have to be a good girl and do what Katrin tells me.'

A gust of wind rattled the window as Amber spoke. 'Did you tell him about Bonzo?'

Ella raised her voice above the wind, 'What did you say?'

Amber spoke louder. 'I said did you tell your Daddy about Bonzo?'

'Ella!' shrieked another voice as Ella's window slammed shut. Then she heard Katrin shouting followed by Ella screaming like she was in pain. Amber banged on the wall. 'Stop. Leave her alone!'

But it didn't stop. It went on for several minutes until finally she heard a door slam.

Then came the sound of Ella sobbing. Deep sorrowful sobbing that broke Amber's heart. She felt so bad. She'd got Ella into trouble with Katrin over the box and now she had made things even worse. All she could do was listen to Ella's sobs and hope things would be better in the morning. When she took the box back she would tell Katrin that talking through the window was her idea. Maybe that would help a little.

Grandad's spiky plant

By Amber Henry

14

More Wrong Than Right

When Amber woke up, it was already nine o'clock. The sun was streaming into the room, bathing it in a warm glow. She ran down the attic stairs and looked into her Grandad's room. He looked up as she came in. He was dressed in his gansey and sitting on his bed but his face was anxious. 'I'm not sure where I am,' he said. 'Is this my bedroom?'

Amber was shocked. How could he not know he was in his own bedroom?

'Yes, this is your room,' was all she could say.

Charlie's face relaxed a little. 'I thought it was my room. There's a photo of me over there.'

Amber looked across at the photo of her Grandad standing with her Granny on the deck of a cruise ship, smiling in the sunshine.

'Who's that woman with me?' asked Charlie.

Amber couldn't answer him. She wanted to cry. How could Grandad forget her lovely Granny. Something was very wrong with him and whatever it was, it was getting worse.

Charlie allowed Amber to take his arm and lead him downstairs to the kitchen. After he had drunk some tea and eaten a slice of toast, he seemed to recover and talked as if nothing had happened. But Amber couldn't wait for her Mum to come home. She was afraid of what her Grandad might do if he became even more confused. But she had something important to do that wouldn't wait. She had to return the box so Ella could get Hoppy back and own up to Katrin that talking through the window was her idea.

'I'm going next door soon Grandad. I won't be long.'

'Yes yes,' said Charlie as he headed for the lounge. 'I'm going to see what's on TV. I think there's a documentary on about sea life.'

Amber didn't have time to correct him. She was on her way upstairs for the box.

By the time she got downstairs Emil was at the door with more food from Julia.

'You need to call the police,' said Emil, when she told him what had happened. 'She's attacked you.'

He clenched his fists as Amber tried to explain why she wanted to keep it secret, but she could tell Emil didn't agree.

'I'm coming with you?' he said, putting down the box of food.

'No Emil. That'll make her more angry and she'll take it out on Ella. You keep an eye on my Grandad 'til I get back.'

'OK, but it's not right. She shouldn't be allowed to treat people like that. Does Charlie know where you're going?'

'Yes, but he doesn't know why. He probably won't remember anyway. He's in his own world at the moment.'

She took a deep breath as she left.

'Good luck,' said Emil. 'You might need it.'

* * *

When she knocked on Katrin's door there was no answer so she knocked again a little louder. A few seconds later Katrin appeared in the doorway wearing a red satin dressing gown. She had a white towel round her head as if she had come out of the shower.

'Oh, it's you,' she said. 'I see you've brought the box?'

Amber handed it over. 'Please don't take it out on Ella. It's not her fault.'

Katrin began to close the door.

'Just a minute. I'd like to explain about last night...'

'I don't have time,' said Katrin.

'It was my idea to talk through the window. It's not Ella's fault.'

'Oh really. Well she's in trouble anyway so it makes no difference.'

'Why? What's she done?'

'She's refusing to eat and if she won't eat, she'll starve. It's not my fault.'

'Maybe she'll eat if she comes to our house. Can she come?'

Katrin thought for a moment. 'I have to take Charlie to an appointment on the mainland this afternoon. There's a car ferry leaving at half past one, so he needs to be ready by one o'clock. I'll bring the child round early, then I can remind him.'

'I don't think he's well enough to go.'

'He has to go. It's important. Tell him I've got the letter.'

'What's the appointment for?'

'Nothing to do with you,' said Katrin, finally closing the door.

Amber shivered. The air felt colder than it should for April. Then she remembered something. The message by the phone said Wednesday 6th April and that was today. That must be the appointment Katrin was talking about.

* * *

'Charlie's been showing me some of his books,' said Emil as she walked into the lounge.

'I still can't find *The History of Legna*,' said Charlie.

'It'll turn up,' said Amber.

Emil looked at Amber's face. 'OK?'

'I'll tell you later.'

She turned to her Grandad. 'Katrin says you've got an appointment on the mainland this afternoon. It'll be that one on the telephone pad. Can you remember what it's for?'

Charlie looked puzzled. 'The notepad in the hall?'

'Yes. I showed it to you before. It said *Wed 6th April Be ready by 1pm* but it didn't say what it was about.'

'Katrin's probably written it on my calendar,' said Charlie. 'It's in the kitchen but I can't remember where.'

Despite looking in all the drawers in the kitchen, they found nothing, until Emil saw an empty hook on the wall above the bin.

'It's here,' he said, reaching behind the bin. 'It must have fallen down.'

Amber took the calendar from him. 'It's still on March. Grandad obviously hasn't looked at it this week.'

'Look,' said Emil as Amber turned it over, 'There's something written in red pen on today's date. It says *Simpson and Grindel 2.30pm.*'

'What does that mean?' said Amber.

'They're solicitors,' said Emil. 'They've got a big office on the mainland.'

'How do you know that?'

'My Mum went there when she divorced my Dad.'

'Why would he have an appointment to see a solicitor?'

'Maybe he's making a will?'

'He made a will last summer,' said Amber. 'I remember because he asked Mum and Dad to check it. Mum was pleased because Grandad said he was leaving her this house. It means a lot to her. She was born here.'

'Maybe Katrin has persuaded him to change his will?'

A cold feeling came over Amber as she thought about what would happen if Grandad left the house to Katrin instead of to her Mum. 'Let's see if we can find out,' she said.

She took the calendar into the lounge and showed it to her Grandad.

Charlie paused before he spoke. 'Ah yes. Now I remember. I asked Katrin to sort it out a while ago. I've got a letter about it somewhere.'

'Sort what out?'

'My will.'

'But you've already made a will. You asked Mum and Dad to check it last summer.'

'Well I want to change it. I want to leave something to Katrin. She's been like an angel to me since she moved in.'

'But you've already given her things. You gave her Granny's jewellery box and she has other things of yours in her house.'

'Those are small things. I want to give her more than that.'

'Like what?'

'I'm not discussing my affairs with you. You're only a child.'

The phone rang in the hall. Amber rushed to pick it up.

'Mum? I'm so glad you rang. I need to tell you something about Grandad.'

Emil followed Amber into the hall. 'Sorry Amber. I've got to go.'

Amber waved her hand as he left. Then she lowered her voice, so her Grandad wouldn't hear.

'Katrin's taking Grandad to see a solicitor this afternoon Mum. He's changing his will to leave something to Katrin.'

'Bring him to the phone,' said Mum. 'I'll see if I can find out what's going on.'

Charlie took a long time to come to the phone. His steps were small and shaky and he held on to Amber like he was going to fall. Amber couldn't hear what her Mum was saying but she was horrified when Grandad denied he was changing his will. When she got back on the phone she could tell her Mum was upset.

'We'll talk later, Amber,' she said, as she rang off.

There was a bang as Charlie collided with the table in the hall, knocking the spikey plant to the floor, spilling soil on the carpet. 'I'm feeling a bit dizzy again,' he said.

Amber took hold of his arm and led him back to his chair by the fire. 'You're not well enough to go to that appointment Grandad.'

Charlie closed his eyes. 'I need a rest that's all.'

When Amber returned to pick up the plant, she heard the key turning in the front door.

'Hello Charlie. It's only me,' said Katrin as she opened the door. 'Oh it's you. What's all this on the floor?'

'Grandad knocked a plant over.'

'Well you'd better clean it up then hadn't you. I don't want soil on my new white trainers.'

'I didn't know you had a key,' said Amber.

'Just goes to show, you don't know everything,' said Katrin stepping round the plant. 'Charlie told me to use it whenever I wanted.'

Fixing her eyes on the large brown envelope in Katrin's hand, Amber didn't notice Ella, standing outside the door until Katrin turned back.

'Don't just stand there like a useless lump,' she said. 'Get in here and watch where you're walking. I don't want you bringing soil back to my house on your shoes.'

'Hello Ella,' said Amber, giving Katrin a knowing look. 'Have you got Hoppy back? I know you lost him for a while.'

Ella nodded as she slipped silently into the hallway, but she said nothing.

'I've come to make sure Charlie knows he's got an appointment later,' said Katrin in a loud voice.

'He's feeling dizzy,' said Amber. 'He's too ill to go anywhere.'

Katrin fixed Amber with an icy stare. 'Where is he?'

Amber nodded towards the lounge.

'Charlie my love,' called Katrin as she entered the lounge. 'I've got the letter for you to sign once we get to the solicitors. You will be ready for one o'clock won't you?'

Amber reached out for Ella's hand, grasping it tightly as they followed Katrin into the lounge. She looked up and smiled at Amber but her face was lifeless. She reminded Amber of a broken doll.

Charlie opened his eyes. 'Katrin. I knew you'd come to see me soon.'

Katrin knelt beside him and held his hand. 'I hope you've remembered about the solicitor. He told us to come back once you'd checked your new will. I've got it here.'

'My new will?'

'Yes. You've got to take this copy of your new will and sign it in front of the solicitor. Otherwise it's not legal.'

'I'm not well. Can the solicitor come here instead?'

'You look fine to me Charlie. All you have to do is sit in my car on the ferry and walk across the road when we get there.'

'I feel a bit dizzy,' said Charlie. 'I think I'd better stay here today.'

Katrin's face hardened. 'It not easy for the solicitor to get here now the bridge has broken.'

Charlie closed his eyes as if that was his answer.

Katrin sighed heavily as she stood up. 'I'll see if I can rearrange it for tomorrow.'

As Katrin headed for the door, Amber saw an opportunity.

'Can Ella stay here for a while. I'm sure you've got plenty to do without looking after her.'

Katrin stopped and looked at Ella. 'Get her back by six, in case Dave rings again. Although why he wants to speak to such a miserable child I will never know.'

When Amber heard the door slam, she put her arm round Ella's shoulders but Ella winced and drew away.

'What's the matter?'

'I've hurt my arm.'

'On what?'

'I... er... banged into a door.'

'Let me see.'

Ella backed away. 'I'm fine. Don't tell Katrin I told you about my arm.

'Why not? What's going on Ella?'

'Nothing.'

'What happened last night? I heard you screaming. Did Katrin hit you? Is that how you hurt your arm?'

'No. No. It was an accident. I banged into a door. Katrin said if I make a fuss she'll send me to boarding school. Don't say anything to her. Please Amber.'

Amber took Ella's hand. 'OK.'

'Thanks,' she whispered. 'Can I see Bonzo now?'

Bonzo moved about in his cage as Amber and Ella opened the door to the attic bedroom. It was as if he knew they were coming. Ella lifted him out and sat him on her lap on the bed.

'I've missed you Bonzo,' she said in a soft voice. 'Katrin won't let me keep you anymore but Amber and Emil will look after you. Be a good rabbit for them won't you?'

Tears welled up in Amber's eyes as she watched the little girl tenderly stroking the rabbit that she loved so much. She hated Katrin for what she was doing to Ella and her Grandad but everyone except Emil thought Katrin was some kind of angel.

* * *

The day passed quickly for Amber and Ella. After eating a good meal, Ella spent some time playing with Bonzo in the garden and playing card games. Amber tried to find out more about what had been happening to Ella, but she still wouldn't talk about it.

Charlie slept in his chair most of the time. He hardly touched the lunch that Amber brought him on a tray. 'Shall I ring the doctor Grandad?'

But he didn't answer. His head was tilted back so his mouth was open. She tried again. 'Grandad?' He opened his eyes slightly and then closed them again. 'I can't breathe,' he whispered.

A terrified feeling came over Amber. Her Grandad needed help and he needed it fast. 'I'm going to ring Mum,' she said.

When Amber's Mum heard what had happened she called the emergency services. Then a friendly woman rang to tell Amber that help was on the way and asked her lots of questions about her Grandad. An hour later, two paramedics arrived in an ambulance car and took Charlie away with an oxygen mask on his face.

Amber's Mum had rung Julia and arranged for Amber to stay there for now. She rang Amber at Charlie's house. 'You can stay with Julia for a while, so you won't be on your own. Julia's going to bring you to see me at the hospital tomorrow. I should know how Grandad is by then.'

'Will I be able to see Dad as well?'

'Yes, but not for long. He's still quite weak.'

'I've got a lot to tell you tomorrow,' said Amber. 'Bye. Love you.'

While all this was going on, Ella had been quietly watching everything unfold, but Katrin was nowhere to be seen. Dave's car had gone, so Amber guessed she had gone to the solicitor by herself to explain about Charlie.

It was after five o'clock when she heard a car turn into Katrin's drive. Ella heard it too. She was sprawled out on the lounge floor, drawing pictures of rabbits.

'I don't want to go with Katrin,' she said, running to Amber. 'I don't like staying in my room all the time.'

'Does she bring food up to your room?' asked Amber, but Ella wouldn't answer. She was clinging on to Amber with an iron grip, but there was nothing she could do to help. No-one except Emil would believe that Katrin was a cruel thief and a liar. No-one, that is, apart from the strangers that had knocked on Charlie's door. How Amber wished she had talked to them a bit more, but it was too late now. They had gone.

After Ella had said lots of goodbyes to Bonzo, she finally agreed to let Amber take her back to Katrin's before six o'clock.

'You need to eat when you're at Katrin's,' said Amber as they walked back hand-in-hand.

'I don't like the sandwich she gives me,' said Ella.

'OK but if you don't eat it you need to eat whatever else she gives you.'

'She doesn't give me anything else.'

'What? Is that all you get all day? One sandwich?'

'Yes and if I don't eat it she brings it back again the next day.'

'You mean you have to eat the same sandwich?'

'Yes. It's not nice cos it's gone all hard. I was once sick when I tried to eat it and Katrin got really cross, so I don't eat any more.'

Amber held Ella's hand a little tighter.

'I wish you were my big sister,' said Ella.

'I wish I was too,' said Amber.

The door opened before they had time to knock. 'Tell Charlie the solicitor can see him next week. I've been to rearrange it today.'

'Grandad was taken to hospital after you left,' said Amber.

Katrin's cold eyes seemed to cut right through them as she spoke. 'Well I hope he'll be home by next week. I don't want to change the appointment again.'

Amber could feel Ella squeezing her hand as if she never wanted to let go.

'I'll call at your house tomorrow,' said Katrin. 'You can let me know how Charlie is.'

'I won't be there. I'm staying with Julia.'

'Well I'll call there then,' said Katrin, pulling Ella into the house by her arm.

As the door banged shut, Amber heard Katrin's harsh words to Ella.

'Get upstairs to your room and stay there. I'll call you if your father rings.'

Amber hurried away. She couldn't bear to hear any more.

* * *

After calling at her Grandad's to collect Bonzo and pack an overnight bag, Amber crossed the road to Emil's house. She knocked on the brightly painted red door and waited.

'Come in,' said Julia, taking Bonzo's cage. 'Your Mum told me you like egg and chips, so I hope you're hungry.'

Amber thought about poor Ella eating a stale sandwich every day. How she wished she didn't have to leave her with Katrin.

Emil opened a cake tin as she came into the kitchen diner. He took out a cake decorated with lemon coloured icing, with flaked chocolate pieces scattered on the top. 'I made this earlier today so I hope you like it.'

Amber was impressed. 'I can't believe you made that Emil. It looks delicious.'

'He wants to be a chef,' said Julia. 'He's great at baking and decorating cakes but he ruined the chunky chips didn't you Emil?'

‘I cut the potatoes too small,’ said Emil. ‘I like baking best but I can make zurek can’t I Mum?’

‘What’s zurek?’ asked Amber.

‘A sort of rye soup,’ said Julia. ‘It’s very popular in Poland.’

Amber didn’t care what size the chips were, it all tasted wonderful.

‘Do you want some ice cream?’ said Emil after they had finished the egg and chips. ‘We’ve got a few different flavours.’ Amber had almost forgotten what it was like to eat a meal with a family. The last few days had been the most difficult days of her life. Emil and Julia were very kind but Amber couldn’t wait to see her Mum and Dad again.

‘Do you think I could use your landline to phone Mum tonight?’ said Amber finishing her ice cream. ‘I want to find out how Grandad is.’

Julia gave Emil a knowing look. ‘I was going to tell you after you’d eaten.’

Amber put the spoon in her empty dish. Something about the way Julia spoke made her feel nervous. ‘Tell me what?’

‘I rang the hospital earlier,’ said Julia. ‘Charlie’s fine. They’ve got him back on his tablets. They think he was forgetting to take them.’

‘So is he coming home soon?’

Julia looked uncomfortable, as if she didn’t want to say any more. ‘He’s very confused,’ she said. ‘He’s going to a care home near the hospital for a few days, so they can do some tests.’

The words ‘care home’ came as a shock. ‘But he won’t like that Julia. Grandad likes his freedom.’

‘He’s too confused to come home,’ said Julia. ‘It’s a good place. I know someone who worked there.’

‘I’d still like to ring Mum later, if that’s alright.’

‘I’m sorry Amber,’ said Julia, ‘but there’s a sickness bug going round the hospital and your Mum has got it. It may only last a day or so, but you won’t be allowed to visit her until they say it’s clear.’

‘What about my Dad?’

Julia put a reassuring hand on Amber’s arm. ‘He hasn’t caught the bug but he’s too ill to talk on the phone.’

Amber looked down as a big tear dropped into her empty dish. She hadn’t realised how much she missed her parents. ‘Sorry,’ she said, fumbling in her pocket for a tissue.

‘It’s OK to cry,’ said Julia. ‘You’ve been through such a lot in the last few days.’

Amber didn’t know why, but the kinder Julia was, the more she sobbed. She was so worried about her family. She wiped her eyes and looked up at Emil. He had a line of white ice cream above his lip.

‘Look at your face Emil,’ said Julia. ‘You look like you’ve got a moustache.’

He dashed up to look in a mirror.

‘He’s like a big baby,’ said Julia laughing.

Emil wiped his face and grinned. ‘Do you want to try my lemon cake now?’

Amber smiled. At least she had some new friends to look after her.

‘We can’t visit your Mum and Dad but we can go and see Charlie tomorrow afternoon,’ said Julia. ‘I rang the care home and they asked us to take him some clean clothes.’

‘I can get those in the morning,’ said Amber, taking a slice of cake. ‘I’ll see if I can find that book he keeps asking about as well.’

‘What book is that?’ asked Julia.

‘It’s called *The History of Legna*. Grandad said it’s got the true story of the Angel’s Child in it.’

‘I didn’t know the Angel’s Child was based on a true story, did you Emil?’

‘There was a child who died in Katrin’s house. She was supposed to be the Angel’s Child. That’s why people say it’s haunted.’ said Emil, ‘But I don’t know any details’.

‘You thought Ella was the Angel’s Child didn’t you Emil?’ said Amber.

Emil stood up to clear the table. He looked embarrassed. ‘No I didn’t. I was only trying to scare you.’

‘I wonder how Ella’s getting on at Katrin’s,’ said Amber.

‘Katrin will take good care of her I’m sure,’ said Julia.

‘Katrin’s two-faced,’ said Emil, running water into the sink. ‘She’s nice to people if she wants something, but she’s really mean to Ella.’

‘Katrin only gives her one sandwich a day and if she doesn’t eat it, she saves it for the next day,’ said Amber.

Julia shook her head. ‘I can’t believe that. Young children sometimes make things up you know.’

‘I’ve seen how scared Ella is when Katrin’s around,’ said Amber. ‘I heard her screaming one night and the next day she had a sore arm. I think Katrin may have hit her. I don’t think she was making that up.’

‘And she made Ella give Bonzo away,’ said Emil. ‘We know that for sure. How cruel is that?’

‘I’m sure there’s a good reason why she can’t take care of the rabbit,’ said Julia, clearing the last dishes from the table.

‘Can’t you ring Dave Mum? If he knew how Katrin was treating Ella, I’m sure he would come home and sort it out.’

Julia carried the dishes to the sink. ‘It’s none of our business. Even if you were right, I don’t think Dave would believe you. I remember what he was like when he used to visit Katrin at my café. He thinks she’s perfect.’

‘Well someone needs to believe us,’ said Emil. ‘Someone needs to save Ella from Katrin. She’s being starved, abandoned and kept a prisoner. Does no-one care?’

'Don't exaggerate Emil. People have different ideas about bringing up children. We may not agree with how Katrin treats Ella, but unless we see bruises or find out she is seriously neglecting Ella, we should mind our own business.'

'But she *is* neglecting her Mum. That's what Amber and I keep saying, but nobody will listen.'

'You don't know anything for certain,' said Julia. 'You only know what Ella has told you and she could be making it up.'

There was a bang as Emil slammed down the plate he was about to wash up and stormed out of the door.

Amber didn't know what to do so she got up to finish the dishes, but Julia stopped her. 'I'll do that Amber. You watch TV.'

There were only two bedrooms, so after Julia had finished the dishes she made Amber a bed on the sofa. The lounge was half the size of her Grandad's but it was clean and bright like the rest of the house.

About an hour later, Emil reappeared, but to Amber's surprise Julia acted as if nothing had happened. 'I'm going for a shower,' she announced.

Emil said nothing for a while. He sat on a large bean bag and stared at the floor as Amber fished in her bag. 'I'm sure I packed my toothbrush but I can't find it now. Ah here it is.'

'I told Mum you could have my room but she said it was too messy.'

'I'm fine here Emil.'

'Sorry I stormed off. I can't take it when no-one will listen to us.'

'No worries Emil. I feel the same.'

'What are we going to do about Ella?'

'I don't know. Maybe we could call one of those child helplines for kids in trouble. They might know what to do.'

'That's a good idea Amber. I'll see if I can get a number tomorrow.'

Grandad's biscuit tin

By Amber Henry

15

Prisoner of the Thief

Next morning Amber awoke to the sound of Julia making breakfast. She met Emil on her way upstairs to the bathroom. He was coming out of his bedroom carrying Bonzo in the cage.

'I thought your Mum said Bonzo had to stay in the kitchen.'

'I think he's missing Ella, so I thought he'd be better sleeping in my room.'

'How can you tell when a rabbit is missing someone?'

'Well he's not eaten much and he seems a bit quiet.'

'I hope he's OK.'

'I'll take him downstairs where it's warm.'

'I'm still worried about Ella,' said Amber.

'Me too,' said Emil. 'I'll try and get a number for the kids helpline later, but I was thinking we could call at Katrin's this morning to ask if Ella can come round for an hour.'

'It's worth a try.'

'Mum said we're catching the two o'clock car ferry, so we'll have plenty of time.'

After eating a huge bowl of cereal and several slices of toast, Amber helped Emil wash the dishes while Julia went to find a bag for Charlie's clothes.

'You do a lot in the house don't you Emil?' she said as she dried a plate with the tea towel. 'I never do anything.'

'Why not?'

‘I don’t know. I always think I can’t do things.’

‘That’s stupid. Of course you can do things. You’ve been looking after Ella and your Grandad since the bridge broke and you helped us get out of the cave didn’t you?’

‘I suppose so. But I’m not doing very well looking after Ella at the moment am I?’

‘You’re trying your best,’ said Emil. ‘What else can we do if no-one believes us?’

Ten minutes later they both set off to Charlie’s house with a bag for his clothes. They had just crossed the road, when they saw Katrin coming down Charlie’s path carrying a large shopping bag.

‘Hello,’ shouted Emil.

Katrin frowned but waited for them to reach her. ‘I’ve been doing a bit of cleaning for Charlie while he’s away,’ she said.

‘Where’s Ella?’ asked Amber.

Katrin hesitated before she replied. ‘She’s sick.’

‘What’s wrong with her?’ asked Emil.

‘She’s got a tummy bug. Probably because she won’t eat the lovely dinners I make her.’

‘We were going to ask if she could come to play with us this morning,’ said Amber.

‘She’s not going anywhere. She’s too ill,’ muttered Katrin. ‘Is Charlie still in hospital?’

‘He’s been taken to a nearby care home for tests,’ said Emil.

Amber wished Emil hadn’t told Katrin where her Grandad was, but it was too late now.

‘How long will he be there?’

‘No idea,’ said Amber.

Katrin turned to go then stopped. ‘Are your parents still in hospital Amber?’

‘Yes, but they’ll be back soon hopefully.’

Katrin gave one of her false smiles. 'Tell them I'll keep an eye on Charlie's house while he's away.'

Emil was quick to reply. 'You've no need to. Amber and I will be going round every day.'

'Well I think Charlie would want me to,' said Katrin as she walked away.

Amber couldn't wait to get into her Grandad's house to find out if Katrin had taken anything.

'Is that tin of money still in the washing machine?' asked Emil.

Amber rushed into the kitchen and pulled out the tin. 'It's still here.'

'Better open it, just in case,' said Emil.

Amber prised off the lid and gasped. It was full of biscuits.

'I knew it,' said Emil. 'She's taken Charlie's money.'

'Maybe Grandad's put the money somewhere else.'

'If he did, why would he put the tin back in the washing machine?'

'He's been doing some strange things lately. But if he did put the money somewhere else, we need to find it before Katrin comes back again.'

They spent the next hour searching everywhere they could think of, but there was no money.

'She's definitely stolen it,' said Emil. 'That's why we can't find it.'

'I've just thought of something,' said Amber. 'There was an identical tin of biscuits in Katrin's kitchen on the day I found Ella. I bet she's swapped them round.'

'If she did that she could say there was never any money in Charlie's tin. She'll say it was full of biscuits.'

'I'm glad I showed you the money Emil. At least two of us saw it.'

‘We need to tell my Mum,’ said Emil.

‘There’s no point. She won’t do anything because we can’t prove Katrin stole it. Unless…’

‘Unless what?’

Amber pulled open a small drawer and looked inside. ‘It’s gone.’

‘What has?’

‘Katrin’s door key. She must have found it and taken it back. I thought if she went out, we could sneak in to see if the money was in her house and check if Ella had been left alone.’

‘That would be a bit risky Amber. If she came back we’d be in serious trouble and anyway she might have the money with her in her bag.’

‘Well the key’s not here anymore, so it doesn’t matter now.’

‘Mum said we should take food out of the fridge in case it’s gone off,’ said Emil. ‘I’ll do that while you get Charlie’s clothes.’

It was a strange feeling going into her Grandad’s bedroom without him being there. It felt like she was entering someone’s private world. She opened a drawer and pulled out some shirts. A book fell out. She looked at the title on the hardback cover. ‘I’ve found it,’ she called.

‘What?’ said Emil from downstairs.

‘The book Grandad was wanting. *The History of Legna*. It was in his shirt drawer.’

After putting some of Charlie’s clothes in the bag, she went upstairs to the attic to fetch some of her own things. But something had happened. One of the lovely wings her Grandad had made her all those years ago, had fallen from the wall. She picked it up gently and placed it on the bed. The paper was wafer thin.

‘Come on Amber,’ called Emil.

She grabbed a clean top and her warm jacket in case it was cold on the ferry and headed back downstairs. 'The house seems strange without Grandad,' she said as they left.

* * *

The car ferry was an old boat with the words *Legna Lady* painted on the side in faded blue. There was room to take two or three cars on the deck, but today their car was the only one.

A man wearing a blue cap came to the driver's window as Julia gave him the fare. He peered into the car. 'I see you've got an extra passenger today.'

'This is Amber. She's Charlie Jones' granddaughter.'

The man nodded at Amber. 'I ferried the ambulance back yesterday. How is he doing?'

'He's OK. He hasn't been taking his tablets,' said Julia.

The man laughed. 'I've known Charlie a long time and he never did like doing what he was told.'

'We're going to see him now,' said Amber.

'Tell him Tom sends his best wishes,' said the man as he moved away. 'We'll be sailing in a few minutes.'

The sea was so calm when they set off that it almost felt like a pleasure trip. Gulls followed the boat as it pulled away from the shore and rays of sun danced on the surface of the sea. But as they came closer to the mainland the weather changed. A grey mist descended, like a cloak, so they could no longer see where they were heading and the waves grew bigger. The boat forced its way through the gloom with a swaying motion that made Amber feel slightly sick, so she was very pleased when the mist cleared and the harbour finally came into view. It was a pretty harbour with brightly painted houses and little shops. Amber used to come here with her Granny. They would sit on a bench watching the boats, eating ice cream cones with chocolate flakes in. It seemed like such a long time ago now.

'That's our café over there,' said Julia as they drove off the ferry. 'What's left of it after the flood anyway. It's the one with the yellow sign.'

'When will it open again?' asked Amber.

'Sadly not for a while Amber. I need to raise some money so I can redecorate it, otherwise I'll have to close it down for good.'

Emil was in the front seat, so Amber couldn't see his face, but she could tell from his silence how upset he was.

'I may not be able to park at the care home,' said Julia as they drove further into the town. 'They only have a small car park at the back. I'll drive in but if there are no spaces I'll drop you off outside, while I look for somewhere else to park.'

'Will we be OK to go in on our own?' said Emil.

'Of course we will,' said Amber.

'They're expecting us,' said Julia. 'That's it on the left. I can see a sign.'

They drove passed an old building with steps leading up to the front door and then turned into a car park at the back. Julia stopped the car and gazed around. 'Looks like it's full. That camper van has taken up two spaces.'

'It's them,' said Emil.

'Who?' said Julia reversing the car.

'That couple Amber and I were telling you about.'

A motorist beeped his horn as Julia drove back into the road. 'You'd better get out,' she said. 'I'm holding up the traffic. I won't be long.'

* * *

The care home was once a grand old building but it now looked tired and worn. They walked up the stone steps and rang the bell. A camera whirred above them as the door opened for them to enter.

A young man in a white coat stood behind a desk. Amber read his name badge. It said *RAJ*.

Amber cleared her throat nervously. 'We've come to see Charlie Jones. I'm his granddaughter Amber Henry and this is his neighbour, Emil… Emil …?'

'Wysocki,' said Emil. 'My Mum Julia will be coming as well. She's gone to park the car.'

Raj smiled. 'Ah yes. We're expecting you.'

He pushed a visitors book towards them. 'Sign this and then come through. He's in room number seven.'

The corridor was narrow with a hand rail on both walls and it smelt of disinfectant. An elderly lady shuffled towards them carrying a very large handbag. She muttered something as they passed but Amber and Emil kept walking until they found room number seven. They knocked but there was no reply so they went in. It was a small but pleasant room with a blue easy chair, a wardrobe and a chest of drawers. The yellow flowered curtains matched the cover on the bed where Charlie lay asleep.

'It seems a shame to wake him,' whispered Emil.

'I'll show him the book another day,' said Amber putting it back in her bag.

Emil gazed around the room. 'It looks empty in here. Like a hospital room. He needs some photos.'

Amber opened the small wardrobe to put the bag inside. There was nothing in it apart from Charlie's gansey hanging on a coat-hanger. 'He won't be here long Emil. He's just having tests.'

She took out her phone.

'What are you doing?'

'I'm taking a photo of Grandad's gansey. I'm going to make a sketch of it for his birthday next week.'

'What will happen to him if he can't go back home? Will he go and live with you?'

'We've only got two bedrooms in our house so I don't know where he'd sleep.'

'There might be a care home near you. Then you could visit him.'

The door opened as Julia burst in. 'I managed to park down the road, but I can only park for half an hour.'

'Shh,' said Emil. 'Charlie's asleep.'

Julia peered at the bed. 'Maybe we should let him sleep then. Where are the clothes?'

Amber pointed to the wardrobe.

'We'll come back another time,' said Julia. 'He might be more awake then.'

They closed the door softly and walked back down the long narrow corridor towards the reception. As they passed a kitchen area, Amber heard a voice she recognised. It was the woman from the camper van. 'Shall I make us a cup of tea Amy? I've brought some biscuits.'

Amber stopped and looked in. The woman was standing next to an elderly lady in a wheelchair, but there was no sign of the man.

'Hi,' said the woman. 'What are you doing here?'

'My Grandad was brought here yesterday.'

The woman looked at Julia. 'Is this your mother?'

'No. I'm Charlie's neighbour Julia and this is my son Emil.'

'I'm Tina,' said the woman. 'You'll know Katrin Morgan then. Is she a friend of yours?'

'Not really. Why do you ask?'

'You'd better come in and sit down,' said Tina. 'There's something you should know.'

She moved the wheelchair to one side to make room. 'This is my mother-in-law Amy.'

The woman in the wheelchair nodded towards them as Tina handed her a plate of biscuits. 'You keep forgetting things don't you Amy, but you remember Katrin Morgan.'

'She's the one who took all my money,' said Amy taking a biscuit from the plate.

'What happened?' said Julia.

Tina switched on the kettle. 'Amy gave Katrin some money to go and stay with her sick sister on Legna Island, but Katrin was lying. She's living with her boyfriend.'

'She told me she had a sister in a nursing home,' said Julia.

'She told Grandad she didn't have any family,' said Amber.

Tina shook her head. 'Who knows what the truth is. The woman tells lies all the time. Amy has dementia and forgot to tell us she'd given Katrin some money. We only found out because Katrin sent Amy a postcard asking for more.'

'I can't believe it,' said Julia. 'Katrin's been so kind to Charlie and yet she's done this.'

'That's the trouble,' Tina said putting a tea bag in a mug. 'She's very nice to old people and they trust her.'

'Grandad thinks she's an angel,' said Amber, 'but we think she may have stolen some of his money and she's taken other things as well.'

'Did you go to the police Tina?' said Julia.

'Rob said there was no point unless we could prove she lied about living with her sister.'

'Is Rob Amy's son?' asked Julia.

Tina nodded. 'He's just come out of the army and he doesn't need this stress. He was so angry when he found out Katrin wasn't really living with her sister, but she won't give the money back, so he's going to tell the police.'

'I found a letter that Amy sent to Katrin,' said Amber. 'It mentions Katrin's sister.'

'That will help if we need more proof for the police,' said

Tina. 'Can you let us have it? If we're not here you can leave it for us at reception. Amy's staying here for a while. She fell and hurt her leg last week and her dementia's getting worse.'

'I'll bring the letter next time we come.'

Amy shuffled in her wheelchair. 'Can I have my tea now?'

Tina poured some water into the mug. 'Rob'll be back soon. He's gone to the shop. He'll be very interested to hear about Katrin.'

Julia looked at her watch. 'I'm sorry we've got to go. I've only got half an hour on my parking ticket and we want to talk to the staff about Charlie before we leave.'

* * *

Raj was still on the desk when they reached reception. He said Charlie was confused but would be seeing a doctor in the next few days.

'We'll come back when we've more time,' said Julia.

'Will he be alright here on his own?' said Amber. 'My Mum and Dad are in hospital and can't visit him.'

Raj smiled. 'Don't worry. We'll take good care of him.'

'It's terrible how Katrin tricked that poor old lady into giving her money,' said Julia as they walked to the car. 'I believed her when she said she took that money from my café because she wanted to help her sick sister, but now I'm wondering if she even has a sister.'

'And now she's trying to trick Charlie as well,' said Emil. 'It's not right.'

'You're quiet Amber,' said Julia as they reached the car.

'I keep wondering how Ella is. I feel like we should be doing something.'

Julia opened the car door. 'Remember what I said about not interfering.'

‘Well we can call and ask if Ella is feeling any better,’ said Emil. ‘That’s not interfering is it? It’s being friendly.’

‘It won’t do any good though,’ said Amber. ‘Katrin won’t let us see her will she?’

‘Ella’s like a prisoner but Katrin knows we’re watching her,’ said Emil.

* * *

The ferry was late, which was lucky because so were they. There had been some problem with the engine but the man said it was fixed now. Amber hoped so. She didn’t fancy being stranded in the middle of the sea. She wanted to get back so she could find that letter to Amy. She thought she had put it in one of her bags in the attic and she hoped she was right.

The ferry took a long time to reach Legna Island, due to the engine cutting out every now and again, so they were relieved when they neared the cliffs.

Julia pointed ahead. ‘Look over there. You can see where Lighthouse Cottage fell into the sea.’

The sight of the tumbled pieces of building amid the rubble made Amber realise how lucky they were to have survived.

When they got back, Amber and Emil went straight round to Charlie’s house to find the letter to Amy.

‘I hope it’s where I think it is,’ said Amber as they climbed the attic stairs.

‘Charlie told me this house and the one next door used to be one big house years ago,’ said Emil. ‘It had servants who probably slept up here in the attic.’

‘Yes that’s why I could hear Ella on the other side of the wall. It used to be one big room.’

'What's that on your bed?' asked Emil, staring at the paper wing.

'One of my Angel wings,' said Amber. 'Grandad made them for me when I broke my leg ages ago but this one's fallen off the wall.'

'Wow they're amazing.'

Amber fished in a bag for the letter. 'It's here. I'd better keep it safe now.'

'What's that noise?'

They listened. The soft moan was something Amber recognised. She dashed to the wall and banged on it three times.

'What are you doing?'

'Ella's crying. Ssh. She might reply.'

There was a pause and then they heard it.

Tap tap tap

Amber went to the window. 'Can you make this open any more Emil? It's stuck.'

Emil banged the catch with his fist and pushed the window open.

Amber leaned out. 'Ella? Knock if you can you hear me.'

Tap tap tap

Amber pushed her face closer to the window so she could lean out further. 'Katrin might hear you if you talk through the window Ella, so just listen. Knock once if you are ill.

There was a pause. Then the answer came.

Tap

'We've got to get her out of there,' said Emil.

'And how exactly are we going to do that?'

Emil leaned out of the window. 'Let me talk to her. Don't worry Ella. My Mum's going to phone your Dad. He'll come back and get you.'

Amber was shocked. 'Why did you tell her that when it's not true. Your Mum said she won't phone Dave unless we can prove something really bad is happening to Ella.'

‘Well this is really bad isn’t it? Keeping a sick little girl trapped in her room all day like a prisoner. How bad does it have to get Amber?’

‘I know it’s bad but if Ella’s ill, people will think there’s nothing wrong with making her stay in her room.’

‘And what about all the other things Katrin is doing to Ella. Like making her eat horrible food, leaving her alone in the house and making her give away her rabbit?’

‘It’s not against the law to give away a rabbit.’

‘No but we think she may have hit her. That’s against the law.’

‘I know all that Emil but Katrin will say Ella is making things up and we can’t prove she isn’t.’

‘Well she definitely attacked you Amber didn’t she?’

‘You promised to keep that to yourself Emil. I don’t want anyone to know about that.’

Emil moved away from the window. ‘I was only trying to make Ella feel better. What else could I say?’

Amber leant towards the window. ‘I’ll tell her we’re looking after Bonzo.’

But before she could say anything they heard a slam and a woman’s raised voice.

‘Katrin’s heard us,’ said Amber.

They listened. More shouting, then a door slammed and then more crying.

Emil’s face reddened. ‘Why did you start calling through the window Amber? You’ve made things even worse.’

‘At least I didn’t tell her a lie. She’ll be thinking her Dad’s coming to rescue her now.’

Emil marched out of the room and stomped down the stairs but Amber didn’t run after him. She was sick of his quick temper. She looked at the wings on the bed. One of the feathers was torn.

Julia's chocolate cake with my butter icing

By Amber Henry

16

Bad Turns to Worse

There was nothing Amber could do to stop Ella crying. She couldn't bear to listen anymore, so she put the letter from Amy in her jeans pocket and went downstairs. The house was empty and silent. She remembered all the summer holidays here when she was younger. She remembered her Granny reading books to her and her Grandad throwing a ball into the paddling pool in the garden and soaking everyone sitting nearby. It all seemed so long ago now. Then she thought about her Mum and Dad and how things could have been much worse if they had been on the bridge when it collapsed and that made her feel a little better.

When she arrived back at Emil's house, Julia was sitting in the kitchen with Bonzo on her lap.

'He's not well,' she said.

Amber sat beside her and stroked Bonzo's ears.

Julia looked up. 'Are you alright?'

'We heard Ella crying in her bedroom.'

'I know. Emil told me he'd stormed off. He's a bit of a hot head like his Dad.'

'He was right I suppose. I shouldn't have called Ella through the window.'

'I know you both want me to phone Dave, but it will make things worse for Ella.'

'Why will it?'

'Katrin will say Ella's making things up and Dave's likely to believe Katrin.'

'I've got the letter from Amy now. Maybe if Dave finds out what Katrin's been up to, he might start believing Ella instead.'

'Maybe. I don't know,' said Julia putting Bonzo back in his cage.

'Do you think Bonzo will be alright?'

'I hope so,' said Julia, washing her hands.

'I hope my Grandad's alright too.'

Julia dried her hands and sat back down next to Amber. 'I'm sorry I can't take you to see him tomorrow. Someone's coming to look at the flood damage in the café and I still have a lot of cleaning up to do.'

'I can help if you like.'

'That's kind of you Amber but it's dirty work and I wouldn't want you to spend what's left of your holiday cleaning up. Besides I need you to stay here and make sure Emil does his homework. He has a project to do and he hasn't even started it yet.'

'I've got some homework too. It's not right when you're supposed to be on holiday.'

'When the teachers hear what you've been through this holiday I think they'll let you off don't you?'

'You don't know some of my teachers. They're slave-drivers.'

Julia laughed. 'That's what Emil says about *his* teachers, but I think he likes them really.'

Amber hadn't thought about school for a long time. It seemed like she lived in a different world now.

'I'll phone the hospital after we've eaten,' said Julia, 'see if I can find out when we can visit your Mum and Dad.'

She took an oven glove and lifted something out of the oven. It smelt delicious. The sound of loud music came drifting down from Emil's room as Julia put a chocolate cake on the table.

‘He says that row calms him down. Since Emil’s not here maybe you’d like to make the butter cream for the cake Amber?’

‘I don’t know how to make it.’

It’s easy. I’ll show you.’

Emil didn’t say anything when he came down for his meal but Julia kept the conversation going by telling Amber how she always wanted to open a café but never had the chance until now.

‘Amber made the butter cream,’ said Julia, passing Emil a piece of cake. ‘What do you think?’

‘Good,’ said Emil as he sank his teeth into a huge slice.

Amber couldn’t finish her cake. She kept thinking about Ella, sitting alone in her room with only a dry sandwich to eat.

‘I’ll wash up,’ said Amber after they’d finished.

‘You’re getting too good,’ said Julia. ‘I’ll be offering you a job at my café soon.’

Emil took out his phone. ‘Put that away Emil. We need to talk about homework.’

Emil groaned.

‘Amber has some to do as well so I thought you could both do that tomorrow while I’m out.’

Emil grunted.

‘I take it that’s a yes then Emil?’

* * *

It was about six o’clock that evening when Julia phoned the hospital.

‘Your Mum’s improving,’ said Julia after she put the phone down, ‘but she can’t have any visitors until they’re sure she’s over the sickness.’

‘What about my Dad?’

'He's recovering well and he hasn't caught the sickness bug so that's good.'

'I'm really worried about him,' said Amber.

'He's in good hands' said Julia standing up. 'Put the TV on Emil. It'll take Amber's mind off things. I'm going for a shower.'

Emil hunted for the remote. 'It's here somewhere.'

'I'm not bothered about TV, Emil. I'm so worried about my Dad, and I can't stop thinking about Ella.'

'I'm the same,' said Emil. 'Sorry I got mad earlier but it gets to me the way Katrin treats Ella and no-one is doing anything to stop her.'

'It's OK Emil. I was thinking we should call on Ella tomorrow but now I think that'll make things worse.'

'We can keep a watch on Dave's car. If Katrin goes out in it and leaves Ella, we can go round to see her.'

'That's a good idea Emil. If that happens it'll prove to Dave that Ella's being left alone.'

'Exactly.'

* * *

The next day went very slowly. Amber and Emil sat at the kitchen table to do their homework, but Emil couldn't concentrate. When he wasn't stroking Bonzo or eating ice cream, he was looking out of the front window to see if Dave's car was still in the drive.

'She wouldn't go out without the car,' said Emil after he'd looked for the sixth time. 'So we know she's still at home. Shall we knock and ask how Ella is?'

Amber looked up from her homework. 'I can't see the point.'

Emil opened the fridge. 'You're probably right. Do you want some more ice cream?'

'No thanks. We've had tons already. You'll make yourself sick if you have any more.'

'You're too sensible,' said Emil as he spooned out the chocolate ice cream.

Amber rolled her eyes. She was finding it hard to concentrate too, but at least she wasn't eating all the time.

'I'm not in the mood for this homework,' said Emil, as he finished his ice cream. 'I'm going for a walk.'

'I know what you're up to Emil.'

'I'm not up to anything. I'm going for a walk that's all.'

'No you're not. You're going to knock on Katrin's door to see if you can see Ella.'

'What if I am? Someone's got to do something.'

'I thought you were going to look for the kids helpline number.'

'I'm not so sure we should do that just yet. I mean we can't prove anything can we?'

'Well you're going to make things worse if you keep bothering Katrin. Wait 'til tomorrow at least.'

'OK,' said Emil, 'but I'm definitely going to call tomorrow.'

Amber put down her pen. 'I wonder if she's still crying.'

'We could go to your attic and find out.'

'I don't want to do that. It upsets me to hear her crying when we can't do anything.'

'Mum'll be back soon,' said Emil. 'I'd better put the kettle on.'

As Emil cluttered about in the kitchen, Amber took out her phone and her sketch pad and began to draw her Grandad's gansey for his birthday card.

* * *

When Julia came home, she had some news. 'I bumped into Tina and Rob when I went to the supermarket. They're keen to get hold of that letter Amy wrote to Katrin.'

'Can we take it tomorrow?' asked Amber.

'We can but I can't stay long,' said Julia, unpacking a bag of food. 'I've got a million things to do tomorrow.'

Emil looked at the food. 'I don't want much to eat tonight Mum.'

Julia raised her eyebrows. 'That's not like you.'

Amber watched Emil's face turn a ghostly shade of white, just before he rushed upstairs.

'What *has* he been eating?' asked Julia.

'Chocolate ice cream,' said Amber. 'Tons of it.'

Amber could hear Emil being sick on and off all evening but by the time she went to bed, all was quiet.

'I'll take Bonzo up to Emil's room,' said Julia as she came in to say goodnight. 'It might cheer him up a bit, but he can't visit a care home if he's feeling sick.'

'But we can still go can't we Julia?'

'If Emil feels well enough to stay on his own, then you and I can still go.'

'Thanks. And thanks for looking after me and Bonzo.'

Julia smiled. 'It's good to have a girl around for a change. But I've never had a rabbit here before.'

'I hope he'll be alright,' said Amber.

'Me too,' said Julia. 'I'm becoming quite fond of him. See you in the morning.'

* * *

Amber slept well considering she was on a sofa and by the time she got up Julia was already making toast in the kitchen.

'I've taken Emil a cup of tea,' Julia said, passing Amber a plate of toast. 'He'll be fine as long as he takes it easy today and stays away from the ice cream.'

Amber took the toast and sat down at the table. 'I don't think he'll want any ice cream for a very long time.'

'I've got so much to do today, Amber. Do you mind if I drop you off at the care home and join you later?'

'No that's fine,' said Amber, but she didn't really mean it. The thought of going into the care home on her own made her anxious. Some of the people there acted strange and she didn't know what to say to them.

'I'll only be gone half an hour. I've got to see someone at the bank.'

'That's fine,' said Amber. 'It's good of you to take me.'

'Don't forget the letter for Tina and Rob. They probably won't be there but you can leave it at reception.'

'I'm taking *The History of Legna* book for Grandad as well. I hope he's awake this time.'

'Mum,' called Emil from upstairs. 'Come quick. Something's wrong with Bonzo.'

Emil was cradling Bonzo in his arms on the bed.

'He was sitting all hunched up, not moving at all,' said Emil. 'He's not even nuzzling me when I sit with him.'

'He's been off his food,' said Julia. 'We'll wrap him up warm and take him to the vets.'

By the time Julia had wrapped Bonzo in a towel and found a suitable box to carry him in, it was almost time to catch the ferry.

'I'll cancel my appointment at the bank,' said Julia. 'I need to make sure Bonzo is alright.'

'I can take Bonzo to the vets if you need to go to the bank,' said Emil.

'You're not going anywhere until you're completely better Emil. And don't tell me you're OK because I can see you're not.'

Emil sighed and rolled his eyes, but Amber could see he wasn't going to argue.

* * *

Amber put Bonzo on the back seat of Julia's car in his new box and wedged it in with cushions. He didn't wriggle out of his towel as he normally would have done. He just looked at Amber with his big eyes. As Emil waved them goodbye from the window, Amber noticed something.

'Katrin's car's gone,' she said. 'I hope she hasn't left Ella on her own. She's not well.'

'Maybe she's taking Ella to the doctors,' said Julia. 'If she is, they'll be on the ferry so we can find out.'

They drove to the ferry in silence. Amber didn't feel like talking. A terrible sense of sadness was creeping over her and somehow she couldn't control it. A large tear trickled down her cheek, then another and another until her body heaved as she crumpled into long sobs.

Julia stopped the car. 'Amber what's wrong?'

'Everything,' cried Amber. 'Mum and Dad are in hospital, Grandad's sick, Ella's crying all the time and now Bonzo's ill. It'll break Ella's heart if anything happens to him.'

Julia put her arm round Amber's shoulders. 'If we can get him to the vets today, he may be OK. You've been through such a lot in the last few days Amber. Stay strong. Everything will turn out alright. You'll see.'

Amber hoped Julia was right. She wiped her eyes. 'Thanks. I'm OK. Let's make sure we don't miss the ferry.'

* * *

Julia was right. Katrin's car was already on the ferry when they arrived. Amber strained her neck to see if Ella was in the car but it was difficult. As they drove on the deck alongside Katrin's car it became clear that Katrin was alone.

Julia got out of her car and went round to Katrin's car window. Amber put down her own window so she could hear what they were saying. She noticed how Katrin faked a smile as Julia approached.

'Hi Katrin. How's Ella? I hear she's not well.'

'A friend's looking after her.'

'Oh that's good. What's been the matter?'

The roar of the boat engine drowned out Katrin's reply and not long after that Julia returned to the car. 'It's OK Amber. Katrin's friend is looking after Ella. The poor child has a tummy bug. I thought Emil had eaten too much ice cream but maybe there's a virus going round.'

Amber didn't bother telling Julia what she thought. She would only say they couldn't prove anything and she was right.

The journey across the sea to the mainland seemed to take longer than before, but maybe it was because they were both worried about Bonzo. Amber kept checking on him but didn't want to lift him out of his box in case it made him worse, so they were both relieved when they drove off the ferry and headed for the town.

Amber watched Katrin speed off ahead of them. 'Did Katrin say where she was going?'

'No. I didn't ask. She has a friend who owns a hairdresser's in town. It's near the care home so we might see her if she goes there. I think she gets free hairdos. That's why her hair always looks so amazing.'

Amber didn't think there was anything about Katrin that looked amazing, but maybe that was because she didn't like her.

'The vets is past the care home,' said Julia. 'So I'll drop you off first and then take Bonzo.'

Amber was about to ask if she could go to the vets with her, when Julia's phone rang. She pulled over. 'It's your Mum.'

Amber's heart missed a beat. Had something happened?

'Hi how are you? …Oh! This afternoon? Yes, that'll be fine. We're on our way to see Charlie now.'

Julia handed the phone to Amber.

'I can't talk long,' said Mum. 'I have to see the doctor about your Dad, but I'm coming home later this afternoon. I've asked Julia if she can pick me up.'

'That's great Mum. I hope Dad'll be alright.'

'He'll be fine Amber. I'm so pleased you're going to see your Grandad this morning. Got to go. See you soon. Love you. Bye.'

'Well that's good news.' said Julia. 'We haven't got much time though. I'll join you in the care home as soon as I've seen the vet and then we can grab some lunch and go to the hospital.'

'What about Bonzo? We can't take him to the hospital with us.'

'I'll ask the vet if I can leave him there until we've picked your Mum up,' said Julia. 'Everyone is pulling together since the bridge collapsed. I'm sure she won't mind.'

* * *

It took longer than usual to reach the care home due to some boxes falling off the lorry in front of them so they couldn't pass. Julia was becoming impatient. 'Why do these things happen when you're in a hurry? Rabbits need to be treated quickly when they're ill. How is he doing?'

Amber looked in the box. 'He seems quiet at the moment.'

'At last,' said Julia. 'Someone's picking up the boxes. We should be off again soon.'

When Amber got out of the car at the care home, she was thinking about Ella. She didn't believe Katrin's friend was looking after her but she knew she couldn't prove it. She rang the bell almost without thinking and entered the building. Raj was on the reception desk. He smiled at her as he passed her the visitors' book, before disappearing into the back office to answer the phone. She picked up the pen to sign her name but, as she did so, she saw a name she recognised. Someone else was visiting her Grandad that morning and that someone was Katrin Morgan.

With her mind racing, she hurried along the corridor towards Charlie's room. An elderly man came out of the kitchen area and nearly collided with her.

'Sorry,' she said as he tottered to a halt.

As she reached Charlie's room, she heard a familiar voice. 'You don't need that old jumper on Charlie, you've got a blanket. It won't take long.'

The door was propped open. Charlie was sitting in a wheelchair, his legs covered in a blanket. Katrin stood behind him, trying to steer the wheelchair out of the door. She glared at Amber.

'I wondered if you were on the way here. Well I'm taking Charlie out, so you'll have to come back later.'

It didn't take long for Amber to work out what was happening. Katrin was taking Charlie to the solicitors to sign his new will. She had to act quickly.

'Are you sure you want to go out Grandad? You look tired.'

'He's going out for some fresh air,' said Katrin.

'I need my gansey on if I'm going out,' said Charlie. 'Where am I going anyway? I don't want to go.'

Katrin tried to push the wheelchair past Amber. 'We won't be long.'

Amber stood in the way. 'He doesn't want to go.'

'Do you want me to tell the police how you stole a jewellery box from my house?' said Katrin.

'You can tell them what you like. I gave it back didn't I?'

The wheelchair jolted as Katrin pushed it towards Amber. 'Get out of the way.'

Amber reached out her hand and gripped one arm of the wheelchair but a violent push from Katrin made her loose her grip.

'What's going on?' said Charlie. But it was no use. Katrin was wheeling the chair down the corridor as fast as she could manage it.

'Stop,' yelled Amber as they neared the kitchen area. 'He doesn't want to go!'

A woman came out. 'What's wrong?'

It was Tina.

'Katrin?' said Amy from the kitchen. 'What are you doing here?'

Katrin stopped for a second and stared into the kitchen as Tina moved towards her.

'Hello Katrin.' said Tina. 'We need a word with *you*.'

There was a pause before Katrin's body jerked into action. Swinging the wheelchair round towards the kitchen doorway, she pushed it violently towards Tina, tipping Charlie forwards and back like a rag doll. Tina yelled out in pain as the metal step of the chair cut into her legs. Then several things happened at once. Katrin left Grandad and disappeared down the corridor like a rat down an alley as two care staff came rushing in from a nearby room.

'Someone call the police,' yelled Tina. 'Katrin Morgan has just attacked me.'

Amber pointed along the corridor. 'She went that way.'

But her words were drowned out by a loud crash, followed by the sound of a woman screaming and a man shouting for help. The two staff in the kitchen left Tina and ran down the corridor, followed by Amber.

Further along the corridor, a large trolley lay on its side with cups and biscuits strewn all over the floor. A member of staff stood beside the trolley rubbing her arm, whilst another tried to quieten the screaming woman. But Amber's eyes were drawn to someone else. Sitting in a heap on the floor was Katrin; her white fur coat stained with brown tea.

'My leg!' she yelled. 'I can't move it.'

Raj arrived and knelt beside her. 'Where does it hurt?'

'I've already told you I can't move my leg. Are you stupid? Can't you see I'm in agony? Call an ambulance!'

Raj stood up. 'OK. Keep still. You'll be fine.'

'I definitely won't be fine. I'll be going to see my solicitor about this. Someone ran into me with the trolley.'

A few seconds later a man in a suit appeared. Amber guessed he was the manager of the care home. He crouched down to talk to Katrin, but the elderly woman started screaming again so Amber couldn't hear what they were saying.

Feeling pleased that Katrin hadn't been able to run away, she returned to the kitchen to see how Tina and her Grandad were. There would be a lot to tell Julia when she arrived.

Tina was holding a towel against her leg. One of the staff had brought a first aid box and was sifting through it as Amber came in.

Tina looked up. 'What's happened?'

'It looks like Katrin collided with someone pushing the tea trolley. She's injured her leg. Raj has gone to phone an ambulance.'

'I'm glad she didn't get away. I'll be able to tell the police where she is when I phone them later.'

'I'm tired.' said Charlie. 'I want to go back to my room.'

Amber pulled the letter out of her pocket and handed it to Tina, who seemed very pleased to have it.

'Come on Grandad. I'll take you back now.'

She was glad Katrin could do no more damage, but she was still worried. She didn't believe Katrin had asked a friend to look after Ella, but she couldn't be sure.

After helping Charlie into the chair in his room, Amber helped him put on his gansey before stepping into the corridor to ring Emil's landline. It seemed ages before he answered.

‘Emil. It’s Amber. I’m at the care home. Can you find out if anyone’s looking after Ella. We saw Katrin on the ferry and she was on her own. She told your Mum a friend was looking after Ella but I don’t believe her. Katrin won’t be going back home tonight. She’s been injured.’

‘What happened?’

Amber started to explain. She managed to tell him about the attack on Tina, but it wasn’t easy with such a crackly phone line.

‘I’ll tell you more later. Can you call at Katrin’s to see if anyone’s looking after Ella?’

‘OK,’ said Emil, just before the line went dead.

* * *

Charlie was still sitting in the same chair when she returned to his room.

‘I’m cold,’ he said. ‘Are you sure this is my gansey?’

‘It’s got the diamond pattern down one side Grandad. That’s definitely the one Granny knitted for you.’

‘So it is,’ said Charlie trying to look at the pattern. ‘But I’m still cold.’

Amber took the blanket from the wheelchair and wrapped it round his legs. ‘Shall I get you some tea from the kitchen?’

Charlie shook his head. ‘How long am I supposed to stay in this place?’

‘They’re doing some tests Grandad. Are you OK after what happened?’

She tried to talk to her Grandad about Katrin, but she could tell he wasn’t really following what she said. He seemed so far away in his mind that in the end she gave up.

‘I’ll have to go soon,’ she said. ‘I’m waiting for Julia. We’re picking Mum up from the hospital today.’

The door opened and a lady with a blue uniform walked in. 'Sorry to barge in Charlie, but the doctor is here to see you.'

'I'll come back another time Grandad.'

'I don't like doctors,' said Charlie. 'They make me feel ill.'

There was no sign of Katrin as she walked down the corridor, so she guessed she must have gone to hospital. Apart from the splashes of tea on the wall, everything seemed back to normal.

She decided to sit in the reception area and talk to Raj while she waited for Julia, but he wasn't there. She could hear him talking on the phone in the back room. An elderly man shuffled past her as she sat in a chair by the main door. He rattled the door and looked surprised when it didn't open. She was about to explain that he needed a code, when her phone rang. It was Emil.

'Did you go to Katrin's?'

'Yes but there was no answer. I shouted through the letter box but no-one came, so I don't know if Ella's there or not.'

'Well of course she's there. Where else would she be?'

'Katrin's friend could have taken her for a walk or something. Don't get mad at me Amber. It's not my fault.'

'Sorry. I'm just so worried.'

'I rang my Mum and told her what you told me. She's still waiting to see the vet, but she's going to ring Dave.'

'At last someone's listening to us.'

'What?' said Emil. 'I can't hear you. See you when you get back.'

Raj came out of the office and guided the elderly man away from the main door just as Julia arrived. She looked flustered. 'Are you alright Amber? Emil has just phoned me.'

'I'm fine. How's Bonzo?'

'He's got some medicine and should recover soon. 'Emil told me Katrin attacked Tina. Is that true?'

Amber nodded. 'She pushed the wheelchair into Tina's legs and Grandad nearly fell out. Then she ran off so fast she collided with a tea trolley and hurt her leg.'

'I can't believe Katrin would do that.'

'Have you phoned Dave yet?'

'Yes, but there was no reply so I had to leave a message. I said it was urgent.'

'Well I hope he calls soon because Ella might be on her own and she's not well.'

'I thought Katrin's friend was looking after her.'

'I think Katrin was lying.'

Julia sighed. 'You could be right. I'd better warn Dave. I'll text him now.'

'I hope he rings soon,' muttered Amber as Julia took out her phone.

'There. It's gone. Now what about Charlie? Is he alright?'

'I think so. He had to see the doctor so I left.

'So, tell me exactly what happened with Katrin.'

The elderly man wandered up to the main door again and rattled the glass. 'Can you let me out?' he said, 'I need to get home to feed my cat.'

Raj came out from behind the desk and took him gently by the arm. 'It's OK Doug. Someone else is feeding your cat today.'

'Let's go somewhere else so we can talk,' said Julia.

After a long time sitting in the car, Amber was satisfied she had explained everything to Julia and it was the first time Amber had seen Julia look angry.

'Can you try calling Dave again?' said Amber.

Julia put her seat belt on and started the car. 'Let's drive to the hospital first.'

The broken Window

By Amber Henry

17

Break of the Glass

It took a long time to find a parking space at the hospital. Julia left Amber in the car whilst she went to search for the pay station. She was gone for several minutes but when she returned she had her phone in her hand. 'Dave's just rung back. I've told him everything I know.'

'What did he say?' asked Amber. 'Is he coming home?'

'He said he knew something was wrong by the way Ella spoke to him on the phone. He said she didn't sound her usual self.'

'So what's he going to do?'

'He said I was to leave everything to him and he would get back to me. I told him we'd look after Ella for a while if he wanted us to. So we'll see what happens.'

Julia put the parking ticket on the car dashboard. 'Let's go to the hospital café. It won't be as good as my café but I'm sure there'll be something we can eat there.'

It was busy in the café but Amber didn't notice. She was looking forward to seeing her Mum, but she couldn't help worrying. She was worrying about Ella and worrying about her Dad all at the same time.

'Not long now,' said Julia as she finished her coffee. 'Your Mum's in Ward Seven. Let's go and find where it is.'

After some confusion over the signs, they eventually found Ward Seven and rang the buzzer. A smiling nurse let them in. 'Who are you visiting?'

'Millicent Henry,' said Julia. 'She's going home today.'

The nurse pointed down the corridor. 'Bay number nine on the left.'

Amber tried not to run in the ward, but she couldn't help it. Milly was sitting in a chair by the side of the bed but when she saw Amber she stood up and hugged her so tightly she could hardly breathe. Julia waited until Amber and her Mum had finished.

'Hello Milly,' she said.

Milly kissed her on the cheek. 'Oh Julia, you're so kind. What would we have done without you.'

Amber watched her Mum saying goodbye to everyone on the ward and noticed how feebly she walked.

'Your Dad's in Ward Ten,' said Mum. 'We'll go there now, but don't hug him. He's got a few broken bones.'

Amber said very little as Julia and her Mum chatted along the corridor. The hospital smells made her feel queasy and the gleaming floors made her dizzy.

'Here we are,' said Mum as they approached Ward Ten. 'She pressed a buzzer and waited. A nurse arrived to let them through. 'Hello Milly,' she said. 'Jim says you're going home today. Is that right?'

Milly smiled. 'Yes, that's right. This is my daughter Amber and our friend Julia. We've come to see Jim before we go.'

'He's been waiting for you,' said the nurse.

Amber wasn't prepared for what she saw when they reached her Dad's bed. He looked so different. He was such a strong man but now he looked frail. His face was marked with cuts and yellow bruises and his eyes looked tired. He was sitting propped up on two large pillows with a bandage on his right arm.

‘Amber,’ he said holding out his left hand. ‘I’m feeling better already.’ Amber squeezed his hand. She wanted to cry but she held it back.

Dad let go of her hand and reached for the box of chocolates on his bedside table. She chose the long thin one, wrapped in gold paper.

‘I knew you’d pick that one,’ said Dad. ‘I’ve been saving it for you.’

Julia chatted about Katrin and what had been happening with Charlie, but Amber didn’t feel like talking. She was just glad to be back with both her parents.

‘We’d better go,’ said Julia after a while. ‘We have to collect Bonzo from the vets before we catch the ferry.’

‘I hope Charlie’s alright in that care home,’ said Jim.

‘Julia’s taking us to see him tomorrow,’ said Milly, ‘but I hear he’s still wearing his gansey so he must be OK.’

Jim laughed. ‘Thanks for everything Julia.’

‘It’s Amber and Emil who deserve all the praise,’ said Julia. ‘Everyone thought Katrin was an angel, except them. If it wasn’t for them, Charlie would have lost all his possessions and his money as well.’

‘When will he start to get better?’ asked Amber.

Milly took out a tissue and blew her nose. ‘Dementia can’t be cured Amber, but we can make things more comfortable for him.’

It didn’t take long to drive to the vets. Julia brought Bonzo out in his box and handed him to Amber in the back seat of the car.

‘I’ve heard so much about this rabbit,’ said Milly. ‘I can’t wait to see him.’

‘It’s best not to get him out until we’re home,’ said Julia. ‘We need to keep him calm while he’s on the ferry.’

Amber looked at her Mum. Her face was so pale.

'Are you OK Mum?'

'I'm fine but I'll be glad when we get home. The doctor said I'll feel tired for a while and should take it easy.'

'You can have a rest when we get back,' said Julia.

As they drove off the ferry towards their houses, Amber wondered if Ella was still in the house or if she had run away like before. 'We need to find out if Ella's at Katrin's,' she said.

'We should wait for Dave to phone,' said Julia as they pulled up outside her house. 'He knows about it now.'

Amber helped her Mum out of the car.

'Come to my house for some tea before you go home Milly,' said Julia. 'You can have some chocolate cake.'

Emil appeared at the door. 'Hi. How's Bonzo?'

Amber made her Mum comfortable in Julia's small lounge, bringing extra cushions and finding a stool so she could put her feet up.

'This is different isn't it Amber?'

'What?'

'You looking after me like this. It's usually me doing all the fussing.'

'Things are going to be different from now on Mum.'

'Really? How different?'

'I'm going to learn to cook for a start.'

'What's put that into your mind?'

Amber shrugged her shoulders. 'I've grown up a lot since you've been away.'

'You certainly have.'

'I'll go and get your tea.'

Amber could tell something was wrong as soon as she went into the kitchen. There was a tense atmosphere and she noticed that Emil was frowning and his face was red.

'Why won't you listen Mum? We need to do something. If no-one's looking after Ella, she'll be on her own all night.'

Julia took some cups from a cupboard. 'I told you we need to wait for Dave to phone back'.

'We can't wait much longer,' said Emil raising his voice. 'She's sick. You need to ring him now. Ella could be dying in there while you're making tea.'

Julia turned to face Emil. 'Alright, I know what you're saying. There's no need to raise your voice.'

'Then why don't you phone him?'

'Because he told me he was dealing with it. He said he was going to ring me.'

'I'm going to ring Katrin's landline,' said Emil. 'If Ella is there she might answer it.'

'Alright,' said Julia as he picked up the phone.

'It's ringing,' he said.

They stood and waited but no-one answered.

Emil put down the phone. 'It doesn't mean she's not there. Katrin told her not to answer the phone.'

'Shall I try calling Ella through the door?' said Amber. 'She might answer if she knows it's me.'

'OK,' said Julia. 'It's worth a try.'

* * *

The light was fading as Amber and Emil walked across the road to Katrin's house.

'Knock as loud as you can Emil then I'll shout through the letter box,' said Amber.

Bang Bang Bang

'Ella! It's Amber. Everything's fine. You can open the door. Katrin's not coming back tonight. Julia's talked to your Daddy… Ella… Are you there?'

‘It’s no good,’ said Emil. ‘If Katrin’s told her not to answer the door, she won’t come down.’

‘Well she doesn’t have to open the door does she? She could call out to us.’

‘Listen,’ said Emil. ‘The phone’s ringing.’

‘Do you think that’s Dave?’ said Amber.

It seemed to ring for ages before it eventually stopped.

‘Maybe she’s not there Emil. Maybe she’s run away again.’

Emil shook his head. ‘She’s in there but something’s not right. I just know it.’

Amber took Charlie’s door key from her pocket. ‘I’ve got an idea. Come on,’

‘Where are we going?’

‘To my Grandad’s.’

Amber led Emil up the stairs to the attic. ‘Be very quiet now.’

She lifted her fist and banged three times on the wall that linked Katrin’s attic to hers.

Nothing.

She tried again. Then they heard a sound like Amber had never heard before. A sort of retching sound.

‘Do you know what that sounds like?’ said Emil.

‘What?’

‘Like someone being sick.’

They listened for a few minutes but they could hear nothing more.

‘Let me knock,’ said Emil. ‘I can do it louder than you.’

Bang Bang Bang

They waited. Then they heard a faint sound.

Tap Tap Tap

‘She’s in there,’ said Amber rushing to open the window. ‘Ella, can you open your window and talk to us?’

‘Ella!’ shouted Emil over and over again. But Ella’s window never opened.

‘She’s sick,’ said Emil. ‘We’ve got to get into the house and get her out.’

He rushed down the stairs and into the hallway.

Amber followed him. ‘How are we going to do that Emil? We’ve no keys.’

‘I’m going to break a window. Is there a hammer somewhere.’

‘You can’t just break in like that Emil.’

In the hallway next to the telephone table was a large painted stone that Charlie used as a door stop. Emil picked it up. ‘This’ll do.’

‘No don’t Emil. Let’s go and tell your Mum.’

‘It’s no good telling her anything. She’s too scared to help. But I’m not.’

Emil opened the door and ran towards Katrin’s house. ‘I’m going to get her out.’

‘Don’t Emil. You’ll get into trouble.’

But Emil wouldn’t stop. He ran up to Katrin’s front door and paused. Amber caught him up.

‘I’m going round the back,’ he said. ‘I can smash the kitchen window and get in that way.’

Amber looked at the stone in his hand and felt a shiver. She had tried to stop him but there was nothing more she could do. Following him round the side of the house she watched helplessly as Emil swung the stone back as far as he could and flung it at the kitchen window. There was an almighty crash as glass shattered in every direction. It fell in splinters onto the path, onto Emil’s hands and onto the sink below the window. But it didn’t break the whole window. There were still jagged pieces of glass around the edge of the frame.

‘You’re bleeding,’ said Amber.

Emil looked at his hands. ‘It’s not much.’

He looked around the garden. ‘I need something to stand on, so I can get high enough to step through the broken glass.’

'Are you mad Emil? Suppose you cut an artery on the glass or something. You could bleed to death before we got you to hospital.'

'OK. I'll get something to smash the rest of the glass then.'

'Don't Emil. Please don't.'

'OK what are we going to do then? Ella could be dying in there.'

'Listen,' said Amber.

'What is it?'

There was a fluttering noise in the distance. Quiet at first, it grew louder as they listened.

Amber looked up at the sky. 'It's a helicopter. It's coming this way.'

It wasn't long before the sound grew so loud it became difficult to hear anything else. They watched it as it circled above them.

'It's coming down behind the houses,' shouted Emil. 'Come on.'

Rushing out of the garden, they ran round the side of Katrin's house into the road as the helicopter hovered above them like a giant moth. Powerful blasts of air rushed across the field next to Katrin's house, bending trees halfway to the ground and flattening the grass. The noise was deafening.

'What's happening?' yelled Julia, running to join them.

The helicopter swayed and tipped, landing in the field like an insect settling on a flower. Then something even more unexpected happened. A dark figure carrying a large bag, jumped out of the helicopter and ran towards them.

'It's Dave,' said Julia.

He jumped over the fence towards them. His voice was frantic. 'Is Ella still in there?'

'We think so,' said Julia.

There wasn't time to say any more. Dave ran to his house, opened the door and shouted. 'Ella?'

Amber, Julia and Emil ran after him.

'We think she's in the attic,' said Emil.

Dave raced up the stairs two steps at a time.

'She's here,' he called.

Fading light from a gap in the curtains shone weakly on the bed where Ella lay.

'Daddy I'm not well,' she whispered as Dave knelt down beside her.

'It's OK,' said Dave tearfully. 'I'm here now. I'm not going anywhere.'

'Is she alright?' said Julia, switching on the light.

Ella lay white faced, her head on a pillowcase stained with vomit.

'I keep being sick Daddy.'

Julia knelt down beside Dave. 'How long have you been like this Ella?'

'For a while.'

'You two go back and let Milly know what's happened,' said Julia. 'I'll stay and help Dave.'

Amber nudged Emil. 'You'd better tell Dave about the window before you leave.'

* * *

Milly was standing in the doorway leaning against the doorframe as Amber arrived at Julia's house. She was watching the helicopter fly away. 'I wanted to come out Amber, but I felt dizzy.'

'Are you OK now Mum? Come and sit down.'

'Yes, I'm fine. Tell me what's going on.'

Amber had just finished explaining everything to her Mum when she heard Emil open the front door.

His face was flushed. 'Dave's OK about the broken window. That helicopter was amazing. I've been talking to the pilot. He's from the oil rig where Dave works. Dave's a great guy isn't he?'

Milly sighed. 'I think we should go to your Grandad's now Amber. I've had enough excitement for today.'

It took Milly a long time to walk across the road. She seemed to sway as she clung to Amber with every step. Julia came out of Katrin's house as they reached Charlie's gate.

'How's Ella?' said Amber.

'She's asleep,' said Julia, 'but she hasn't been sick again. She's had a drink and a dry biscuit. Hopefully she'll be fine in a few days.'

Dave came out whilst Julia was speaking. 'Thanks for all your help everyone. I was such a fool to think Katrin would make a good step-Mum for Ella.'

'She fooled everyone except Amber and Emil,' said Julia.

'What will happen to her now?' said Amber.

'I've called the police,' said Dave. 'They're going to talk to her at the hospital. She won't be able to lie her way out of all this.'

Milly shivered in the cold. 'We'd better go in.'

'Ella's been asking for Bonzo,' said Julia. 'I'm going to get him so he'll be there when she wakes up.'

'Good idea,' said Amber. 'Tell her I'll be round to see her when she feels better.'

'She told me you've been like a big sister to her,' said Dave. 'I can't thank you and Emil enough for helping her.'

Amber opened the door for her Mum. 'She was pleased Ella was safe, but with her Grandad and her Dad still sick, anything could happen.'

* * *

The next day, Amber called to see Ella, armed with her sketch book. She had woken early that morning and had decided to sketch things that would remind her of everything that had happened during this Easter holiday. Ella liked drawing and Amber hoped it would be something she would like to look at.

'How's Ella?' asked Amber as Dave opened the door.

'Improving,' said Dave. 'But she's still very tired. Thanks for coming. She's been asking to see you.'

When Ella saw Amber, she held out her arms for a hug.

'How are you feeling Ella?'

'I'm a lot better and so is Bonzo. Daddy's going to make him a big rabbit hutch.'

Dave smiled. 'I was going to make a start on it today but it's pouring with rain.'

Ella was sitting on the sofa, surrounded by sheets of paper that she'd been drawing on.

'I've been trying to draw Bonzo but it's too hard,' she said.

Amber pushed aside the sheets of paper and sat down beside her. 'I've brought my sketchbook to show you.'

Ella's eyes lit up as she turned the pages. 'Wow Amber. You're so good. I wish I could draw like you.'

'You will when you're older,' said Amber. 'Maybe you should try drawing Hoppy instead of Bonzo. Toy rabbits are easier than real ones.'

Ella sighed and leaned back on the sofa. 'I might do it later.'

'Tell Amber about Mummy,' said Dave.

Ella grinned. 'She's getting better and she'll be well enough to see me soon.'

Amber didn't like to ask what was wrong with Ella's Mum. She guessed it must have been serious if she couldn't look after Ella and hadn't even been in touch.

Dave sat down in the chair opposite Ella. 'You're going to stay here with me for a while, aren't you Ella? There's a lovely primary school on the mainland.'

Ella frowned. 'It's not a boarding school is it?'

'No of course it's not.'

'What about your work at sea?' asked Amber.

'I've given up my job on the oil rig,' said Dave. 'I don't need to save up for a bigger house any more. This one is fine for the two of us.'

Amber felt sad at the thought that Ella and Emil would be staying on Legna without her. Next week they would both be going to good schools on the mainland, while she would be at a school she didn't like, two hundred miles away. She knew she would miss both of them and strangely enough she would miss this little Island too.

'Can you draw Bonzo in your book?' asked Ella.

Amber looked at Bonzo sleeping in his cage in the corner of the room. 'I'm not sure I can draw a rabbit.'

'Please Amber. Just try.'

She was about to ask Dave if her Granny's jewellery box was still in the red bag in the wardrobe, when he suddenly left the room, so she picked up her sketch book and began to draw an outline of Bonzo. A few minutes later he came in with his coat on, carrying a biscuit tin.

'Can you stay with Ella a while?' he said. 'I need to give this to your Mum and Julia wants to see me about something. I think she has a surprise for Ella.'

Amber recognised the tin straight away. 'Is that Grandad's savings?'

Dave nodded. Julia told me what happened. Katrin must have swapped them round so Charlie thought he still had his savings.

'But all he had was a tin of biscuits,' said Amber.

'Anyway, how is your Dad?' asked Dave, changing the subject.

Amber had the feeling he didn't want to talk about Katrin any more.

'He's getting better thanks.'

'Good,' said Dave. See you later.'

Amber knelt on the floor with her sketch book to get a better view of Bonzo. It wasn't easy sketching a rabbit but she tried her best.

Ella watched with interest. 'I like playing with you Amber. We can pretend we're sisters can't we?'

'I always wanted a sister,' said Amber.

'So did I,' said Ella.

'I'm going to write a story in backwards writing when I feel better?' said Ella. 'It's about a lonely little girl who comes to live on Legna and finds a friend. I'm going to call it Legna's Child.'

'Are you going to write the title in backwards writing as well?'

Ella took a piece of paper and a pencil and wrote out the letters one by one. 'DLIHC S'ANGEL'

Amber's eyes widened in surprise. 'LEGNA!' she said. 'I never realised. LEGNA is ANGEL spelt backwards. I've been coming here since I was little and I never knew.'

Ella thought for a moment then laughed. 'Legna is a back-to-front Angel.'

'I like that Ella. A back-to-front…'

She stopped mid-sentence.

'What's wrong Amber?'

'I thought I heard a car,' she said moving to the window.

Ella climbed off the sofa to join her. Peering through the raindrops on the window they watched a hooded woman step out from the driving seat of a small red car into the rain. A lock of long fair hair blew out from her hood as she lifted a large suitcase from the boot. Amber felt a sudden pang of fear. The woman looked a lot like Katrin.

'She's coming up the path,' said Ella.

Rap Rap Rap

Ella made a move towards the door, but Amber stopped her. 'Wait. We don't know who it is?'

Rap Rap Rap

'What shall we do Amber?'

The letter box rattled. 'Dave?' said a voice.

Ella grasped Amber's hand. 'It sounds like Katrin.'

Amber shook her head. 'It can't be. She's in hospital with a broken leg and anyway she has a key.'

'Look through the spy hole in the door Amber. I can't reach it.'

Standing on her tip toes, Amber pressed her eye to the spy hole. The woman's hood was pulled down, shielding her eyes from the rain, but the rest of her face was visible and for a fleeting second Amber too thought it was Katrin. And yet there was something different about her.

'Dave. I need to speak to you,' said the voice again.

Amber jumped back, pulling Ella away. 'I'm going to ring your Dad,' she whispered.

But the sound of raised voices in the street made them rush back to the lounge window.

'It's Daddy. He's by the gate talking to that woman.'

They couldn't hear what they were saying but Dave stood talking to the woman for some time, his face tense and angry. After a while they both turned and headed up the path. Then the key turned in the door.

'First door on the left', said Dave gruffly.

He put his head round the door. 'Stay there you two.'

‘Who is it?’ asked Amber.

‘Katrin’s sister. She’s come for Katrin’s things. I’m going to make sure that’s all she takes,’ said Dave closing the door.

‘So she does have a sister after all,’ said Amber. ‘But she doesn’t look sick to me.’

Ella looked puzzled. ‘I don’t know what you mean.’

‘Never mind,’ said Amber. ‘It’s not Katrin. That’s all that matters.’

‘Katrin has lots of things.’ said Ella. ‘Lots of clothes and lots of shoes and bags.’

Amber felt suddenly sick. If the red shopping bag in Katrin’s wardrobe still had Granny’s box in it, Katrin’s sister might take it away and she would never see it again.

She ran up the stairs to find Dave standing outside Katrin’s room watching the woman pack the suitcase. ‘Go back downstairs Amber,’ he said. ‘It’s OK.’

‘Dave I need to talk to you.’

‘Later Amber.’

‘No Dave. I need to talk to you NOW.’

Dave stepped away from the bedroom door. ‘What is it?’

‘Grandad got mixed up and gave Katrin my Granny’s jewellery box. It was in a red shopping bag in the wardrobe, but she might have put it somewhere else now. I don’t want her sister to take it.’

‘OK,’ said Dave. ‘I’ll see if I can find it. Go back and stay with Ella. I don’t want you two mixed up in all this.’

Amber did as she was told but she couldn’t relax. She tried to tell Ella about the box and how important it was to her but she wasn’t sure she was making much sense. All she could do now was wait.

It wasn’t long before they heard Dave raising his voice again and Katrin’s sister shouting back, but the words were muffled through the closed door. The shouting seemed to go on for ages but eventually they heard footsteps coming down the stairs, followed by the sound of the front door banging shut.

There was a pause before Dave opened the lounge door. 'I've got it,' he said.

As her hands reached out for the precious jewellery box, she felt as if her Granny was smiling at her. 'Thank you so much,' she whispered.

'So much for this sick sister Katrin was supposed to have,' said Dave. 'I wondered why she never took me to meet her.'

'She told my Grandad she was an only child,' said Amber.

'Yet more lies,' muttered Dave. 'I'd better go and tell Julia. She'll be wondering what's happening. Can you stay with Ella a bit longer Amber? I'll be as quick as I can.'

When Dave returned a short while later, he was carrying a cake tin. 'Emil made this for you Ella. It's a work of art.'

There was a gasp from Ella and Amber when Dave lifted the lid from the cake tin. It was the most beautiful cake Amber had ever seen. On the top was a rabbit made of fondant icing, sitting on some green icing that looked just like grass and round the edge were outlines of trees and plants.

'It's lovely,' whispered Ella. 'Put it on the table Daddy. I'm going to draw a picture of it.'

Amber smiled to herself as she left. She remembered how suspicious Emil was when he first met Ella, and now he was making her beautiful cakes. She decided to ask Emil for his cake recipe. She could never decorate a cake as well as Emil but maybe she could try.

Ella's drawing of Emil's rabbit cake

Grandad's legna Gansey

By Amber Henry

18

Truth of the Story

It was early afternoon when Julia, Milly and Amber took the car ferry to the mainland. The weather was fine for once and the ferry seemed to glide across the sea like a skater.

Amber watched the gulls dipping and swooping overhead and she felt good. She was still worried about her Dad and her Grandad but she didn't have to worry about Ella any more. 'Do you think the police will arrest Katrin?'

'I hope so,' said Milly. 'She'll be charged with a string of things: attacking Tina, neglecting a child and stealing from elderly people for a start.'

Amber wondered if she ought to tell her Mum about what happened when she took the jewellery box from Katrin's house but she decided not to. The box was back on Grandad's shelf now and that was all that mattered.

'What makes someone do bad things like Katrin did?' said Amber.

Milly shrugged her shoulders. 'A woman in the hospital used to live near Katrin and her sister. She told me they'd been mistreated by their parents and been in and out of trouble since they were teenagers. It's very sad really.'

'I thought she was such a caring person,' said Julia. 'And I believed everything she said about her sick sister.'

'People are not always what you think,' said Milly.

'I was scared of Rob when I first met him,' said Amber. 'But I like him now.'

Julia nodded wisely and held her face up to the sunshine. 'I love the sun. Did I tell you Dave's going to help me redecorate the café in time for the summer season?'

Milly looked pleased. 'I'm glad something good has come out of all this trouble.'

As the boat chugged effortlessly towards the harbour, Amber thought how beautiful this place was.

'Do you ever miss living on Legna, Milly?' asked Julia.

Milly nodded. 'All the time. Once you live on an island it gets in your blood.'

'Do you think you'll ever come back? Charlie's house is big enough for all of you.'

'Jim and I have been thinking about moving back for a while now.'

'You never told me,' said Amber. 'Why do grown-ups never tell you anything?'

'We need to talk to Grandad first.'

'How would you feel about living here Amber?' said Julia.

The boat swayed gently as it drew alongside the harbour wall. Amber breathed in the salty sea air. 'I'd love it.'

'Well that's a surprise,' said Milly.

'So are we going to move here then Mum?'

'If Grandad agrees then I think we will.'

'Hurray,' said Amber. 'Something good's happening at last'.

'We'll soon be there,' said Milly. 'Have you got that book your Grandad wanted? I'll have to read it myself one day.'

Amber nodded. 'It's in my bag with his jelly babies.'

They arrived at the care home just as Tina and Rob were leaving. Her mum spent so long talking about what happened with Katrin that Amber thought she would never stop. Grandad was right, her Mum did talk a lot, but for once Amber didn't mind. She was pleased her Mum was more like her old self again.

'I'm going in to see Grandad,' said Amber after a while.

'OK,' said Milly, barely stopping for breath. 'I'll be there soon.'

'Hello again,' said Raj, pushing the visitors book towards her.

Amber signed the book with all their names. 'My Mum's outside with Julia. They're talking to Tina and Rob.'

'Good,' said Raj. 'I need to tell your Mum what the doctor said about Charlie.'

Making her way down the corridor, Amber passed the kitchen area where Amy was sitting with another lady, drinking tea. When she arrived outside Charlie's room she noticed his name was now on the door, with a photograph of him trying to smile.

Charlie was propped up in bed, surrounded by pillows. He looked thin and pale but when he saw Amber he sat up a little. 'A visitor at last. About time.'

'Mum won't be long. She's talking to someone.'

'Have you brought me any sweets?'

Amber pulled the jelly babies from her bag and opened them for him.

'Good girl. You're an angel.'

'I found that book you asked for: *The History of Legna*.'

'Ah yes,' said Charlie. 'The story of the Angel's Child. It's in Chapter Three.'

'How come you can remember which chapter it's in?'

Charlie coughed loudly before he spoke, wheezing as if he couldn't catch his breath. 'I do remember some things. I'm not completely crazy you know.'

Plunging his hand into the packet of jelly babies, he grabbed a handful and stuffed them into his mouth in one go.

'Careful Grandad.' She waited for him to finish chewing. 'Do you want the book now?'

He lay back on his pillows. 'You read it to me. I'm feeling so very tired today.'

Amber sat in the blue armchair and began to read aloud. But as she read, she began to realise the story of the Angel's Child wasn't just a story after all.

Chapter 3

Angel's Child

On 1st April 1852, a twelve year old girl was accused of stealing a baby. The girl's name was Angel Savage. She was the daughter of the lighthouse keeper on the Island of Legna. Her father discovered the baby in one of the tunnels leading to his cottage.

This is a written record of Angel Savage's confession on the night she was arrested:

> *'I was standing in the cave, waiting for my father and brother to return from fishing, when I saw a sailing ship crash on the rocks.*
> *A woman swam towards me, carrying a baby in a shawl on her back.*
> *I helped them into the cave.*
> *Before the mother died, she asked me to look after her baby.*
> *I took the baby girl up through the cave to our cottage.*
> *I knew my father would not allow me to keep the baby, so I hid her in a chamber in the tunnels. Each night I creep away and sleep in the tunnel with the baby.*
> *I love the baby and she loves me. Please do not take her away.'*

Amber was curious. She wanted to find out what happened to Angel, so she turned the page and read the next few lines.

> Angel was pardoned for her crime but her family moved off the Island and she never saw the baby girl again.
>
> The baby's father could not be found, so she was given to a couple living on the Island. They named her Bella, in memory of the Bella Rose ship.
>
> Sadly, Bella died of a mysterious illness when she was seven years old.

When Amber had finished, she looked up. Her Grandad had fallen asleep. She put the book back in her bag and thought about what she had read. It wasn't a story about an angel from the sky who stole a child. It was about a lonely girl called Angel Savage, who promised to look after an orphaned child and cried when the child was taken away.

Grandad was right. '*Stories always have some truth in them, if you look hard enough.*'

Then an unexpected thought struck her. The girl who took the baby was called Angel Savage. Ella's last name was Savage. Grandad said Dave's family came from Legna many years ago. Was Ella descended from the same family as Angel Savage? Amber never did believe Ella was the ghost of the Angel's Child, but maybe she was related to the girl who took the baby.

The sun shone through the window, bathing the room in a warm golden light and Amber felt peaceful. She had been through such a difficult time but things were getting better now and she couldn't wait to tell Emil and Ella she was moving to Legna.

Looking across to her Grandad, she noticed one of his arms dangling over the side of the bed. She walked over and put his hand under the covers. It felt so cold. She pulled the duvet further up over his chest, like he used to do for her when she was little. She hoped he would be well enough to come home soon.

As she turned away, her eyes caught sight of the bag of jelly babies lying on the floor. She picked it up. Taking the jelly babies out one by one, she placed them in a row on the bedside table.

But none of the yellow ones were left.

Angel's Child Quiz

Notes for Teachers

- These questions have been written in a similar style to that of the Year 6 SATs reading test.
- They focus, in particular, on retrieval and inference.
- There are 10 questions for each chapter.
- The questions are ordered so that question 1 references the earlier part of each chapter, through to question 10 which concerns the latter part.
- You can find out about more comprehension questions and extracts through @Y6SUPPORT on Twitter.

Note from the author:

The majority of these quiz questions were written by Elliot Morgan (@_mrmorgs), an experienced Year 6 teacher from London. Elliot is a local authority writing moderator, SATs marker and maths subject lead. He has a keen interest in teaching reading skills and explicit vocabulary instruction.

Quiz: *Are you a super reader?*

There are ten questions for each chapter of *Angel's Child*. Check your answers on page 245.

Chapter 1 Cry of the Thunder

1. 'Amber thought his words sounded like a machine gun' (page 1). What does this suggest about how the man was talking?
2. Why do you think Amber was starting to feel nervous?
3. How can you tell the man and woman were in a rush? There are clues in the entire first passage.
4. How did Charlie know a storm was coming?
5. How old was Amber?
6. 'Amber stifled a yawn' (page 4). What does the word 'stifled' mean and what does this tell you about how she was feeling?
7. What was missing from the glass shelf?
8. 'Amber pulled a face' (page 6). Why do you think she did this?
9. What did Charlie reveal about Katrin?
10. 'I'm sure this wasn't forecast' (page 11). What does 'forecast' mean in this sentence?

Chapter 2 Sounds in the Dark

1. 'They could be injured, or worse' (page 13). What did Amber mean by this?
2. Where did Amber find the torches?
3. Which word shows that Charlie was impressed by the storm?
4. 'Amber took a torch and stormed off to the kitchen' (page 17). What does this suggest about how Amber was feeling?
5. What did Amber put in the sandwiches?
6. 'A sound so shrill it made their ears hurt' (page 19). Which word is closest in meaning to shrill?
   Quiet Sharp Deep Noisy
7. What was making the scratching noises?
8. What impression do you get of Katrin so far?
9. Where was Amber sleeping?
10. How good is your memory? Number these events from 1–5 in the order they happened. The first one has been done for you.
    a) Amber makes sandwiches. ___
    b) Amber thinks she sees a hand at the window. ___
    c) Emil knocks at the door. ___
    d) They find a rabbit in the kitchen. ___
    e) Charlie tells Amber to get the torches. **1**

Chapter 3 Face at the Window

1. Why was it strange that the back door was open?
2. How was it possible that the potential burglar was still on the Island?
3. Why did Amber doubt how helpful Katrin was?

4. 'Amber had a horrible feeling that all the boxes were empty' (page 31). What do you think Katrin has done with the ornaments?
5. How do we know Charlie's memory is getting bad?
6. Fill in the blanks to show what impression you get of Emil from the text.

   I think Emil is ______________________________

   because he ________________________________
7. What was making the whirring sound?
8. Why was Katrin's house said to be haunted?
9. Why is it unlikely that it was Dave that Amber saw in the window?
10. 'I knew she was still there' (page 35). Who do you think Charlie was talking about?

Chapter 4 Tears on the Cliff

1. Why do you think Amber wanted to cry when she heard her mother's voice?
2. How do you know Charlie was interested in the phone conversation?
3. Amber gently 'squeezed' her Grandad's arm (page 44). Why do you think she did this?
4. What had changed about Charlie since last summer?
5. Why did the Irish families leave Ireland?
6. Why hadn't Amber seen the bench before?
7. What does the word 'engraved' mean?
8. Why didn't Amber think Benny died from the curse?
9. What were the tunnels used for?
10. 'I don't like the look of those clouds at all' (page 46). What do you think this suggests will happen next?

Chapter 5 Blood on the Floor

1. Why did Charlie ask Amber to lead them back?
2. Why did Charlie say Katrin gave him her key?
3. What did the couple in the camper van want?
4. What could have happened if Charlie had used the gas oven to dry his slippers?
5. Why did Amber wait until Charlie was asleep to check the boxes?
6. How do you know that the tin hadn't been opened in a while?
7. What was inside the tin?
8. Why didn't Emil like Katrin?
9. Why was Amber shocked when they entered Katrin's lounge?
10. Why did Amber and Emil think there was someone in the house?

Chapter 6 Silence of the Child

1. What did Amber think might be in the supermarket bags?
2. What familiar item did Amber recognise?
3. 'Wishing she had brought a torch…' (page 66). Why do you think she wished she'd brought a torch?
4. How do you know Amber was scared when she was in the attic? Find two pieces of evidence.
5. Who could the girl be at this point in the story?
6. Why did Amber only pretend to read the collar?
7. Was the girl being looked after well?
8. How did Amber know her Grandad had gone out?

9. What is a parka?
10. Why do you think Charlie might not have realised how dangerous the situation was?

Chapter 7 Wings of the Angel

1. 'Amber's knuckles whitened as she gripped her torch' (page 79). What does this tell you about how Amber was feeling?
2. What does 'stoop' mean?
3. What did Amber's heart sound like?
4. How old did Emil think a Bronze Age well might be?
5. What was scratched onto the wall of the cave?
6. 'There was no point saying anything' (page 81). Why not?
7. How did Amber and Emil know that Grandad's condition was getting worse?
8. Who did Charlie think the little girl was?
9. How had Charlie changed since Amber was a child?
10. How did they find out the little girl's name?

Chapter 8 Fall of the Rocks

1. What time was it when Emil looked at his phone?
2. Why do you think Amber didn't go to sleep?
3. What did Amber's Mum think was wrong with her Grandad?
4. Why wouldn't Charlie go to the doctors?
5. Where was Emil's Dad?
6. Why did Emil think they'd never get out of the cave?
7. What did Amber believe about the curse?
8. How do we know Emil was annoyed after the rocks fell?

9. Why didn't Amber trust Charlie to find the way out?
10. What did Amber suggest to make sure they found their way back?

Chapter 9 Out of the Gloom

1. 'Amber felt a stab of fear in her stomach' (page 97). What was she afraid of at that point?
2. 'This was not the time to cry' (page 97). Why did Amber not want to cry?
3. What word shows that Ella did not want to do something?
4. What was in Ella's pocket?
5. Why did Ella scream?
6. Why did the daylight sting their eyes?
7. Why did Ella think Katrin wouldn't come back?
8. Why did the woman in the camper van frown at them?
9. How do you know Emil was angry at what Katrin said to Ella?
10. Who had arrived at the house?

Chapter 10 Words of the Cruel

1. What surprised Amber about Katrin?
2. 'She needs a firm hand' (page 114). What does this suggest about how Katrin treats Ella?
3. What did Katrin say was wrong with Ella?
4. What did Amber see on Katrin's bed?
5. What reason does Katrin give for wanting to get rid of Bonzo?
6. Why did Amber take back the jewellery box?
7. Who sent the letter?

8. Why did Julia think the letter could be written by an elderly person?
9. What did Amber find in her Grandad's room?
10. What had gone missing?

Chapter 11 Pain of the Missing

1. 'She ran around the house in a frenzy' (page 127). What does *in a frenzy* mean?
2. What word in this part of the story means 'to be filled with wonder'?
3. 'There was a rattle as the windows quivered in the wind' (page 129). What does *quivered* mean in this sentence?
   Danced Bounced Shook Waved
4. What happened to Lighthouse Cottage?
5. Why was Ella limping when she was found?
6. What did Charlie give Ella to cheer her up?
7. Who was on the phone later that morning?
8. How do you think Amber felt after all the adults told her to stop accusing Katrin?
9. How do we know Charlie's book was old?
10. What was Ella planning to read whilst Amber went to see her Grandad?

Chapter 12 Curse of the Angel

1. How did Charlie say Benny died?
2. What did Charlie's mother believe caused Benny's death?
3. What did Ella read out to Amber and Charlie?
4. What had Charlie forgotten how to do?
5. Why did Emil say his Mum was too nice sometimes?

6. Who won the least amount of card games?
7. Who was Hoppy?
8. What did Amber draw that evening?
9. What time was it when Bonzo woke Amber up?
10. Why do you think Charlie ripped up the book?

Chapter 13 Talk Through the Window

1. Why was Charlie looking for the book, *The History of Legna*?
2. Why was Katrin annoyed at Ella's dirty clothes?
3. 'Emil coughed and pretended to blow his nose' (page 151). What does that say about how Emil was feeling?
4. What was different about how Katrin talked to the children and how she talked to Charlie?
5. What time did Amber plan to call Ella?
6. Why did Amber want to draw the cave?
7. Why was Katrin's face 'thunderous' when she answered her door?
8. What did Katrin take away from Ella?
9. What was Charlie doing in the greenhouse?
10. What did Amber plan to do the next morning?

Chapter 14 More Wrong Than Right

1. Why did Amber want to cry?
2. 'He's in his own world at the moment' (page 160). What do you think this phrase means?
3. 'I'll bring the child round' (page 161). What does this choice of words suggest about what Katrin thought of Ella?
4. What is a will?

5. What do you think Charlie planned to leave Katrin in his will?
6. 'Katrin's face hardened' (page 165). What does this suggest about how Katrin was feeling?
7. Why didn't Ella want to talk about how Katrin was treating her?
8. What did Katrin give Ella to eat?
9. What does 'two-faced' mean?
10. How do you think Amber and Emil felt when Julia said 'We should mind our own business' (page 173)?

Chapter 15 Prisoner of the Thief

1. Why did Emil think Bonzo was missing Ella?
2. What do you think was in Katrin's large shopping bag?
3. Why did Amber wish Emil hadn't told Katrin where Charlie was?
4. Why was Katrin giving a 'false smile'?
5. Why did they think Katrin had stolen the money?
6. Why did Tom think it was funny that Charlie hadn't taken his tablets?
7. What was the name of the receptionist?
8. Why did Amber take a photo of her Grandad's gansey jumper?
9. How was Katrin able to take advantage of Amy and Charlie?
10. Why did Emil lie to Ella about contacting her Dad?

Chapter 16 Bad Turns to Worse

1. Why was the house 'empty and silent' (page 189)?
2. What is a 'hot head'?
3. Why did they believe Katrin was still at home?

4. What did Amber make for the chocolate cake?
5. Why couldn't Amber finish her cake?
6. Why was Emil feeling sick?
7. How do you think Amber felt when she realised Katrin was alone in the car?
8. Where was Katrin taking Charlie when she saw Amber at the care home?
9. Why didn't Julia speak to Dave on the phone?
10. Why do you think Julia wanted to drive to the hospital first?

Chapter 17 Break of the Glass

1. What did Dave say when Julia told him everything?
2. What ward was Amber's Mum in?
3. What was different about Amber's Dad?
4. Why didn't Amber feel like talking in the hospital?
5. What did Amber say she was going to do in the future?
6. What did Emil use to break the window?
7. Who arrived in the helicopter?
8. What did Ella want Amber to draw for her?
9. Why did Dave give up his job?
10. What did Emil send over for Ella?

Chapter 18 Truth of the Story

1. What words tell us the ferry was moving smoothly?
2. How did Amber feel about moving to Legna?
3. What did Amber have in her bag for her Grandad?
4. Why did Amber go to her Grandad's room alone?
5. What was the name of the young girl in the story who stole the baby?

6. Why was the baby girl named Bella?
7. What happened to Bella when she was seven years old?
8. Why did Amber think Ella might be descended from the same family as Angel Savage?
9. How has Amber changed since the beginning of the story?
10. Why did Amber place the jelly babies in a row?

Quiz Answers

Chapter 1 Cry of the Thunder

1. 'Amber thought his words sounded like a machine gun' (page 1). What does this suggest about how the man was talking? **(Loudly or quickly)**
2. Why do you think Amber was starting to feel nervous? **(They were asking a lot of questions)**
3. How can you tell the man and woman were in a rush? There are clues in the entire first passage. **(They banged at the door three times, he sighed impatiently, he spoke like a machine gun and asked a lot of questions)**
4. How did Charlie know a storm was coming? **(A flash lit up the room)**
5. How old was Amber? **(Twelve)**
6. 'Amber stifled a yawn' (page 4). What does the word 'stifled' mean and what does this tell you about how she was feeling? **(She stopped the yawn from happening. She was bored at the thought of reading one of her Grandad's books but didn't want him to know)**
7. What was missing from the glass shelf? **(Granny's jewellery box)**

8. 'Amber pulled a face' (page 6). Why do you think she did this? **(She thinks eating sweets off the dusty table is disgusting)**
9. What did Charlie reveal about Katrin? **(That she says she is related to Granny)**
10. 'I'm sure this wasn't forecast' (page 11). What does 'forecast' mean in this sentence? **(Predicted)**

Chapter 2 Sounds in the Dark

1. 'They could be injured, or worse' (page 13). What did Amber mean by this? **(They could be dead)**
2. Where did Amber find the torches? **(Under the kitchen sink)**
3. Which word shows that Charlie was impressed by the storm? **(Spectacular)**
4. 'Amber took a torch and stormed off to the kitchen' (page 17). What does this suggest about how Amber was feeling? **(Annoyed)**
5. What did Amber put in the sandwiches? **(Cheese)**
6. 'A sound so shrill it made their ears hurt' (page 19). Which word is closest in meaning to shrill?
   ~~Quiet~~ **Sharp** ~~Deep~~ ~~Noisy~~
7. What was making the scratching noises? **(A rabbit)**
8. What impression do you get of Katrin so far? **(Very controlling over Charlie, always telling him what to do, e.g. wrapping all of his ornaments up, locking his back door, she tells him off for being untidy, she will get mad if the paper with the appointment on it isn't left by the phone etc.)**
9. Where was Amber sleeping? **(In the attic)**

10. How good is your memory? Number these events from 1–5 in the order they happened. The first one has been done for you.
    a) Amber makes sandwiches. **3**
    b) Amber thinks she sees a hand at the window. **5**
    c) Emil knocks at the door. **2**
    d) They find a rabbit in the kitchen. **4**
    e) Charlie tells Amber to get the torches. **1**

Chapter 3 Face at the Window

1. Why was it strange that the back door was open? **(Amber locked it the night before)**
2. How was it possible that the potential burglar was still on the Island? **(They cannot leave as the bridge has collapsed)**
3. Why did Amber doubt how helpful Katrin was? **(The house doesn't look tidy or clean and the fridge was nearly empty)**
4. 'Amber had a horrible feeling that all the boxes were empty' (page 31). What do you think Katrin has done with the ornaments? **(Either genuinely taken them to clean them or sold them – she may be interested in money as she told Charlie to let her look after his savings)**
5. How do we know Charlie's memory is getting bad? **(Twice he has wanted to make a cup of tea while forgetting there is no power to do so)**
6. Fill in the blanks to show what impression you get of Emil from the text.
   I think Emil is (**very thoughtful/selfless/caring**) because he (**offered to give them sandbags and food**)

7. What was making the whirring sound? **(A helicopter)**
8. Why was Katrin's house said to be haunted? **(The Angel's Child died there)**
9. Why is it unlikely that it was Dave that Amber saw in the window? **(He is away a lot for his job)**
10. 'I knew she was still there' (page 35). Who do you think Charlie was talking about? **(Either Katrin or the Angel's Child)**

Chapter 4 Tears on the Cliff

1. Why do you think Amber wanted to cry when she heard her mother's voice? **(She was so relieved to hear she was alive)**
2. How do you know Charlie was interested in the phone conversation? **(He stood beside Amber, craned his neck to listen in, asked Amber what's happened afterwards)**
3. Amber gently 'squeezed' her Grandad's arm (page 44). Why do you think she did this? **(To comfort him)**
4. What had changed about Charlie since last summer? **(His body was thinner; his steps were now shorter)**
5. Why did the Irish families leave Ireland? **(There was a famine)**
6. Why hadn't Amber seen the bench before? **(She had never been on this path before because she was too young)**
7. What does the word 'engraved' mean? **(Carved into, inscribed)**

8. Why didn't Amber think Benny died from the curse? **(She didn't think you could die from a curse, she questioned why Charlie was still alive if he went into the cave too)**
9. What were the tunnels used for? **(Smuggling brandy and rum to avoid paying tax)**
10. 'I don't like the look of those clouds at all' (page 46). What do you think this suggests will happen next? **(A storm is coming)**

Chapter 5 Blood on the Floor

1. Why did Charlie ask Amber to lead them back? **(He said he couldn't see very well with rain in his eyes but there was no rain so he may have been crying)**
2. Why did Charlie say Katrin gave him her key? **(To look after the Angel's Child)**
3. What did the couple in the camper van want? **(They wanted to know if Charlie had heard from Katrin)**
4. What could have happened if Charlie had used the gas oven to dry his slippers? **(They would have set on fire and then the house might have caught on fire too)**
5. Why did Amber wait until Charlie was asleep to check the boxes? **(She didn't want to upset him, she didn't want him to know that she was suspicious of Katrin)**
6. How do you know that the tin hadn't been opened in a while? **(It was covered in dust)**
7. What was inside the tin? **(Two glass marbles, a small blue fish-shaped button and a folded piece of paper)**

8. Why didn't Emil like Katrin? **(She stole money from his mother's café)**
9. Why was Amber shocked when they entered Katrin's lounge? **(Charlie's painting was on the wall)**
10. Why did Amber and Emil think there was someone in the house? **(The dish was still wet and so was the blood)**

Chapter 6 Silence of the Child

1. What did Amber think might be in the supermarket bags? **(Grandad's ornaments)**
2. What familiar item did Amber recognise? **(Granny's jewellery box)**
3. 'Wishing she had brought a torch…' (page 66). Why do you think she wished she'd brought a torch? **(Turning on a light switch meant she might be seen in the house or that people would know she was in the house)**
4. How do you know Amber was scared when she was in the attic? Find two pieces of evidence. **(She felt her breath catch in her throat, her legs trembled, her hands were sweating, her heart gave a thump)**
5. Who could the girl be at this point in the story? **(Either the Angel's child or the daughter of Katrin or Dave)**
6. Why did Amber only pretend to read the collar? **(She already knew the rabbit's name)**
7. Was the girl being looked after well? **(No – she was left alone; her hair was matted and her clothes were creased and grubby)**

8. How did Amber know her Grandad had gone out? **(His coat and white hat were missing and his shoes were gone)**
9. What is a parka? **(A coat)**
10. Why do you think Charlie might not have realised how dangerous the situation was? **(He was very forgetful and may have forgotten that the tide could come in and hurt him or his mind was focused on finding Benny and not on how dangerous the area was)**

Chapter 7 Wings of the Angel

1. 'Amber's knuckles whitened as she gripped her torch' (page 79). What does this tell you about how Amber was feeling? **(Scared)**
2. What does 'stoop' mean? **(To bend)**
3. What did Amber's heart sound like? **(A bat)**
4. How old did Emil think a Bronze Age well might be? **(Four thousand years old)**
5. What was scratched onto the wall of the cave? **(Angel's wings)**
6. 'There was no point saying anything' (page 81). Why not? **(Charlie would just forget anyway)**
7. How did Amber and Emil know that Grandad's condition was getting worse? **(He didn't know who Dave was)**
8. Who did Charlie think the little girl was? **(Bella, the Angel's Child)**
9. How had Charlie changed since Amber was a child? **(He used to be strong and clever and now he was like a child)**
10. How did they find out the little girl's name? **(It was engraved on her locket)**

Chapter 8 Fall of the Rocks

1. What time was it when Emil looked at his phone? **(Two o'clock)**
2. Why do you think Amber didn't go to sleep? **(She was too worried, anxious, scared)**
3. What did Amber's Mum think was wrong with her Grandad? **(He has dementia)**
4. Why wouldn't Charlie go to the doctors? **(He said they make him feel ill)**
5. Where was Emil's Dad? **(Poland)**
6. Why did Emil think they'd never get out of the cave? **(He thought the girl was the Angel's Child and the Angel won't let her child out of the cave)**
7. What did Amber believe about the curse? **(It was something the smugglers made up to keep people out of the cave)**
8. How do we know Emil was annoyed after the rocks fell? **(He kicked the stones around)**
9. Why didn't Amber trust Charlie to find the way out? **(He is so forgetful)**
10. What did Amber suggest to make sure they found their way back? **(To put a pile of stones along the walls)**

Chapter 9 Out of the Gloom

1. 'Amber felt a stab of fear in her stomach' (page 97). What was she afraid of at that point? **(That her Grandad could have wandered off and be lost forever)**

2. 'This was not the time to cry' (page 97). Why did Amber not want to cry? **(She wanted to stay strong for the others)**
3. What word shows that Ella did not want to do something? **(Defiantly)**
4. What was in Ella's pocket? **(A frog torch)**
5. Why did Ella scream? **(She saw a rat)**
6. Why did the daylight sting their eyes? **(They had been in darkness for so long)**
7. Why did Ella think Katrin wouldn't come back? **(She thought she was dead)**
8. Why did the woman in the camper van frown at them? **(She didn't believe they had gone for a walk)**
9. How do you know Emil was angry at what Katrin said to Ella? **(He clenched his fists)**
10. Who had arrived at the house? **(Katrin)**

Chapter 10 Words of the Cruel

1. What surprised Amber about Katrin? **(She was younger than she imagined)**
2. 'She needs a firm hand' (page 114). What does this suggest about how Katrin treats Ella? **(She was strict)**
3. What did Katrin say was wrong with Ella? **(She tells lies)**
4. What did Amber see on Katrin's bed? **(Granny's jewellery box)**
5. What reason does Katrin give for wanting to get rid of Bonzo? **(Caring for a rabbit was too much for her to cope with as well as looking after Ella and having had a fall)**

6. Why did Amber take back the jewellery box? **(Katrin was going to sell it)**
7. Who sent the letter? **(Amy)**
8. Why did Julia think the letter could be written by an elderly person? **(The writing was shaky)**
9. What did Amber find in her Grandad's room? **(Benny's notebook)**
10. What had gone missing? **(Ella's locket)**

Chapter 11 Pain of the Missing

1. 'She ran around the house in a frenzy' (page 127). What does *in a frenzy* mean? **(In a wild manner, wildly)**
2. What word in this part of the story means 'to be filled with wonder'? **(Marvelled)**
3. 'There was a rattle as the windows quivered in the wind' (page 129). What does *quivered* mean in this sentence?
   ~~Danced~~ ~~Bounced~~ **Shook** ~~Waved~~
4. What happened to Lighthouse Cottage? **(It fell into the sea)**
5. Why was Ella limping when she was found? **(Some bricks had fallen on her leg)**
6. What did Charlie give Ella to cheer her up? **(Jelly babies)**
7. Who was on the phone later that morning? **(Amber's Mum)**
8. How do you think Amber felt after all the adults told her to stop accusing Katrin? **(Annoyed because nobody was listening to what she had discovered about Katrin)**

9. How do we know Charlie's book was old? **(It was faded with age and the staples were rusty)**
10. What was Ella planning to read whilst Amber went to see her Grandad? **(Benny's poem)**

Chapter 12 Curse of the Angel

1. How did Charlie say Benny died? **(He slipped and fell off the cliff while they were playing soldiers)**
2. What did Charlie's mother believe caused Benny's death? **(The curse)**
3. What did Ella read out to Amber and Charlie? **(Benny's poem about the Angel's Child)**
4. What had Charlie forgotten how to do? **(Turn off the TV)**
5. Why did Emil say his Mum was too nice sometimes? **(She let Katrin off when she stole money from her)**
6. Who won the least amount of card games? **(Amber – She won 2)**
7. Who was Hoppy? **(Ella's toy rabbit)**
8. What did Amber draw that evening? **(Lighthouse Cottage)**
9. What time was it when Bonzo woke Amber up? **(Midnight)**
10. Why do you think Charlie ripped up the book? **(Out of anger, he didn't like the memories it reminded him of)**

Chapter 13 Talk Through the Window

1. Why was Charlie looking for the book, *The History of Legna*? **(There was some information in it about the Angel's Child)**

2. Why was Katrin annoyed at Ella's dirty clothes? **(Because her Dad spent good money on them)**
3. 'Emil coughed and pretended to blow his nose' (page 151). What does that say about how Emil was feeling? **(Upset because he felt like crying)**
4. What was different about how Katrin talked to the children and how she talked to Charlie? **(She was more polite and nicer to Charlie)**
5. What time did Amber plan to call Ella? **(Midnight)**
6. Why did Amber want to draw the cave? **(She wanted to show how dark and scary it was)**
7. Why was Katrin's face 'thunderous' when she answered her door? **(She thought Amber had taken the jewellery box)**
8. What did Katrin take away from Ella? **(Her toy rabbit Hoppy)**
9. What was Charlie doing in the greenhouse? **(Looking for tomatoes)**
10. What did Amber plan to do the next morning? **(Take the jewellery box to Katrin and explain it was her fault Ella was talking through the window)**

Chapter 14 More Wrong Than Right

1. Why did Amber want to cry? **(Grandad had forgotten his wife)**
2. 'He's in his own world at the moment' (page 160). What do you think this phrase means? **(Unaware of what is going on around them)**
3. 'I'll bring the child round' (page 161). What does this choice of words suggest about what Katrin thought of Ella? **(She didn't really care about her as she wouldn't even use her name)**

4. What is a will? **(Something people write to tell everyone what they want after they die, e.g. who they want to give their money and belongings to)**
5. What do you think Charlie planned to leave Katrin in his will? **(The house maybe?)**
6. 'Katrin's face hardened' (page 165). What does this suggest about how Katrin was feeling? **(She was getting annoyed)**
7. Why didn't Ella want to talk about how Katrin was treating her? **(She was afraid of being sent to boarding school without Bonzo if Katrin didn't look after her)**
8. What did Katrin give Ella to eat? **(One sandwich each day)**
9. What does 'two-faced' mean? **(Dishonest)**
10. How do you think Amber and Emil felt when Julia said 'We should mind our own business' (page 173)? **(Frustrated as she wasn't listening to what they were saying / annoyed she didn't believe them)**

Chapter 15 Prisoner of the Thief

1. Why did Emil think Bonzo was missing Ella? **(He hadn't eaten much and was quiet)**
2. What do you think was in Katrin's large shopping bag? **(More ornaments, the money in Charlie's biscuit tin)**
3. Why did Amber wish Emil hadn't told Katrin where Charlie was? **(She could go and see him and change the will)**
4. Why was Katrin giving a 'false smile'? **(She was pretending she cared about Charlie and Amber's parents)**

5. Why did they think Katrin had stolen the money? **(The tin was now full of biscuits and they could not find the money anywhere)**
6. Why did Tom think it was funny that Charlie hadn't taken his tablets? **(Because Charlie never did like doing what he was told)**
7. What was the name of the receptionist? **(Raj)**
8. Why did Amber take a photo of her Grandad's gansey jumper? **(To sketch it for his birthday card)**
9. How was Katrin able to take advantage of Amy and Charlie? **(Katrin was nice to elderly people like them so they trusted her. They also both had dementia)**
10. Why did Emil lie to Ella about contacting her Dad? **(To console her and make her feel better)**

Chapter 16 Bad Turns to Worse

1. Why was the house 'empty and silent' (page 189)? **(Charlie wasn't there)**
2. What is a 'hot head'? **(Someone who gets angry easily)**
3. Why did they believe Katrin was still at home? **(Dave's car was still there)**
4. What did Amber make for the chocolate cake? **(Butter cream)**
5. Why couldn't Amber finish her cake? **(She was thinking about Ella only having a sandwich to eat)**
6. Why was Emil feeling sick? **(He had eaten too much ice cream)**
7. How do you think Amber felt when she realised Katrin was alone in the car? **(Worried as she would believe Ella was still at home alone)**

8. Where was Katrin taking Charlie when she saw Amber at the care home? **(To the solicitors to change the will)**
9. Why didn't Julia speak to Dave on the phone? **(There was no answer so she left a message)**
10. Why do you think Julia wanted to drive to the hospital first? **(To confront Katrin / to speak to Amber's parents / to give Dave time to sort out the problem)**

Chapter 17 Break of the Glass

1. What did Dave say when Julia told him everything? **(He suspected something was wrong and told Julia to do nothing yet as he would sort things out)**
2. What ward was Amber's Mum in? **(Ward Seven)**
3. What was different about Amber's Dad? **(Frail, cuts and bruises, tired)**
4. Why didn't Amber feel like talking in the hospital? **(She was happy just to be with her parents again)**
5. What did Amber say she was going to do in the future? **(Learn to cook)**
6. What did Emil use to break the window? **(A painted stone that Charlie used as a door stop)**
7. Who arrived in the helicopter? **(Dave)**
8. What did Ella want Amber to draw for her? **(Bonzo)**
9. Why did Dave give up his job? **(He didn't need the money to buy a big house anymore)**
10. What did Emil send over for Ella? **(A cake with a rabbit on)**

1. What words tell us the ferry was moving smoothly? **(it 'seemed to glide across the sea like a skater' (page 225))**
2. How did Amber feel about moving to Legna? **(She loved the idea)**
3. What did Amber have in her bag for her Grandad? **(The book *The History of Legna* and a packet of jelly babies)**
4. Why did Amber go to her Grandad's room alone? **(Her Mum and Julia were busy talking to Tina and Rob)**
5. What was the name of the young girl in the story who stole the baby? **(Angel Savage)**
6. Why was the baby girl named Bella? **(She was named after the Bella Rose ship that she was rescued from)**
7. What happened to Bella when she was seven years old? **(She died of a mysterious illness)**
8. Why did Amber think Ella might be descended from the same family as Angel Savage? **(Ella's last name was Savage)**
9. How had Amber changed since the beginning of the story? **(She was scared to do things but was more confident at the end)**
10. Why did Amber place the jelly babies in a row? **(That's what her Grandad always did)**

Acknowledgements

I have been very lucky that so many people have helped me in the writing of this book. So many in fact that I almost don't know where to start.

So I will start with the **children**:

> Thanks to my granddaughter Ivy Campbell for being the brilliant model on the cover, and for designing and sketching Emil's rabbit cake.
>
> Thanks to my granddaughter Esther Campbell for illustrating the book with her wonderful sketches.

Thanks also to the following children who read an early draft of this book and gave me such useful feedback. As a result of their comments and those of the few adults who also read the draft, I changed the title and added another 5,000 words, along with some illustrations:

- Imisi Greensides
- Ryco Attwood, Jack Bailey, Grace Halsall, Logan Mann Tighe, Jemima Wright (Ackworth Mill Dam Junior & Infant School, Pontefract)
- Ben Bayliss, Faye Harper, Edward Helks, Cameron Rogers (Normanton Junior Academy, Wakefield)

- George Birch, Jay Morgan, Katy Muncaster, Neeve Perry, Alicia Robinson (Sharlston Community School, Wakefield)
- Georgia Bloomer, Millie Gulliford, Lilly Hardcastle (South Kirkby Academy, Pontefract)
- Manahil Ali, Nibaa Fahim, Aleena Faizal, Jessica MacKenzie, Elieza Sagabaen, Benazir Satti (Wexham Court Primary, Slough)
- Mia Jones, Jake Reeves, Jacob Roclawski, Isobel Watson (Wrenthorpe Academy, Wakefield)

Thanks also to the following **adults**:

- Rebecca Coggins (teacher, Wexham Court Primary, Slough) for co-ordinating the children's feedback in her school.
- All the teachers from the five Waterton Academy Trust schools in Wakefield and Pontefract, who kindly collected feedback from the children.
- Dave Dickinson OBE (CEO, Waterton Multi Academy Trust) for his support and for taking the time to give me detailed feedback on an early draft.
- Elliot Morgan (teacher and KS2 SATS moderator) for his hard work and expertise in devising most of the questions for the 'Quiz'.
- Tony Morris for his song 'Mulberry Smuggler' and for sharing his background knowledge on the subject.
- All the members of Agbrigg Writers, Wakefield, for their support and encouragement, especially Sharyn Owen for providing such detailed and useful feedback.
- Jane Simpkins (School Improvement Officer, Waterton Multi Academy Trust) for her continual

encouragement, but also for her hard work in co-ordinating the feedback from the Waterton Academy Trust Schools.

- Sam Thompson (Head Teacher, Ackworth Mill Dam J & I School) for her positive and constructive comments on an early draft.

Thanks to the following **organisations** for information on dementia:

- The Dementia Network – https://dementia.network
  See their articles on 'How to talk to children about dementia' and 'The impact of dementia on children'.

- The Alzheimer's Society – www.alzheimers.org.uk
  See their Fact sheet 515LP: 'Explaining dementia to children and young people'.

And finally… thanks to my **family…**

I would like to thank my family for taking the time to read early and final drafts of *Angel's Child* and offering such supportive and constructive comments. However, in addition to my grandchildren mentioned earlier, I would particularly like to thank:

- my daughter Kate Campbell for professionally editing the book with such a forensic eye for detail;
- my son Kerry Harrison for shooting and producing such an amazing cover photo; and
- my daughter-in-law Debby Lewis-Harrison for skilfully designing the book cover, postcards and bookmarks and for organising the website.

But most of all I would like to thank my husband Martyn for all the support, encouragement and advice he has given me during the many hours I have spent on my writing over the past few years.

About the Author

Larraine Harrison is a former teacher and school inspector. She has written several books for teachers on using drama to help children learn. She now writes stories for children and likes to involve her grandchildren and local schools in the production of her books.

Angel's Child is Larraine's second novel. Her first novel, *Red Snow*, received great reviews from experts and children alike.

Larraine lives in Yorkshire with her husband and, when not writing, likes to play saxophone.

Red Snow: 'A compelling tale'

Northern Life Magazine 2018

Larraine's first novel, *Red Snow*

When Megan and Ryan find two wild cats in the woods, they decide to keep their existence a secret.

But they soon discover there is a link between the cats and the death of Megan's mother several years ago.

No-one in their village will talk about it, so Megan and Ryan must solve the mystery on their own.